GONE IN THE STORM

BOOKS BY B.R. SPANGLER

DETECTIVE CASEY WHITE SERIES

Where Lost Girls Go

The Innocent Girls

Saltwater Graves

The Crying House

The Memory Bones

The Lighthouse Girls

Taken Before Dawn

Their Resting Place

Two Little Souls

Our Sister's Grave

Her Last Hour

DARK SKIES APOCALYPSE

When the Sky Falls

When the Dawn Breaks

B.R. SPANGLER

GONE IN THE STORM

bookouture

Published by Bookouture in 2025

An imprint of Storyfire Ltd.
Carmelite House
50 Victoria Embankment
London EC4Y 0DZ

www.bookouture.com

The authorised representative in the EEA is Hachette Ireland
8 Castlecourt Centre
Dublin 15 D15 XTP3
Ireland
(email: info@hbgi.ie)

Copyright © B.R. Spangler, 2025

B.R. Spangler has asserted his right to be identified as the author of this work.

All rights reserved. No part of this publication may be reproduced, stored in any retrieval system, or transmitted, in any form or by any means, electronic, mechanical, photocopying, recording or otherwise, without the prior written permission of the publishers.

ISBN: 978-1-83525-764-7
eBook ISBN: 978-1-83525-763-0

This book is a work of fiction. Names, characters, businesses, organizations, places and events other than those clearly in the public domain, are either the product of the author's imagination or are used fictitiously. Any resemblance to actual persons, living or dead, events or locales is entirely coincidental.

PROLOGUE

The stones were first. The pebbles were next, smaller ones placed on top of the larger. He packed them tight, daylight poking through the cracks. Some of them were a plain gray and had spots of brown. There were others which were glossy white like a pearl. They were the most attractive, and he saved them for the top like candles on a birthday cake. In a way, it was like her birthday. Each stone was carefully selected, picking only the round ones. They'd been smoothed by the river, the years washing away the coarse surface. Fifty was the right count, the pile near the center of this arrangement.

The twigs were next. Starting with the larger that were nearly half the length of his arm. They were placed on the bottom first, the collection evenly spaced. Crisscrossed perpendicular, he aligned them to the four cardinal directions, not a degree more or less. He pinched the tips of his fingers, some of the bark still wet, pleased by the progress. But the satisfaction was fleeting. It wasn't enough.

Bothered, he pawed anxiously at his chin. It was the gap near the center of the collection. It needed something bright. The smell of snow hung in the air. It was distinct and told him he'd have to hurry. The weather agreed with a whisper, its cold breath touching the back of his neck. Flower petals. He thought of the colorful, silky petals of a bloom. His eyes grew wide, the idea of flowers gnawing like hunger. They would have been the perfect selection. It was the gut of winter though and he couldn't chance a visit to a flower shop.

"This won't do." He paced impatiently, taking care of where he stepped. He didn't dare leave any of himself behind. That included footprints. In the distance, dark clouds lumbered quietly. They weren't charged full of electricity like the ones at springtime or the late afternoon summer storms. It wasn't a tropical storm either with its eye set to travel up the coast. These clouds were barreling in from the west and were heavy with moisture. And in the cold, that meant snow. They were going to bring a lot of snow. "Cancel?" The question was raised, tense pace increasing.

"I can't. It has to be today!" He nodded, agreeing, and glanced at his watch. It was six hours between now and when he'd take her. "It will be today."

"Bright. That's what is missing..." His focus returned to the collections and the blank space in the middle. Shoes grating, he spun around. "Would shiny work?"

With the thought, he returned to his bag, the sides bulging, stuffed heavy from years of collecting. Digging through the plastic, he found the one he was looking for. Bottle caps. His spirits lifted and he held the bag up to the sky. These weren't just any bottle caps either. They were vintage, the small collection dating back decades. He'd found them at a yard sale, a hundred or more stuffed in an old navy-blue shoebox, the cardboard frayed and turning pulpy. The seller tried haggling, speaking of their dead father's love for them. He haggled back some but couldn't stomach the negotiating. He gave up a few more dollars than he'd wanted but got the collection to add to his. It was the colors, the shininess and variety, and now he had a use.

She'll love them. How could she not? After all, he'd cleaned the bottle caps too, using hot water and that gentle soap they use on animals when they were fouled by an oil spill. He'd seen the commercials. Sunlight escaped the encroaching clouds, a beam striking the bottle caps. There were ones that looked like silver and gold. Some that were yellow and red. The green colored ones were an instant favorite—the soda pop they'd been used for had tasted like apples. Shame they don't make that one anymore.

Without a moment to spare, he knelt and swept the ground, knuckles tightening around the broken end of a broom. He raked the dirt, the bristles leaving faint impressions. When the area was ready, he placed the bottle caps one by one. When he was done, he stood to look, the tiniest snowflake wetting his cheek. It melted and raced away like a tear. The decorations were in place, the site made ready. There was only one thing left to get now. His victim.

ONE

Snowflakes. The chunky kind that drifts gracefully like royalty entering a ballroom. There were hundreds of them. Maybe thousands. They fell without a sound and planted cold, wet kisses on her face. Jill Carter could barely blink, her gaze fixed on the gray sky while a wish that she'd never gotten in that car rose on a weak breath.

This isn't so bad. Dying that is. Not really.

The terror and horror of what was happening to her had passed already. He'd taken it with him when leaving her alone. *Did he think I was dead? Probably.*

She was still alive. For now. But there was an unfamiliar feeling she instinctively recognized. It could only be one thing. Death. The body and mind know when it's nearby. Thankfully, the pain had eased. Had she ever felt anything like it before? Not that it mattered now. Her senses were slipping quickly into nothingness, fading like the flakes melting on her lips.

My killer, she thought distantly with a shallow breath. *Why? Why did he do this?*

Oddly, she felt grateful her eyes were still open. The snowfall was a pretty thing to watch. And she thought it was okay if it was the last thing she'd ever see. Mind stirring, the neurons and whatever else in her brain beginning to starve.

Hold on. Just for a little longer.

It had all started with a question. One simple and short question. "Where are you going?" That's what her killer had asked from the car window.

"I'm headed home," she'd answered immediately, excited to have him talking to her. She answered fast as well. Maybe it was to impress him. Didn't she always want to impress him? "So, where're you headed?"

Jill could smell that moment, the frosty air mixing with the fumes from his car. He'd slowed down until matching her gait, the car tires crunching the unpaved road's snow. He'd flashed a smile, answering, "Hop in and I'll drop you off."

Why didn't I just walk? The question pestering, her body dying and her eyes too dry to produce a tear. *Why would he do this? I had a life!*

Frigid air swooped down from the north during the night, the weather people forecasting some breezy flurries. By the time the school's second-period buzzer stung her ears, those flurries had accumulated to more than an inch. The early release announcement that came next had kicked off the short stampede for the doors. This was the Outer Banks, a beach town. How often does the snow actually stick?

What was worse, knowing that you're about to die or knowing how terrible those left behind were going to feel? Thoughts returned to her killer. *My killer.* He'd opened the car door, eyes inviting, the expression on his face the same. And wasn't she cold? Her toes and fingers aching painfully with another mile to go. Jill remembered thinking she'd invite him inside her home where she could fix him a cup of hot chocolate with the tiny marshmallows. A thank you for the ride. But when they reached the corner of her street, he turned left instead of right. That's when she should have known.

"I've got to show you something," he'd explained, brow bouncing with excitement.

"But my house—" she began to ask, a smile replaced by confusion.

"It'll only take a couple minutes," he continued, dipping his head to check a windshield wiper. The rubber on the tip was split, hanging loose. A frown formed, his muttering, "I gotta fix that."

"What is it you wanna show me?"

Excitement returning. "It's a new collection." She didn't know what that meant. "You're the first person I'm showing it to."

"I'm the first?" That meant something. Didn't it? A left turn. Jill wiped the moisture from the window. They weren't in her neighborhood anymore. The houses here were set far apart, the ocean further away. Her teeth began to chatter, the cold biting. "Where is it?"

"It's just up ahead," he answered, turning right onto a gravelly road, rocks spitting beneath the car. He glanced at her, his gaze remaining. Her mouth went dry, the look on his face making her feel uncomfortable. She made herself busy and tried warming her hands. He saw and turned up the heat. "That'll help."

Air poured from the vents, tepid and stinking of the car's rusty age. The brakes let out a chirp when they stopped. "This is it?"

"Over there a bit," he answered without looking back. The door opened, cold rushing in. Jill hesitated, uncertain what to do. He noticed and put on that inviting smile again. She could see his breath while coaxing her. "It's really cool, you'll love it. Especially with the snow and all."

"Okay," she said, following. The weather was getting worse. It had taken the sun with it, a hard shiver making her tremble. "How much further?"

"Right here," he said, passing through a gate that was topped with spiraling wire. There were old cars piled high to one side and heaps of scrap metal on the other. He began to jog, shouting over his shoulder, "Follow me. Keep up."

"What's here?" A worry set in. The place he'd brought her to was filled with junk. There were narrow, winding footpaths that reminded her of the cornfield mazes they'd enjoyed the past Halloween. She tried to hurry and followed the footsteps in the snow. The cold was turning unbearable, but the stacked cars were tall and helped to soften the wind. When she reached him, he was standing tall, hands on his hips while looking at something proudly. The smile on his face was contagious and she couldn't help but return it when their eyes met. She gazed ahead, a breeze blowing her red hair. She searched, seeing some stones and sticks and what looked like bottle caps. "What? What am I looking at?"

"My collections," he answered, eyes growing wider.

She pegged a toe in the snow-covered dirt, realizing they were far from the road. They were far from anywhere.

He moved closer, saying, "Isn't it wonderful?"

"Yeah, I guess." Jill shivered badly. Trembling uncontrollably. But it wasn't just the cold. Uncertainty confused her and she didn't want to be rude, forcing a smile, nodding with him. "It's-it's really very nice."

"Oh jeez."

He saw that she was cold and took her hands in his, which were surprisingly warm. He cupped them gently and lifted them to his mouth, blowing a warm breath over her fingers. His eyes never left hers and at once she realized she shouldn't be here. The hairs on the back of her neck stood with fright, his asking, "Does that feel better?"

"Uh-huh," she tried to say, words stuck in her throat. The look on his face changed. Fright filled the pit of her stomach and told her to run. It was the instinct she should have listened to.

He nodded his head, an ugly sneer forming. Jill stepped back, shaking and saying, "I really gotta go. My dad's gonna be mad if I'm not home on time."

"It's okay." His eyes bulged. "I know your dad isn't expecting you until later."

"Oh, right."

His grip tightened with a squeeze, the tips of her fingers turning wet in his humid breath. She jerked her hands from his mouth, certain she felt him kissing one of her fingers. The tears were coming, her voice rising, "I got to go!"

"But we just got here," he tried to explain, a hurt look on his face.

Concerns of being rude were gone in a flash, Jill spinning around, muscles in her legs tensing to run. She was fast. Probably one of the fastest in her class, always beating the other kids in every schoolyard race.

Only, he was faster, and before she knew what was happening, he'd pinned her to the ground, his attack vicious. Terror flooded through every part of her with the sound of clothes ripping and the touch of junkyard dirt and grime against her bare skin. She glimpsed his angry face once or twice during the fight and saw an evil rage beaming from his eyes. Over and over he'd said, "For my collection."

He'd rolled over after he was done, one hand like a vice around her wrist, painfully tight.

"Please let me go," she remembered begging. "I won't tell anyone what happened. I swear it."

Her pleas went unanswered while he got up and tidied himself. The cold air replaced where he'd been and she tried covering herself, a strange daze making her light-headed. There was a content look on his face which was eclipsed by a new look. Jill scurried backwards, elbows cutting against the frozen ground, his hands suddenly around her throat.

"I already told you. You're for my collection."

Why? Jill snapped back from what had happened and distanced the remaining minutes of her life from the reality of his actions. The consequences too. It happened and I'm going to die.

A wiggle. It was weak and barely noticeable. Jill felt the tip of her finger move and jabbed it into the fresh snow. When the cold registered in her thoughts, she told herself to smile, but could only do so in her mind. *His name, I'll write his name.*

It was the last thing Jill would do, give the world the name of her murderer. Try as she might to think of happier thoughts, she couldn't help but focus on what he'd said. "For my collection." It meant there were others.

TWO

Investigating death wasn't always a part of my life, not like it is now. I had a normal childhood. Pretty much, anyway. In fact, it wasn't all that different from any other kid's. Back then, we'd shared the same questions about dying. Nothing too heavy or ponderous, just the basic stuff like: what happens when you die? What happens to your body? Where do you go? Do you really become worm food? But then there'd been that first time when death touched close enough to feel it. And I remember it being so much more than seeing insects scorched on the pavement.

It was a body, alive, panting fast, heart beating hard, their eyes gazing frightfully. And then, like the snap of a finger, it was over. To this day, I'm sure I felt every bit of that final, living moment. It wasn't a person or anything like that. It was a small bird, and it had flown into our kitchen window.

The strike came with a sharp thwack that made us all flinch. My mother yipped embarrassingly and covered her mouth while my father took to looking outside, eyelids peeled. A dusty imprint on the window's glass showed us what happened. The feathery wingspan was unmistakable, and I remember thinking how much it looked like an angel we'd used to top our Christmas tree.

My father said nothing and went to check the yard. I felt compelled to see it too and followed him outside. A chill shook me, my bare feet wet from the morning dew, the sky a hazy orange and purple to warn of the afternoon storms. Beneath the kitchen window, the bird was heaped in a pile of rumpled feathers, mottled brown and gray colors specked on a black coat.

"It's a starling," my father had told me, gaze rising to the trees. "They're the birds that make the shapes in the sky called a murmuration."

"This one is alone though." The surrounding trees were empty, the branches bare.

A slow nod. "It was probably a hawk on the hunt. The other starlings scattered, and this little guy flew straight into the house."

"Poor thing," I remember saying, choking up when my dad put his arm around me. The starling was gasping by then, an eye bulging. We moved closer, slowly so we wouldn't scare it. Its breathing began to ease, and I remember a cool breeze racing through me. I think it was death passing by to take the bird, the starling's life ending swiftly. My father looked at me then as if death had taken some of my innocence. And in a way, maybe it had. Just a little of it, but enough to always remember that morning.

When I asked why the bird flew into our kitchen window, pressing for an answer, my father explained how the morning sun had fooled the bird. He hoisted me into the air, my hands on his broad shoulders, and then showed me the window. In it, I saw the backyard and the trees behind us, the reflection as clear as if it was a mirror. There was no way for the bird to know that it was flying straight into death.

While the bird's life was over, a brief tear wetting my cheek, what happened that morning was all but forgotten by the evening. Thinking about it now, the dead bird was my very first homicide case. It was the first time I'd ever investigated a cause of death: the starling was the victim, and the hawk was the murderer. I know that's a stretch, and I know it was nature being nature with the food chain and all that. Still, it was a case, and it was mine.

Homicide cases are different to me now, but the hawks haven't changed, they lurk and hide in the shadows like the boogeymen living beneath my bed. While they hunt the innocent and chase them toward death, it's not the food chain or nature being nature. It's murder. Plain and simple.

"Earth to Casey White?" Tracy Fields asked, leaning closer to the windshield. Heavy snowflakes bounced off the glass, her eyes following the windshield wipers back and forth. "I think the snow might be lifting some."

"You've lived here a lot longer than me. Have you ever seen snow like this in the Outer Banks?" I jabbed the car's dashboard and cranked the heat. My toes ached, the cold nipping at them since leaving my apartment on the beach. Tracy started to shake her head but then nodded. Teeth chattering, voice wavering, I asked, "Yes?"

"A couple times, maybe?" she said, blowing a long breath into her cupped hands. "Flurries though. Nothing like this."

"The crime scene is gonna be a mess," I commented, nudging my chin toward her phone. "See if the medical examiner is already there?"

My car was newer, but the heater was a disappointment. Days earlier, a cold front crept in and dropped the temperatures enough to freeze everything. It carried a few inches of snow with it too, which had never been an issue in Philadelphia. But for the Outer Banks, the sudden blanket of white stuff was debilitating. We were on the tail end of it now, seeing just the promised flurries, storm passed. I thumped the car's dash to motivate the heater. It didn't work.

Tracy snickered when I waved my hand, grimacing. "Yeah, I bet that stung."

"Just keep trying Samantha," I answered, refusing to admit it. The car's rear swung wide, the tires spinning, I gripped the steering wheel and turned into the swerve.

"Whoa!" an officer hollered, the car fishtailing into the crime scene. I stomped the brakes, sliding, breath stuck in my throat. The officer jumped out of the way, the bottom of his yellow raincoat flinging open like an umbrella. I raised my hand, eyelids wide with apology, and stopped short of the crime-scene tape. He gave me a stern look and snorted a misty cloud from his nose and mouth.

"That was too close," Tracy said, letting go of the console, color returning to her fingernails.

"I told you I'd get us here," I said, shifting the car into park and breathing fast. "Snow, or no snow."

"Holy shit," Tracy shrieked, the wind catching the door. She braced herself, a gust lifting her wavy brown hair and twisting it like the crime-scene tape edging the perimeter. The air was frosty, her nose and dimples turning red in an instant. Shock shined in her baby-blue eyes, winter's cold hand reaching into the car. She shook her head, yelling, "I didn't think it'd be this bad!"

"I've got some gear for us," I said, and led her to the back, the trunk opening. We huddled beneath the lid, the inside filled with the tools of our trade. There were multiple forensics kits and enough camera gear to process three crime scenes. Tracy found the heavy coats and snowsuits, grabbing them eagerly. "Rule number one?"

"Come prepared," she answered, voice carried on a puff of smoky breath. She looked up, shaking badly, and added, "Thank you."

"The winters in Philadelphia trained me good," I answered with a nod, jerking the pantsuit over my legs.

"You mean well," she chirped, correcting my grammar, a habit of hers.

"Nah. I mean good," I said, putting on my best Philly accent, gaze fixed on the crime scene. We were downwind and I lifted my nose out of habit. Sometimes we could gauge the time of death before seeing the body, but I could only smell the cold air.

"I'm not getting anything either," Tracy said, fluffy snowflakes on her long eyelashes. She blinked fast and grabbed the camera gear. "Any chance you have plastic bags and rubber bands?"

"There's a bundle behind the extra coats," I answered, shivering. "Shouldn't you have those?"

"I usually do." The camera flash went off, Tracy testing the charge. "I've got no excuse."

"No excuse," I repeated, sleeving an arm into the heavier coat and searching the gated entrance of the vehicle salvage and scrap metal property. From the looks of it, I'd call it a junkyard. There were cars stacked ten-high, flattened, their original identities lost. Scrap metal edged the fence line where razor wire kept trespassers out. I didn't know what kind of money was in scrap but wondered who'd go in willingly. It was morning, though the winter months brought the dark skies early. Checking the time, I added, "Let's get moving before we lose whatever light we've got."

The officer I'd nearly hit approached us, my belly stirring with embarrassment. "Gotta watch them roads, Detective."

"Sorry about that," I told him. He wasn't much older than Tracy, the uniform poking out from beneath the rain gear, the sight of it reminding me of my time back in Philadelphia. "Who found the body?"

"Not sure. I'm just guarding the entrance," he said, tipping his hat against the weather. "Maybe check over with the medical examiner."

GONE IN THE STORM 15

"Thank you, officer."

Snow crunched beneath my boots, and I shined a flashlight onto the footpath. It bordered the crime-scene tape, the number of footprints too many to count. We'd have issues finding anything usable. I gave the okay and Tracy went ahead of me, Samantha Watson standing near the medical examiner van. She was the Outer Banks medical examiner, and close friends with Tracy.

At the crime scene

I texted my husband Jericho. I'd met him my first days in the Outer Banks, when I'd unexpectedly been drafted to help with a homicide case. We've been together ever since. A lifelong resident and one-time sheriff, Jericho is retired now, taking on the role of stay-at-home father to two adorable children. But even in retirement, his mind still works cases. He's a cop like me.

When I was close enough to the gate, I saw a faded red and yellow sign, the cursive writing telling me the name of the place. I texted it.

Patsy's Junkyard?

I know the place

The dots bounced as he typed, the text appearing.

Patsy and his wife died years ago. The place is owned by his children.

Good to know

Samantha and Tracy were waiting. Bodies shivering.

Gotta run, give the kids hugs and kisses.

Will do

He answered with a thumbs up.

"I'm coming." The cold reached inside my jacket and made me shake. I zipped the front and waved to my team. "Go ahead, I'll catch up."

They entered the junkyard, Derek following. A bear of a man, he was the medical examiner's assistant and was as gentle as a mouse. They peered around at the mountain of torn and twisted metal lining both sides while taking care to stay on the path leading to the body. I'd seen my share of crime scenes, but none in a junkyard. The closest had been a dump, a body found rolled up in an old rug. It was one of my first homicide cases, back when I'd lived north of the barrier islands. Sometimes that case feels like it was just yesterday. Other times, it feels like it was a lifetime ago. In a way, it was a lifetime ago, a life I often try and forget.

THREE

In my years of working homicide, I couldn't recall a single time where the crime scene was covered in snow. Not sure how I'd escaped that particular scenario. But here we were, the four of us standing side by side in front of what looked like a snow mound. If not for the single, petite hand, little more than a finger, nobody would have known there was a body until after the snow had melted.

"How do we proceed?" Derek asked, hoisting his pants. Steam rose from the top of his balding head, a breeze catching thin hair. He was quick to comb over the strays and tuck them behind an ear. "I mean, like, do we just brush it off?"

"There's the risk of brushing away evidence," Tracy commented, her voice muffled behind the camera. She stung the air with a flash, snowflakes momentarily seeming to halt their descent. I saw the image on the rear of the camera, slightly underexposed, fooled by the snow's brightness. The victim's palm was colored like a bruise, rigor having set. Tracy flipped through a series, dimples appearing with a frown. "I'm guessing a day?"

"At least," I agreed and glanced at Samantha for her opinion. She nudged a wool cap over her short black hair, tufts of it jutting from beneath. Her lips were a pale blue like her eyes, which stood out against her snowy complexion.

"Getting an accurate body temperature might be out of the question," she said, leaning into a breeze. She took Derek's arm while he helped her kneel. From inside her coat, she held up a pair of latex gloves, the empty fingers flapping. I took the cue and did the same, my fingertips freezing instantly. Tracy considered it, but held on to the camera, deciding what her role in this assessment would be today. Derek thumbed the *Record* button of an audio recorder, the end of it shaking. Samantha's teeth chattered while she carefully brushed the snow from the victim's arm, exposing the skin up to the elbow. "The victim is presenting with rigor mortis, blanching and discoloration consistent in the hand and arm, pooling beneath."

"No coat?" Tracy questioned. Carefully brushing aside the snow, the victim's shoulder and a breast were exposed, the skin gray. "Female. Where are her clothes?"

"Victim is a female," Samantha spoke into the recorder. Clearing the snow from her face, a pretty, young woman appeared, her eyelids stuck open, the lashes frozen. "An adolescent, clothing is missing."

"Her neck," I said, finding ligature marks where snow had been removed. I searched Samantha's face for approval. She nodded, Tracy joining, the camera's nose appearing over my shoulder. Gently sweeping more snow from the victim's neck, the cause of death became clear. Before announcing it, I shined a pen light in the victim's eyes, the pupils hidden behind a cloudy film. Tiny rivers of blood vessels had flowed over, pooling as the life was taken.

"Signs of petechia in the eyes indicate strangulation as the possible cause of death."

"I agree," Samantha answered. Snow crunched beneath her knees while she moved to the victim's middle and swept the remaining snow. She sat back on her heels and slowly closed her eyes, the finding bothersome. "The victim has no clothing. The skin around the victim's waist has scratches and welts, indicating clothes were forcefully removed."

"Sexual assault?" Tracy asked, her voice thin. I nodded, my stomach turning. It didn't matter how many years were behind me. How many cases. Or how many atrocities I'd seen. This was a young woman who'd been sexually assaulted and murdered. The day that doesn't bother me is the day I know it is time to quit this job. On Tracy's face, I saw how horrible I felt. The horror turned to disgust, her commenting, "In a junkyard?"

"Tracy," Samantha said, waving her over.

The victim's legs were together, one knee raised as if in a defensive posture. Tracy photographed the body, understanding what was coming next. The camera batteries whined slowly, the cold challenging them. When she finished, Tracy slipped on latex gloves, a poof of dust joining the snowflakes. She took an ankle and helped spread the victim's legs just enough for Samantha to make an assessment. I saw confirmation near immediately, Samantha motioning to Derek. He lowered the recorder.

"Abrasions and bruising found on the inside of the victim's thighs."

A breeze gusted between the walls of cars, turning into a harsh icy wind that blew the loose snow toward us. We turned away from it, covering our faces, snow pelting. When it was over, more of the victim's body was exposed. She was young, possibly early teens, with fiery red hair. While her eyes had clouded with death, there was enough blue remaining in them to note the color. Though faint, her complexion faded by death, there were freckles across her cheeks and chest. I followed her hand, the one extended, the index finger crooked like she was holding a pencil. The wind had blown away the fresh snow, revealing a letter. Possibly two, frozen in the frost beneath.

"Over here. I think the victim was writing something."

"Let's see," Tracy answered, rushing over, pant legs swooshing. Batteries straining, they whined near my ear when she fired off a few pictures. There were two letters. Unreadable though, the edges too soft. A third letter was barely started, the victim dying before she could finish.

Tracy shook her head. "A letter O and E?"

"Could be a D or Q," I replied, focusing on the first letter.

"Uh-huh. That's a G," Derek countered. He cocked his head, adding, "Wait, it's a Q, like you said."

"We're not going to guess it out here," Tracy commented, shutter firing rapidly. "I'll grab multiple angles. That way we can work it on the computer."

"Casey?" Samantha asked, her voice sharp. I turned around to where she was pointing and followed her gaze. It was a neat pile of rocks, arranged in a pattern and nothing you'd find in a junkyard. "Those rocks don't look like they belong here."

"Agreed. I think they're from a river and they've no right place here."

"Stones," Tracy said, brightening the scene with her camera's flash. "Small, like pebbles."

"How do you know?" Derek asked, lifting his chin to see. "They're just rocks."

"They're all rocks. Pebbles and stones. But I think these might have been collected like someone would collect seashells. The edges are smoothed by water erosion. That's why I think they're pebbles." He acknowledged my answer with a grunt. I heaved a strong breath, emptying my lungs to clear the powdery snow. Stars zipped across my vision, the exertion too much. Blinking it away, I continued. "The colors and size of them too. That can't be random."

"It's in a sequence. Each one of them purposefully placed." Tracy stepped back, metal crunching beneath her heel. "Shit."

"Wait! Don't move." I fanned the snow from around her

foot to expose another pile. This one was shiny with rainbow colors, a pair of old-style bottle caps sticking out. I stood up and raised my voice. "I want everyone to follow your footsteps back the way you came."

One by one, we stood and stepped into the impressions we'd left behind. For a moment, it looked like an odd game of Twister, bodies contorted, legs wide, arms stretching to catch our balance.

When we reached the outside perimeter and I motioned it was safe, Derek said, "I've got a leaf blower in the van. We've used it at the beach to move dry sand from bodies."

"Yes!" I nearly shouted, having forgotten about the past beach recoveries we'd performed. "Get it."

Sometimes I feel like an archeologist in the sands of an ancient temple, standing ankle deep in the ruins of a city that's no more. And with each sweeping pass, the layers representing the time between life and death are removed, revealing the truth I'm after. That was true this morning with a young woman who'd been sexually assaulted and then strangled. Sadly, Samantha shared which of the two had occurred first and that the victim was surely awake and aware. There was tissue beneath one of the victim's fingernails, the signs of a struggle that resulted in evidence for us to gather and analyze.

While Derek struggled to kick over the leaf blower, I sealed an evidence bag around the victim's left hand. It was to protect that single, precious cracked fingernail and the skin which could potentially have come from the killer. We wouldn't attempt to collect it until the victim was transported indoors, out of the elements. I flinched when the blower's motor turned and spewed the stink of fuel and smoke.

"Gently!" I yelled over the noise.

Derek's hair stood like an arrow pointing up while he throttled back and tested the grounds away from the body. I motioned to go even lower. He obliged, setting the blower safely.

"That's good. Start over there."

"Gotcha!" he yelled back, easing the nozzle around the body. It was the piles of stuff near the victim which looked both impossibly random and very specific. They could have been placed there by kids, but my gut was telling me there was more to them than just kids fooling around with pretty rocks. When the snow blew away to reveal another pile, some sticks, thick on the bottom, thin on top, my heart sank. This wasn't the work of children playing. Derek stopped suddenly and shut off the blower. I looked at him curiously. He pointed, "I think that's a pile of leaves."

Between the bottle caps and the sticks, one heavy rock weighed down a small pile of leaves. I took to one knee, Tracy's camera flashing double-time. The obvious conclusion struck me like a slap when I recognized the leaves. There were some trees edging the junkyard, but none of them were tall enough or mature enough to produce the likes of these. And none of them were sycamores or dogwoods or a Japanese maple, which I'd known from my time living in Philadelphia. "These are from the autumn season. Most likely, they were brought here."

"Look how perfectly arranged they are," Tracy commented, an expression of awe on her face. She shook her head, adding, "Is it a message?"

"Sticks and stones may break my bones," Samantha began. She joined us while Derek continued clearing the snow from the victim. "But words can never hurt me."

"Do you think?" Tracy asked, uncomfortable, even a bit disgusted. "The killer is using rhymes?"

Metal clanking softly, I studied the walls surrounding us. They were built using piles of scrap metal and crushed vehicles.

"The killer didn't just choose this place for the seclusion." A deep breath, and like the archeologist on the verge of discovery, I was seeing what the killer saw. I motioned to the pile of pebbles and leaves, the sticks and bottle caps. Samantha and Derek and Tracy turned to face what the killer had built. "Piles of junk. The killer picked this place specifically."

"Junkyard. Piles of junk," Samantha answered quickly, repeating what I said and gazing.

I looked at the victim, sickened and angered by the lack of regard for this girl's life. "That's how the killer treated her. Like junk."

FOUR

The morgue seemed colder than usual. Inescapable might be a better word for it. I pulled a third lab coat across my shoulders to stave a shiver. Tracy was already suited, the two of us in the basement of the municipal building, waiting for the medical examiner to give the okay to enter. The elevator and stairwell were behind us, along with a row of lockers and shelves that carried everything needed to meet the morgue's strict protocols. Metal clanked with an echo when I shut the locker and spun the lock to safeguard my firearm and other belongings. That was part of the protocol too, stowing gear, suiting up, and then spending an afternoon in the only place where the dead had a voice.

With the evidence collected and helping to pose the questions, the morgue and its rituals was the place where we listened to the victims and heard them, the science explaining what happened in the moments leading to their deaths. Samantha was our guide, and as the medical examiner, she translated what was beyond us. All parts of an investigation were important, but this was one of the more critical. This was where we had to get it right, the victim's body in our custody for only a brief period before releasing it to the family. I'd already received no less than three text messages from the district attorney and our chief of police. Both were waiting to learn more too, the homicide bad, the news breaking this evening.

Having completed the preliminary autopsy, Samantha had scheduled the meeting with the victim's family. We would pay our condolences and answer their questions, including the hardest of them which involved how their daughter was killed. Nerves stirred in my gut, the angst an unfortunate part of our jobs. I checked my watch and saw they'd be arriving soon, our time shorter than I'd like.

Tracy helped close my front, hurrying when footsteps shuffled from behind a pair of thick rubber doors. Frosty air slipped beneath them, a shadow appearing in the plastic windows, the height telling me it was Derek. He jarred one of the doors, poking his head out. "Samantha is ready for you."

"Thank you, Derek," I answered and shook out my hands. My fingers felt tight inside the gloves, the latex doubled.

"Any luck on a replacement?" Tracy asked, clumsily working the camera gear. Her expression said all I needed to know about how she was feeling. We'd usually have three of us working a case but we were left shorthanded after a recent new hire decided this wasn't the field for them. When I didn't answer immediately, she frowned. "Any applicants?"

"Might be the winter months," I answered, shaking my head. "It's slow."

"Doesn't seem to have slowed crime," she commented, the tone of her voice cold like the morgue.

I didn't reply, the words and what to say escaping me. Derek held the door, and I followed Tracy inside, paper slippers scraping, the added cover ensuring the field remained sterile. I keep a clean house, is what Samantha told us. We didn't dare compromise it either. Tracy walked ahead of me, the camera gear whining with a charge from the battery pack slung around her shoulder.

Multiple autopsy tables stood near the center of the room, the tables fixed to the pedestals that seemed to sprout from the floor like plants. Above each, a myriad of electronics, sensors, screens, lights and recording devices, the morgue having recently leaped forward in technology, the view like something out of a science fiction novel. To my right was the large body refrigerator, the original and likely the oldest piece of equipment in the entire building. It hummed methodically, preserving the dead who lay in wait for their session with Samantha.

I followed Tracy to an autopsy table as Samantha dragged a step stool from beneath and climbed it. The equipment inside the table's pedestal hummed and large screens above flashed. At the other end of the morgue, the once cinder-block wall was covered by large screens, a full-sized body X-ray showing, the victim's name brightly displayed in the lower right corner.

Samantha adjusted the step stool, her height on the shorter side, the tables fixed in place. Even with the stool, she got onto her toes and moved the microphone, commenting, "This is the preliminary autopsy review of Jill Carter, female, fifteen years of age."

The victim was naked like she had been when first discovered, an evidence sheet lying in wait at the end of the autopsy table. The victim's clothes had been taken. Every stitch of them. From her socks and shoes to her pants and shirt and even her undergarments. All of it was gone, not a trace of them found in the surrounding areas either. The immediate question asked was why? The answer sickeningly simple. The killer had removed any risk of leaving behind their DNA evidence. However, they'd overlooked something, and it was beneath one of the victim's fingernails.

I did a cursory walk around the table while Derek and

Samantha continued with the formalities. It was the evidence bag on the victim's hand that was of interest. But it was the victim's toes I saw first. At the crime scene, they'd been covered by the snow. And in the morgue's lights, the colors stood out hideously bright against the victim's gray-blue skin. Every toenail was painted differently. There was electric pink and green and yellow and orange, all of them vibrant. I saw the rainbow, along with other shades too, the polish shiny and newer.

"Her toenails," I said, speaking when Samantha clicked off the recorder. Tracy joined me, noticing them for the first time also. "It looks like she might have had a recent pedicure."

"Or she did them herself?" Tracy offered, leaning close and focusing with her camera. She nodded with approval, adding, "They are nicely done."

"But not her fingernails?" I asked, having seen them at the crime scene. "There's no polish on them."

"Just a second," Samantha said, her eyes hidden slightly behind straight bangs. She blew a puff of air, her black hair clearing her face while she moved a camera over the right hand. On one of the screens, she zoomed in to show the nail bed and cuticles of the middle finger. Chipped, peeled and ragged along the edges, there'd been neon-orange nail polish recently. "Looks like she was a peeler."

"Yeah, I know the type," Tracy commented, dangling her fingers, old polish in a similar state. "I do that too, paint them, let them dry and then peel it for days. It's kinda satisfying."

"It was only a matter of time before she'd have done the same to her toenails."

Samantha moved the camera out of the way and directed her focus to the injuries around the neck area. The skin was littered in dark bruises the colors of a violent rainstorm. There were more now than when we first saw the victim. That can happen, bruising postmortem. The scale of what the killer did to this girl was horrific.

"Sam, you were able to confirm strangulation?" I asked, verifying the initial assessment, which had also been conveyed to our chief. Her eyelids closed slowly as if stuck half-lidded. I'd seen the look before, and it said she couldn't confirm. "What is it?"

Shuffling the stool toward the front, Samantha attached a scope to the camera, saying, "There's bruising around the neck and signs of petechia in the eyes and on the victim's face."

"Strong indications of strangulation," Tracy said, taking a picture of the blood-red rash on the victim's eyelids. "You found something?"

"Take a look," Samantha said, opening the victim's mouth, a white light shining on the end of the scope. When the scope traveled inside, I would have expected the victim's cheeks and neck to glow a blood-orange color. It didn't. The dead don't bleed, the vessels drained and already pooling. Samantha thumbed another monitor, the scope relaying a picture from the back of the victim's throat. "With the extensive bruising, I was looking for damage to the larynx or further down into the windpipe, maybe even a fracture in the neck."

"The bones in her neck? Were they damaged?" I asked. Samantha nudged the point of her chin at the wall showing the X-rays, the bones intact and without injury. Confused by the level of bruising found around the victim's throat, I asked, "The cause of death might not be strangulation?"

Eyes flashing with a nod. "Certainly, it contributed to her death." She removed the scope, the victim's jaw fixed open. Samantha closed the mouth slowly and with care, touching the side of the victim's face gently. "The writing in the snow, the way it was scribbled, I suspect the victim was suffering from cerebral hypoxia."

"A lack of oxygen to the brain," Tracy commented, brushing past me. "Not asphyxiation?"

"Good question. Generally, in the case of strangulation, the airways are blocked, leading to asphyxiation," Samantha began to answer, running her fingertips over the bruising. "But these bruises, it's like the killer was careful and squeezed hard enough to interrupt the blood flow to the brain."

"Like a string tied around your finger, cuts the circulation off," Derek said, adding to the explanation.

"Causing the bruises and hypoxia, low levels of oxygen in the blood," Tracy said, continuing around to the front, adding pictures of the bruises. "Her brain was starved."

"Starved? The writing—" I began, unsure about the differences discussed. Shifting back to the snow, the letters in it. "We still have to review the writing and make sense of what was written."

"Well, that's just it," Samantha replied. "To the victim, the letters might have made sense. But to anyone else, they were scribbles."

"Because of the hypoxia," I said, beginning to understand. "But if the victim fell unconscious, how was she able to write anything?"

Samantha frowned, lips pinched. She had an idea and from the look on her face, it was bad. She shined a light on the victim's eyes, continuing. "Petechial hemorrhages, which occur in both asphyxia and hypoxia." It wasn't an answer to my question, and I narrowed my focus. Samantha took a breath, "With the high number of bruises around the neck and the significance of petechial hemorrhages, I believe the victim lost consciousness, woke up, her mind already altered as she attempted to write in the snow."

"The killer didn't notice the writing but saw that she was awake," I said. Tracy's camera shutter clicked in rapid succession. "That's when they continued with the strangulation?"

"Possibly. It's still unclear exactly what happened," she replied, shaking her head. "But this level of petechia and bruising, whatever occurred in that junkyard, it lasted a long time."

I leaned in, sickened by an idea. "Do you think the killer stopped on purpose, like they were relishing in the act and didn't want it to end?"

Her brow rose, eyes widening as she regarded the question. "Detective, I can tell you the science. I can tell you everything about what caused this girl's death," Samantha answered with a deep sigh. "But I can't explain the motives of who killed her."

"Fair," I said, searching the victim's neck, my eyes locked on the bruises. "The science then. Can we get anything else from these injuries?"

"Well, I believe our killer's initial attack was a strangulation, the air passage blocked which caused the petechia. But then they pulled back. They stopped. It could be they got distracted before returning to start again."

"Or, the killer was adjusting their position," I said, moving to join them and re-enacting. Sentiment slammed deep inside me, realizing the battle this poor girl endured. Voice breaking, I continued. "What else?"

"I'll know more with a full autopsy," she began, running her gloved fingers through the victim's hair. "This was a prolonged torture. Whether it was on purpose or the victim fighting back, I can't say."

Goosebumps rose like the hairs on the back of my neck, a sticky heat beneath my arms. I hated to think it, but there were cases when I was glad to know death came swiftly. The idea of being awake and extending the suffering on purpose sickened me. I cleared my throat and asked the hard question, "If she did regain consciousness, how long?"

"Injuries were severe enough to end her life. I would think it was seconds, possibly a minute," Samantha answered. "There would have been terrible confusion, severe listlessness, an inability to move. But thankfully, brain injuries aren't generally associated with pain."

"Casey, that's when the killer took the victim's clothes,"

Tracy said, painting a timeline. She shook her head. "The killer would have thought she was already dead."

"Would she have been alert enough to understand what was happening?" I said, questioning and hoping the victim didn't know.

Samantha could only shake her head again. After a moment, she answered, "If she was aware enough, she may have believed this was survivable and held the hope of escape."

"God, how terrifying," Tracy replied.

"I'll have more answers to share once the full autopsy is performed," Samantha said, stepping down and shoving the step stool toward the victim's midsection. The stool's rubber feet screeched, the noise alarming. It didn't faze Samantha as she climbed back with a grim look on her face. "I've also confirmed there were signs of a sexual assault."

"Was there any evidence collected?" I asked, the hopefulness fleeting. With the killer having removed the victim's clothes, I couldn't believe they'd be inept enough to leave behind any other physical evidence.

"We collected what may be spermicide." Samantha seemed to glare at the victim's body, bothered, the subject always a difficult one. "The lab results will be included in the full report."

"That'll get us a list of condom brands that have spermicide," Tracy suggested. She ducked behind her camera, checking the battery. "Kinda sick but I think we've already got that list."

"I think we do," I commented. I went to the end of the table, assessing the violence. "This assault is as ugly as they get."

"I would agree with that," Samantha said while lifting the evidence sheet to end the preliminary review. "It's one of the worst I've seen in my career."

FIVE

I pushed open the door to the station, the wintry air following like an uninvited guest. Tracy was right behind me, her boots squeaking against the wood floor, each step echoing in the near-empty station. She shook herself in an attempt to rid the cold, but the heating had been out for days, and the chill had turned biting like the morgue. We'd traveled from cold to colder and then even more cold. My breath clouded in front of me for a second before disappearing while Tracy wrapped her coat tightly. I did the same, deciding to leave it on while we tended to the work.

"Hi, Alice," I began, stopping to shiver.

"Hi, Casey," Alice called from behind her desk, her voice muffled slightly by the thick wool scarf she'd wrapped around her neck. "Karl's at it again, trying to fix the damn heater."

"Gosh, any hope of it working soon?" Tracy asked in a stutter through chattering teeth.

"Afraid not, dear," Alice replied, her bonnet of thick hair unmoving as she poked a pencil into it. She put on a helpful grin, adding, "I put a small space heater in the conference room."

"Then it's the conference room we'll work in," I replied.

I glanced toward the hallway where Karl Levkin, our station's handyman, was staring hard at the thermostat. Expressionless, his gaze fixed, he had his hands against the wall like he was holding it in place, his focus beaming on the appliance controlling the heater. He wore his usual faded dungarees and a plaid shirt that looked older than some of the evidence boxes stacked in the back room. He broke his stance to give us a wave and courteous smile. It didn't last, his brow returning to a furrowed concentration, thick fingers taking hold to carefully fiddle with a spaghetti mess of wires that I was sure had seen better days.

"That does not look promising?" I said, asking, and rubbed my hands together for warmth.

Alice shrugged, her eyes rolling just enough to show how fed up she was. "I'm not holding my breath. The heater's been on the fritz since last Tuesday."

Karl, hearing our conversation, straightened up, cracking his back with an audible pop. "It's an old system, Casey. They don't make 'em like they used to." He flashed me a grin, wrinkles spreading across his dark skin, the heater likely adding a few today. "But I'm getting close. Shouldn't be long now."

I smiled despite the cold. "Thanks, Karl. Appreciate it."

Tracy nudged me with her elbow. "At this rate, we'll be wearing snow boots at our desks."

Alice snorted. "Speak for yourself. I've already got my thermal socks on."

We shared a laugh, a rare moment of lightness in a job where laughter was often scarce. But that was the thing about this station—it had its quirks, but it was home. The wood floors were worn smooth from years of traffic, the walls a pale beige, the paint chipping in some of the corners, and a few ceiling tiles were discolored from some recent water damage that Karl hadn't gotten around to fixing yet. It wasn't perfect but it was our station; it was our place where I felt at home and where I belonged, despite some of the chaos that came through its doors.

Tracy and I made our way past Alice's counter and stepped through the small wooden gate that separated the front of the station from the desk area where we worked. Our cubicles were tucked in the back, near the fishbowl, a nickname I'd given the conference room because of its floor-to-ceiling glass walls. You could see everything and everyone inside, very little privacy, just like being trapped in a fish tank.

As we reached our cubicles, I dropped my gear onto my desk and chair with a heavy plunk. My crime-scene gear and the evidence collected from the junkyard weighed heavy in my bag, both physically and mentally. It had been a long day already and it wasn't nearly over yet. Tracy followed suit, unceremoniously tossing her coat onto the back of her chair, a laptop bag onto the desk, and heavy camera gear slipping down her arm to rest on the floor.

"I need a gallon of coffee," she said, offering, and rubbed her arms for warmth. "Want some?"

"What do you think? Yes," I replied emphatically. The thought of something hot was too good to pass up.

We headed into the conference room where its large table dominated the center of the room, the surface scratched and worn from years of use. On the front wall, massive monitors waited for us to plug in and pull up the photos from the junkyard. Tracy returned with coffees in hand as I snapped a pair of latex gloves over my hands and then spread the evidence bags across the conference room table. The smell of coffee filled the room, mingling with the scent of paper and ink and latex gloves which always seemed to linger here.

"Here," Tracy said, handing me a steaming cup before settling into a chair. "Let's get this laid out."

I took a sip of the coffee, feeling the warmth spread through me as I continued to arrange the evidence bags, separating each of the item types we'd found. River stones. Bottle caps. Leaves. Sticks. All were found in neat little piles, carefully placed like some twisted offering. Was that what they were? An offering? Questions mounted.

Tracy powered up her laptop, a soft hum breathing from it as she connected the back to a cable snaking toward the center of the table where it disappeared. The front screens flickered to life, flashing white before the pixels came to life, too. "Let's start with the photos."

The first image appeared on the screen and instantly gave me pause. It was a close-up of the bottle caps, arranged in a perfect pyramid. Its shape was both odd and deliberate and had zero meaning in relation to anything else we saw in the junkyard. I pinched the corner of the evidence bag containing the bottle caps, opening it and removing a green one, the name on its face barely legible. "Who takes the time to do something like this?" I muttered, my stare returning to the screen. "Maybe it's a ritual?"

"Or maybe it's just fanatical or crazy," Tracy offered, leaning back in her chair.

I squinted and motioned for her to zoom in. She did and I moved closer, saying, "Look at the precision. Whoever did this wasn't in a rush."

"That means they had time?"

"Which means it wasn't a spur of the moment, the piles were there before the murder." I reached for the evidence bag again, the bottle caps rattling as I searched them. "These were collected and then arranged intentionally."

"Move on to the next one?" Tracy asked.

"Wait," I said, the heater unit clamoring a raucous bang from the vents. I flinched, saying, "There was snow on the bottle caps. Derek cleared it from the piles."

"Uh-huh?" Tracy agreed, questioning. When she understood, she added, "That suggests the piles were already there."

"We just don't know how long."

Tracy clicked to the next photo, pixels shifting to a pile of river stones this time. "What do you think the stones mean?"

"Stones can be symbolic. At one time, certain types were thought to ward off illness and unhappiness," I said, carefully opening the evidence bag and removing one of them, holding it up to the light. "Or it could be nothing at all. Sometimes a stone is just a stone."

Tracy frowned. "I don't know, Casey. Look at how they're arranged. Stones, bottle caps, leaves, sticks. I'd think there has got to be meaning here. An intention or a message maybe?"

"But what?" I asked, nodding slowly. She had a point. Everything about this scene felt calculated, like the killer was trying to tell us something. Frustrated, I asked, "If there's a hidden message here, then what the hell is it?"

"I have no idea," Tracy answered, shaking her head.

"Let's try to break it down some more," I said, returning the stone to the next evidence bag. I picked up another evidence bag, the leaves inside, which I believed to be cattail leaves, dried and brittle. "Why leaves? And why these leaves? It's winter, so these had to have been collected during the summer."

"Were there any chutes around the junkyard?" Tracy asked, filling a third screen with pictures of swampy grounds, red-winged blackbirds perched on the fronds of a cattail plant.

"None. Junkyards aren't exactly known for their lush vegetation."

Tracy crossed her arms, staring at the screen as if the photos might start telling us their secrets. "The leaves had to have come from somewhere else then. He brought them with him, but from where?"

"I don't think it'll help the case. There must be a thousand places around the islands," I said, adding a complication. "Still, it feels like a lot of effort for something like cattail leaves."

Tracy clicked to another photo, this one showing the sticks. They were mostly piled but a few seemed to have been arranged in a subtle starburst pattern, radiating out from a central point. "I almost missed this when Derek was blowing the snow from them."

"It almost looks like a compass. Doesn't it?"

Her brow rose with a nod. "Yeah, a compass."

"You know what else?" I leaned closer to the screen. "Nothing random here either. That pattern is precise."

"What if the killer is trying to make it look like it means something when it really doesn't?" Tracy countered. "It could be misdirection."

I regarded what Tracy said, a hint of pride rising in me. She was thinking like a detective. I went with it, asking, "So you think the killer is playing with us? Trying to lead us down a rabbit hole?"

"Sure. It wouldn't be the first time either." Tracy shrugged, pulling up the final image on the monitor. "This is a killer who seems to really like dressing up a crime scene, and keep us guessing."

"That they do." The last photo was of the entire scene, an aerial shot she'd managed using a drone. It let us see far and wide, confirming no cattails in the vicinity. It also showed the victim at the center of the crime, and how all the piles were placed in the junkyard. I'd wanted the picture, hoping to see if there was something in the placement, like a map, the piles positioned at intervals, forming a kind of pattern. "Let's take a look at the spacing."

Tracy leaned forward, narrowing her eyes. "You think the placement of the piles is important?"

"I don't know yet." I sighed, rubbing the back of my neck. "But I want to cover everything we can think of."

Tracy stood up, pacing around the room as she thought. "Okay, let's assume for a second that the killer is trying to tell us something and the language used implies meaning in the piles, the types of materials selected?"

"The types," I muttered, staring at the bags of evidence, running through every possible scenario in my head. "Stones, bottle caps, leaves, sticks... What connects them?"

"How about three natural materials and a single man-made object?" Tracy suggested.

"The sticks are broken so the lengths are the same, which is the same with the other piles. The stones are relatively the same size as the bottle caps." I frowned, feeling like the killer had our number and led us to the lip of the largest rabbit hole there ever was. We had to speculate and throw every idea out there though. It was like wading through rough waters to reach the truth. "But if it is three natural materials and a man-made material, then why mix them? If this was just about nature, why add the bottle caps? Is he saying there's a collision between nature and industry? That's why he picked the junkyard?"

Tracy raised an eyebrow. "Junkyards are places where the man-made world meets decay."

"Could be," I said, though the theory didn't sit quite right with me. "I don't know. That feels a bit too philosophical. Don't you think?"

"Yeah, maybe we're reading too much into it," Tracy admitted, dropping into her chair. "Maybe the items don't mean anything. Maybe they're just there."

"Or maybe it's about leading us to think there's no connection, same idea as what you said earlier," I said softly, staring at the photos. "Maybe the point is to make us question everything."

Tracy looked at me, looking tired, daylight fading in the nearby window. "So what's our next move?"

"It's getting late." I glanced at the clock. We were running out of time. The longer we spent chasing these theories, the colder the trail would get. But something about this crime scene gnawed at me. There was a message here, hidden in plain sight, and we had no idea what it was. "We'll keep digging."

"Digging," she replied, both of us standing up and grabbing the next bag of evidence. "Want to start fresh in the morning?"

"Fresh in the morning," I agreed, repeating her words. "One piece at a time, we'll make sense of whatever chaos this killer is up to."

SIX

Love struck us like lightning. It sounds corny, but that's what I tell people when they ask how we got together. It's not far from the truth either. Not really. I mean, there may not have been some heavenly flash shooting through the clouds, but in my heart, I felt it. Almost immediately too, I just didn't recognize what it was until I was head over heels in love.

I'd come to the Outer Banks with a clue in hand. It was the final clue in the case of my missing daughter. But there had been a murder, a body found on a boat, and the chief needed an experienced detective. The chief of police offered a trade, Jericho's time for my time. I didn't know the Outer Banks or the surrounding areas and accepted the help. That summer, we worked closely on two cases, solving both and falling in love.

February winds bit at the tip of my nose and chin, the walk from the car to our place taking longer than usual. I stopped midway when I saw the heart-shaped sign on the door. It warmed me instantly. It was wrapped in a shiny red bow with the words "Love of my Life" in the middle. While it was sappy and even a bit over sentimental, I loved it. After a day like today, it helped.

Jericho had been busy. The sign wasn't store-bought: I recognized the cellophane and the ribbon used to make it. Not that I needed store-bought, it was the thought that meant most to me. The evening was late, and the day had gone five hours past a typical shift. I'd missed dinner and cleaning up and helping to tuck the kids into bed.

I was late but why the heart? There was an envelope taped to the door too, a pretty card inside reading *Be My Valentine*. My heart dropped. Shit. I grabbed my phone as if my checking the date on the screen would magically roll it back a day. It wouldn't. Valentine's Day was only a few hours from being over too, and I'd completely forgotten it. Jill Carter?

Tracy

I texted, hitting send immediately. My hands shook from the cold while I took the Valentines from the door.

You awake?

Yup, she replied. *What's up?*

It's about Jill Carter's murder.

I stopped texting and braced against a strong ocean breeze, the scent of sea salt faint in the colder air. Working the house keys, fingertips numb, I got inside and shut the door, finishing the text.

It's Valentine's Day.

That's right! It could be significant?

The dots bounced while she continued typing, stopping a

moment. I slipped my bag and coat off, unfurling my scarf and plopping them onto the kitchen table. My firearm was next, stowing it securely, alongside my badge, the tin sweating from the sudden change in temperature.

What are you thinking?

Jill Carter's murder occurring on this day. I don't think it's a coincidence.

Until I saw the Valentine on the front door, we didn't have a motive in mind. There was premeditation though, given the crime took place in a junkyard, along with the collections displayed around the body. While we suspected the pile of stones and bottle caps were there prior to the murder, we had no evidence to support it. Only speculation. Still, the existence of them supported premeditation.

Coffee. Instant. Not ideal, but my day wasn't done yet. There was another case I was working and I needed to check on it before going to bed. I ran the water until it was hot and reached for a spoon, my fingers landing on another Valentine. I went weak immediately. This Valentine's card was from Thomas, the letters spelling my name made scribbly, along with a heart and an XOXO for hugs and kisses. I had to put my phone down and joined his Valentine with Jericho's. If there was one from Thomas, then there was one from Tabitha too.

"Where would she—" I began, searching the kitchen. On the counter where the can of instant coffee was, I found Tabitha's Valentine. She was a few years younger than Thomas, the children becoming our family recently. We'd been their foster parents briefly after their parents were brutally murdered. Adoption was next, the idea of living without them in our lives quickly becoming impossible. Her heart was wobbly and shaped more like a circle, but still a wonderful surprise.

"You found them," Jericho asked, wrapping his arms around me and planting a kiss on my cheek. Half-lidded, his eyes sleepy. I glanced at the clock on the microwave, the time early. He noticed that I noticed and answered fast, "Getting old. After schoolwork and baths and cleaning up, I couldn't stay awake."

"Thank you," was all I could say. Since his retirement from the Marine Patrol, he'd been doing the heavy lifting. His days were filled with being a stay-at-home dad, the career in law enforcement behind him. Sometimes I worried he was going to miss it, but that hadn't happened yet. Not once. He was enjoying this new life with me and Thomas and Tabitha.

It bothered me that I'd completely forgotten what day it was, coming home late and empty-handed. I could do better. His eyes were deep and puffy from sleep, gray pouches surrounding his blue-green eyes. There was a week's worth of stubble too, which I liked on him. It wasn't so scraggly that it hid the dimple in his chin, but gave him that rugged Indiana Jones look that turned a few heads whenever we went out. I took his face in my hands and kissed him long and hard, ending it with an apology, "I'm sorry."

"About?" he asked, confused.

"I forgot it was Valentine's Day."

He didn't reply and turned toward the canister of instant coffee. From the cabinet, he got my mug and began to make it. That was his way. He'd get busy doing something in the kitchen versus telling me how he was feeling.

"Cream?" he asked.

"Babe? You're mad?" I asked. But Jericho wasn't the type to get mad. Especially over something like a missed Valentine. He shook his head and worked the stove's burner to heat the water. "Talk to me."

"The kids." He tapped the Valentines. "They were really looking forward to seeing you."

I cringed, hating that I'd disappointed them. "The time on

the case got away from me," I answered, heat rising in my voice. The guilt had put me a bit on the defensive, but it was only a reaction. I was mad at myself. "It's a bad case. You remember what that can get like?"

"I do, which is why I think it's a concern," he said, steam rising from the cup while he scooped the coffee, shaking his head. I knew it was his son he was talking about. Their relationship was better now. But for a long time, they weren't good. Jericho handed me my mug, taking my hands in his while I held it. I froze, saying nothing. It was those eyes of his, like he'd known me forever. "I just don't want you to make the same mistakes I did."

"I can do better," I told him, setting the coffee aside. My eyelids sprang open with an idea, a giggle slipping from my lips. "How about heart-shaped pancakes in the morning. I'll dress them up with whipped cream and some chocolate chips?"

"Bribery?" He laughed. "Yeah, they'll love it."

I looked past Jericho, at the small room in our apartment we used as office space. It wouldn't be that way much longer, the shared bedroom for Thomas and Tabitha needing a split. That, or we'd have to find a new place. "Mind if I catch up on the other case?"

"Tonight?" he asked, frowning.

Like the chief, the FBI, the US Marshals, and a few other government agencies, neither Jericho nor any one of them approved of my off-hours work on a case for which I had zero jurisdiction. I didn't need jurisdiction though. Not when it was my fault. A woman was dead, and an evil was released upon the world. Indirectly, both were my fault. His name was Dr. P.W. Boécemo, and while working as a detective in Philadelphia, I'd put him behind bars. When there was an opportunity for parole, I successfully nixed his chances to keep him behind bars. Only, he'd orchestrated an escape which included the murder of an innocent woman.

Dr. P.W. Boécemo was a psychiatrist and when I'd put my guard down, he got into my head. I can still hear our conversations. The deep discussions about my daughter. The guilt. The blame. A shiver ran down my spine, planting goosebumps on my arms. Had I been that easy to read? Or was the doctor really that good? I'd like to think the latter but none of what we talked about mattered now. If the doctor was free, that meant there were lives in danger.

"You won't stay up too long?"

"Thanks, I won't be long," I said, pecking Jericho's cheek with a kiss, the stubble tickling. Before leaving, I brushed his face and kissed him longer. "Happy Valentine's Day."

The apartment was warm. The thermostat set high. The shoes and socks came off. And then the bra, ditching every stitch in favor of some cotton pajamas. We were barely making it in the small apartment. The bedrooms taken. The rest of the rooms filling fast with toys and clothes and the dozens of other things children need. I had a corner that was mine. A whiteboard installed, along with a computer, desk and chair. There was a repurposed nightstand with bundles of yarn and thumbtacks, and a short stack of index cards. These were the ingredients I'd used when working my daughter's missing persons case. The recipe for them was on the wall. Every clue about Dr. Boécemo's whereabouts, the last sightings, the original police reports, even notes from the guards in prison. All of it was on the wall with yarn strung from one to the next, a colorful pattern emerging.

There was an online sleuthing group working the case with me which included an old friend, Nichelle Wilkinson. She'd been a member of the team, her technical expertise spotted by the FBI, who were quick to recruit her. Thankfully, she still had time to help online, and I thumbed the switch on the monitor, the pixels warming until they were bright enough to make me squint.

"Nichelle, sorry it's late, you on?" I asked, the chat window showing that we hadn't talked in a few days.

"You're up late," she replied.

"I could say the same about you." Sipping the lukewarm coffee, the bitterness made me cringe. It was the caffeine jolt I was after, needing at least an hour of time online. *"Did you guys get hit with the snow too?"*

"Couple inches. Not bad though," she answered. The chat dots danced, stopping briefly. When they started and stopped again, I knew what Nichelle was going to ask. She'd been close to Tracy. Very close. The two had shared their lives briefly, Nichelle ending it when she accepted the FBI job. *"Tell Tracy I said hi."*

"Did you lose her number?" I asked, the question carrying a bit of snark. They were good together and, in my heart, I thought they'd be able to make a long-distance relationship work. When Nichelle didn't reply, I followed up with, *"Just text her a heart emoji and Happy Valentine's."*

"Well," she wrote back. *"Not sure it's a good idea but I'll think about it."*

"Maybe, just a hello then? It'd lift Tracy's spirits. She hasn't been herself," I typed but didn't hit send. I wasn't sure how much I should share. It was true that Tracy had been off since Nichelle's move to Philadelphia. But it wasn't just the breakup that had her down. There was more going on. I slowly closed my eyes as if eliminating the pixel-light could hide the truth somehow. It was the kidnapping that bothered her. My daughter was remembering more of what had happened to her. Her kidnappers were gone, and with them, they took the weeks and possibly months that went unaccounted for. Only Tracy

knew what happened and she was remembering more of it. Having second thoughts, I pressed the backspace, erasing what'd been typed. Instead, I sent, *"It'd be good to say hi."*

Nichelle replied with a smiley emoji, typing, *"The doctor?"*

"We picked up a new case today. This killer's M.O. may have something to do with collecting things."

"Collecting victims?" she asked. I knew where she was going. *"Serial killer?"*

"Unconfirmed, but I'll keep you updated," I entered fast, not wanting her to run a report up through her directors. *"Anything in your area?"*

"I picked up local chatter about a suspicious man lurking around the Oxford Valley Mall."

"Bucks County?" I asked, leaning forward. It was a suburb of Philadelphia and one of the places the doctor had called home. *"Arrests?"*

"None," she answered. *"The description matched the doctor though."*

"Send it to me?" I asked, uncertain if the chatter was public or secured through the FBI. *"If you can."*

"Sent," she typed. *"Gotta run. I'll catch you later?"*

"Always and thank you."

An email emoji popped out of the lower corner of my screen, the clue sitting in my inbox. Before Nichelle was gone, I reminded her, *"Don't forget to say hi to Tracy."*

A thumbs-up emoji flashed briefly before her status showed she was gone, the green online status shifting to offline.

The email was short, containing a paragraph with a description of a man standing around the mall's food court and talking to some girls. They were all twelve and thirteen, one of them calling their parents when the man wouldn't leave them alone. He disappeared by the time the police arrived, but the descriptions given were consistent and without contradiction. Better yet, it matched the doctor. I updated the wall, adding a new index card with the time and location and circumstance, along with a length of red yarn, the clue hot and new. Sitting back, eyelids heavy, sleep was tempting me to end the long day. I'd give in to it in a few minutes but for the moment, I looked at the clue-wall, feeling content that some progress had been made.

SEVEN

The heart-shaped pancakes were a hit, Thomas and Tabitha barely making eye contact while they gobbled the sugary goodness. Batter and butter and tons of syrup, the sticky mess was everywhere, and thankfully, Jericho was a good sport about helping me clean up after.

I'd stayed up later than I should to work on the Dr. P.W. Boécemo case. But it was Jill Carter's murder that had me tossing and turning. Every hour on the hour, it stirred me awake. I'd flip my pillow and watch the icy rain sliding down the window, their shadowy globs appearing on the far wall.

It was the meeting this morning that was putting knots in my stomach. Samantha met with the Carters yesterday, performing the duties of medical examiner to offer a preliminary report about their daughter's death. This had to include the morbid details about the attack. As a courtesy, she'd also called later to let me know what questions the couple asked. It was what I'd expect to hear this morning, and it was going to be difficult.

"Anything stick out?" I asked.

Tracy grunted, her focus sticking to the laptop screen where the crime-scene pictures showed the bottle caps and the pebbles. She joined me for the interview, the drive taking us north to Corolla. The rains had stopped, the temperature warming, steam rising from the mounds of plowed snow. "The victim's home is walking distance to the school."

"I noticed," Tracy answered, tucking her hair behind her ear. I didn't say anything, but she looked tired. Restless was a better word. I didn't think it was the case, given it was new, still fresh with us just getting started. Maybe it was the breakup with Nichelle? I let out a sigh, trying not to worry. She turned her laptop enough for me to see a map with three pins dropped. "Jill Carter's home is a fifteen-minute walk from the school. The junkyard is at least ten minutes more in the opposite direction."

"To your right," I said, passing Jill's school. It was a set of three red and brown brick buildings with hallways connecting them. School buses were lined up outside, a dozen or so, the tailpipes puffing gray smoke, the day's students already attending their first class. "The victim would have walked along here and then made a left at the intersection."

"What if—" Tracy began to say, laptop sliding while she unbuckled and twisted.

"Cameras?" I asked.

"Uh-huh." She ducked her head to look forward and back, shaking it. "I don't see any municipal ones, other than what the school has for security."

I squinted, finding the cameras tucked up near the roof. "I'd say we'll want to visit the school this morning too."

"We're not getting anything from those," she replied, her tone hard. She saw that I noticed and followed with, "I mean, you know, the distance."

"I know what you meant," I answered, softening my voice. I wanted to ask what was bothering her, but we had a case to work, the priority set. "Doubtful we'll identify the victim walking along here. But we might see if any students were picked up?"

"A car," Tracy replied, understanding. She leaned forward, searching outside the driver-side window. "Those houses, they might have a doorbell camera that picked up something too."

The brakes squealed when I slowed to a stop at the intersection, the school property ending. "We're going to get our steps today. Door to door."

"From here, a right turn takes us toward the junkyard," Tracy said, zooming in on the map, the image's pixels turning blocky. It cleared up to show the intersection, the trees and shrubs in full bloom, the pictures on the map taken during the summer. "Turn left, and we're a block from the victim's house."

I spun the wheel left, accelerating forward, the houses set further back from the road. They were larger and expensive, the neighborhood affluent. "What do you have on the parents?"

"Let's take a look," Tracy said, the clickity-clack of the keyboard filling the car. "I found them, Carter and Evans Esquire."

"Lawyers? Both?"

"Real estate from the looks of it," she replied. Tapping through a web page, reading. "Commercial primarily, some residential too."

"Nice place," I said, turning to park in a long driveway. Two cars were parked beneath the house, both SUVs, limited editions with all the trimmings. The house was stilted, as many were in the area, the front door a level above the driveway, the steps cleared of snow. Cedar tiles that were painted sunshine yellow; the shutters and door were farmhouse red. The curtains were drawn in all but one of the windows, a woman staring out of it, a cup of coffee in her hands. "They're waiting."

"Here we go," Tracy said, closing the laptop and tucking it into a bag. For a moment I thought to ask her if she was up for the interview. She must have sensed it, turning as if to say something. She didn't and opened the car door, cold sea air rushing inside. "I swear it's colder here."

Zipping my coat, I braced for the outside and rushed to the steps. It was cold enough to see my breath and I clutched Tracy's arm, the steps creaking while we ascended carefully. The front door opened slowly, a man and woman appearing. They were a good-looking couple, as was their daughter. I could see Jill Carter in their faces, the resemblances shared between them. His with the large eyes and a thin nose, and hers with the auburn hair, high cheekbones and a narrow chin.

"I salted the steps," the man said, the door opened wide.

When our eyes met, he put on a welcome smile, the kind we don't even think about, the basic instincts and muscle memories driving for us when our brains are elsewhere. The woman next to him sipped from her cup, eyes vacant, brow narrowed with grief. Extending a hand, he continued, "Sam Carter. My wife, Janine Evans."

"Detective Casey White," I answered, slipping off a mitten, the cold replaced by his warm hand. Tracy did the same. "And my colleague, Tracy Fields."

"Please, come inside," Jill's mother said. The couple looked to have been in their early forties, possibly younger. We followed them indoors, the foyer large with a tiled floor and tall ceiling. A rack of shoes was to the left, a sign above it, reading: "We kindly ask you to remove your shoes." I began to slip my snow boots off, the victim's mother, saying, "That's very nice of you. Given the circumstances, I don't mind if you leave them on."

The floors were pretty. Clean and polished. I didn't need guilt weighing on my questions. My left boot came off with a burp. "I don't mind at all."

"I've made coffee and tea," she continued, and turned to lead us into a short hallway. The walls were lined with photographs, family portraits and school pictures of the victim. I searched each of them, looking for anything that'd strike me as odd. None did.

A whiff of warm coffee and pastry reached me when we entered the kitchen. The counter was made up as if a conference were taking place. There were cups and saucers, two carafes with pumps, one of them labeled *decaf*. I stopped short at the breakfast nook, a breath stuck in my throat.

The chairs were pulled away and placed against the wall. A sizable armory was on the table, lights gleaming from a stash of firearms and ammo covering most of the table. There were rifles and shotguns, pistols big and small. Some of them I recognized, the types common. But there were others which I'd never seen before, the collection broad and impressive. None of the ammunition was loose, which might indicate none of the guns were loaded. Still, the sight of it gave me pause, my instincts having me step in front of Tracy. When Jill Carter's father went to the table, I abruptly asked, "Sir?"

"Damn things," Jill's mother said, annoyance flaring. She proceeded to fill a coffee cup, the pump wheezing. She stopped and looked up, eyes wet. "All that protection. A lot of good it did."

Jill's father grunted and cleared his voice. "I read that the police would accept firearms if I wanted to turn them in?" His neck and face had turned blotchy, a light sheen on his brow. He was nervous, which made me nervous. When I didn't answer immediately, he straightened himself, adding, "I assure you, they're all legally purchased. I-I just don't want them anymore."

"I believe you're asking to forfeit your firearms?" I asked, nodding in Tracy's direction. It wasn't a common practice, but as a courtesy, under the circumstances, we could help. Jill's father nodded, face cramped with anguish. Tracy took to the task, making the arrangements. It occurred to me, a collector was apt to hold on to one or two. "Is this all of them?"

"Yes, ma'am. It is," he answered, wiping his face dry. "Jill went with me to the range all the time. She was steady and strong. A great shot, you know."

"A lot of good they were," Jill's mother repeated.

"You're right," he replied to his wife. "I couldn't protect her."

"I am deeply sorry for your loss," I said, offering my condolences. I wanted to tell them it wasn't their fault, that it wasn't anyone's fault, except the killer's. There were questions that needed to be answered first. Jill's mother nodded and handed me a cup. I accepted, though hadn't asked for one. "Would now be a good time to ask questions and to see your daughter's room?"

"Yes, certainly," Jill's father answered, shoving fingers through his hair, grays littering the dark brown color. "Anything you need. Anything at all."

"A squad car is on their way," Tracy said, accepting a cup from Jill's mother. Tracy approached the table, eyeing the firearms. "It will take some time, they'll index the serial numbers and have you sign a release."

"Sure. Sure. Yes," Jill's father answered. He moved a few chairs from the wall, legs scraping. Jill's mother went to sit on one, her eyes fixed on the firearms. "The medical examiner was... well—" Jill's father couldn't finish. He stood abruptly and went to a window, the glass streaked with rain.

"The medical examiner explained what may have killed our daughter." She dangled her fingers around her head, finishing, "My daughter's brain was deprived of oxygen. The damage severe."

"Yes, ma'am. It is our belief that the killer may have thought your daughter had died from strangulation. However, that was not the case."

"Fucking animal," Jill's father barked, fingers splayed against the window as he leaned into it. "She was our baby—"

Jill's mother got up, moving swiftly to join her husband. My stomach hurt for them, the pain inconsolable. After a moment, they returned to their seats. "We'll keep this short?" Jill's mother asked.

"Certainly. A few questions and we'll look at your daughter's bedroom?" I asked, not wanting to delay too long. "We can follow up with any additional questions later."

"Thank you," she answered, crossing her arms and legs. She closed her eyelids and remained that way.

"You both saw your daughter that morning?"

Jill's father looked past us toward a staircase. His wife opened her eyes.

"Before school?"

"We would have?" he said, asking his wife, a flash of guilt on his face. "Right?"

"Jill came downstairs... we talked about..." Jill's mother looked like she was about to cry. She covered her mouth and sucked in a breath. A moment passed and she broke down. "Why can't I remember?"

"It's okay, ma'am. Mornings with school and work, they're routine." I was speaking without thinking, trying to console what was inconsolable. Jill's clothes. We had nothing to work with. "How about your daughter's clothes? Could you tell us what she was wearing when she left the house?"

Blank faces. The question was met with empty expressions and wide eyes. And I regretted the question almost immediately. They didn't know. I'm sure they saw their daughter but didn't notice her or what she wore.

"Wait!" Jill's father said. He held his phone up. "We left together."

"Security footage?" Tracy asked. She opened her laptop, adding, "If you can send it, that'd be helpful."

"I'll do that," he replied, tapping his phone, pinching the screen. Brow rising, he exclaimed, "I got it."

"Text or email is fine," I told him, handing them our cards.

The reprieve softened his face. I wasn't here to make Jill's parents feel worse than they already were. "We'll review the footage."

"Did your daughter have a cell phone?" Tracy asked, continuing to type. Jill's parents nodded. "Any chance she shared an account with you? Cloud based?"

"It is," Jill's father answered, his focus pivoting to his phone, swiping eagerly. "We... well, we monitor her text messages and phone calls."

"We'll want to review them," I said, insisting. "If the account is shared, the messages will have been saved as long as there was a connection. When your daughter didn't arrive home, you called and tried to locate her phone?"

"Of course," Jill's mother answered gruffly, offended. She shrugged with a sigh, saying, "Sorry, I didn't mean... yes, we set up the phones under one account."

"When we called the police, we explained that Jill's last known location was the school," Jill's father explained. "I'm not sure what happened but with the storm, the cell connection was spotty."

"There was an outage that afternoon," Tracy said, turning her laptop around. "It was brief but certainly unfortunate."

"What if her phone was turned off?" Jill's mother asked.

"That's a possibility as well," I told her. "Which is why it's important for us to review her messages and see who she's been talking to."

"I can work with you to forward access," Tracy said, speaking softly.

"You think Jill was meeting someone without our knowing?" Jill's father asked, a shocked look on his face. "She'd never do that."

"It's all part of the investigation," Tracy assured him. "Can you provide us with a list of her friends?"

Jill's parents exchanged a look, his saying, "There were a few from school."

"A lot from school," Jill's mother explained. "They'd come here and go to her room."

"Claudia, or was it Cameron?" her father said, asking. "No! Shay. Shay was one of her friends."

"Shay?" Tracy asked, typing. When the silence came, she looked up from her laptop. "We'll get it."

"We're visiting the school next," I said, sensing the discomfort. "We'll get the names."

"Wait, I don't understand something. Earlier, you mentioned Jill's clothes," Jill's mother questioned, a frown deepening. She looked at me squarely, voice breaking. "Where are my daughter's clothes?"

"Ma'am," I began, my heart sinking like a stone. The spit in my mouth went dry, realizing Samantha hadn't shared the details about the crime scene.

"Could you tell us what happened to our daughter?" Jill's father asked. He glanced at his wife, seeking her permission. She nodded. His focus returned. "Please, Detective. The medical examiner told us some, but not all of it."

"Understand, we're working to fill in the gaps," Tracy answered.

"We understand," he replied.

"What we know so far is that the schools let out early due to the weather. We don't know who your daughter was with yet or where she went."

"She never came home," Jill's father said, staring blankly ahead. "I called the police."

"You did, and there was a patrol nearby," I replied, steering them from seeking fault in the police response. "An Amber Alert was issued when the patrol was unable to find your daughter."

"She was taken by then," Jill's mother said, looking up from her coffee. "They got her. Didn't they?"

"Yes, ma'am. That is our belief." I hated this part of the job. But as a parent, having gone through it too, I understood the need to know. It was more than knowing though. Impossible as it might seem, a mother wants to take every bit of pain their child felt. "We think that Jill was abducted soon after leaving the school grounds."

"And her clothes?" Jill's father asked again, his complexion growing pale. Fidgeting. Struggling to speak, his wife covered her mouth as he continued. "The medical examiner told us that there were signs of an assault... sexual. Our daughter was raped?"

"Yes," Tracy answered, glancing over briefly. I gave her a short nod. "Your daughter was taken to a salvage yard where she was assaulted. We believe her clothes were removed as a means of removing any evidence from the crime scene."

"You mean their DNA," Jill's mother said, disgusted. "Animals."

"Yes, ma'am," I replied.

With sharp concern, she said, "I know my daughter."

"Of course, you do—" her husband began.

"Shh! Lemme finish!" she snapped. "It's not about what she was wearing or said. I know my daughter. She wouldn't have gotten in a car or gone with someone without telling us first."

"That's good to know," I answered, Tracy noting it. "She regularly notified you of her whereabouts?"

"Always," Jill's mother replied like it was the law. And perhaps it was. "We keep a family calendar, every appointment and event. All of it."

"Could we get a copy of that too?" Tracy asked. Jill's father raised his phone, acknowledging.

"You said the salvage yard. Patsy's Junkyard?" he asked, his focus shifting to his phone. I nodded. He began to blink fast and swiped the screen a few times. When he found what he was looking for, he turned it around to show a picture of the junkyard, the front of it, the gates with the razor wire and sign, the trees green, the sky cornflower blue. "We're handling the sale of that property."

"With Patsy's children?" I asked, recalling what Jericho had said about the owners passing, the children taking over.

"Do you think it's related?" Jill's mother asked. She shook her head, saying, "I mean, we only started the paperwork the other day."

I glanced around the house, sizable for three people, Jill being an only child. From the outside, I'd seen a second path around the side, leading me to ask, "Your office?"

"It's a home office, but with a separate entrance," she answered. "An old in-law suite we converted after buying the house."

"We'll want to interview anyone who might have come into contact with your daughter," I said, carefully selecting my words.

"Certainly." I could see on their faces, the word selection didn't help, the conclusion immediately jumped. "You think the owners of Patsy's know something?"

"It's standard procedure to question everyone who could have been in contact with your daughter." I didn't share with them what I was thinking. The distance from the school to Patsy's Junkyard was too far to have walked in poor weather. That told me Jill Carter did get into a car. What I didn't know was whether she'd been abducted or that she knew her killer.

EIGHT

I understood the guns Jill Carter's father had put on display and wanting to forfeit them. His wife might not have recognized what it meant. Tracy as well. But I got it. It was about rage and the potential of it like water pressure building behind a dam. This wasn't about turning in something he no longer believed in. It was about his no longer trusting that he wouldn't lose control. I got it. I'd been there. I'd lost a daughter too. It was a long time ago and in some of the darkest moments of my life, I believe I could have seriously harmed or maybe even killed a person if they'd been responsible when my daughter went missing.

I wasn't always a homicide detective. That came much later for me. I'd started my career as a cop in Philadelphia where I wore a uniform and walked a daily beat. But I'd also been a wife and mother to a beautiful little girl too. Hannah was her name, and she was my heart and soul. She was my everything. And then one morning, she was gone. She was three when she'd been kidnapped. It happened in a flash like a bullet ripping through my heart. I'd be lying if I said it felt like anything less. Losing her tore a hole through me. But the real damage came after, when our lives fell apart. Truth is, there's only unrest, the kind that leaves you barely existing, which is a short step above a nightmare. That was where Jill Carter's parents were now and there was nothing we could do to relieve the hurt and pain they were going through.

Everyone said my daughter was gone, including her father. But I never stopped looking. Not once. They told me to close Hannah's case and salvage some normalcy in my life. I couldn't do that. I wouldn't do that. Just how do you do such a thing when nothing feels normal anymore? Not the birthdays. Not the holidays. Not the family visits. Not even the simple things like daylight and dusk, or the sunshine and rain. In a world without Hannah, none of it seemed normal anymore. Yet, every once in a while, peace found me. It teased with a hint of what life should feel like. I'm careful when I say that it found me because I refused to seek it out while I kept Hannah's missing person case open. In my heart and soul, I knew she was still alive.

Years after I became a detective, I followed the very last clue I had in Hannah's case. It'd been overlooked. Missed really. A slip of paper about the size of an index card that had fallen from my clue-wall. On it, I had a name and a phone number, and it had brought me to the Outer Banks, the barrier islands along the coast of North Carolina. It took every single clue I'd ever followed to reach that last one and finally reunite with my daughter. Fifteen years had passed since losing her, and that cheeky and giggly and cuddly toddler I once knew had grown into a beautiful young woman.

Nearly all the questions and nightmares had been put to rest too, the ones haunting me day in and day out. Where was she? Who had her? And the worst of them, what were they doing to my baby? There were some black holes though. There were some memory blocks, chunks of time that Hannah couldn't recall. But mostly, her memories were good ones, filled with a family she'd been a part of much of her life.

My daughter's name is Tracy now, the same Tracy Fields working alongside me. I don't know if serendipity is a thing or not, but a small miracle brushed our lives for the better. It hurts a bit whenever the urge to call her Hannah surfaces. I pinch my lips and bite my tongue and then take a breath, hoping she doesn't notice. Sometimes she does and I'll get a short look and then feel guilty for a past we'd no control over. If I'm being honest, I've gotten used to calling her Tracy, but in my heart, she'll always be baby girl Hannah.

Tracy walked past me as we entered Jill Carter's bedroom, leaving her parents alone in the kitchen with two officers. I expected an hour, possibly two to index each gun's serial number and then for Jill's father to sign each of them over, forfeiting the registrations. Our efforts shifted to the victim's bedroom which was everything a young teenage girl's bedroom could be. There were leftovers from her childhood such as stuffed bears and posters. There were also signs of adolescence and becoming a teenager, a stack of magazines for young women, a pile of romance novels mixed with fantasy and teenage angst.

"Didn't know anyone still read these," I commented, sifting through one of the magazines. "Thought everything was online."

"I still do," Tracy replied, surprising me. "Glass of wine or cup of tea. The end of the day and relaxing with a book or magazine."

"What a romantic," I said, a wave of nostalgia hitting me. "That was your father's thing. He loved his books."

"Where do we start?" Tracy asked, gloving her hands,

acknowledging mention of her father with a nod. It was time to get to work and I did the same, powder from the gloves drifting. I fixed my stare on the bedroom window, Tracy following. She studied the lock and raised the window, poking her head outside to inspect the roof. "There are no signs out here that the victim was sneaking in and out."

"No secret rendezvous," I commented, the window grating when Tracy closed it. The closet door hinges let out a chirp, the clothes inside typical. I shoved the bulk of them aside as if expecting to find a skeleton or two hidden in the darker recesses. "Let's see what else we have in here."

"Do you think she knew her parents were reading her messages?" Tracy asked. She'd moved to a tall oak dresser, opening the top drawer. "I mean, it's invasive, don't you think?"

"I think it was more about being protective than nosey," I answered without hesitating. "Think about some of our cases. You've seen first-hand what's out there."

"Yeah, but still. I'd want my privacy," she continued, shuffling through a handful of clothes.

"The kids these days will find a way. When they want privacy, they get it." I nudged my chin at a laptop next to the bed. It was thin and looked as if it might be newer. "Could be she had another account on there that her parents don't know about. We've seen that before."

"I'll see what I can find," Tracy answered, opening the laptop, a login prompt greeting her. "Locked, but that was expected."

"Can you get around it?" I asked, and immediately knew better. She gave me the look, one brow raised with a sneer. "Yeah, I know you can. Let's get permission first."

"I'll have to," she answered, leaving toward the door. "I didn't bring my gear."

Tracy was gone, silence descending into the room. I wanted to find something that stuck out. That had us exploring wild ideas of a secret life this young woman might have had that her parents didn't know about. My gut was saying that wasn't the case though.

"Well, hello," I grunted, my foot bumping a box in the corner. It was buried deep in the corner of the closet, too dark to have been seen. I dragged it into the bedroom's gray daylight, opening it. My nose itched from the dust, the box filled with school papers. Tests and reports, nearly every one of them scoring an A. "She cared enough to keep them." I sifted through some of the papers which were dated more recent, catching sight of one of her exams, a heart shape penned at the top with initials inside it. I closed the box and stood, my hands on my hips, turning around to find anything that'd tell us something.

"I got permission," Tracy said, the suddenness of her voice making me jump. She let out a laugh, apologizing, "Sorry."

"Sure, you are," I replied while she continued giggling. I held up the exam paper and handed it to her.

She cringed at the sight of it, reading the questions. "Science class. I was so bad at it."

"I thought you got straight As?" I asked, regretting the implication immediately.

Her brow popped, irritated. "Sure, I always got the top grades. But I had to work for them." She glanced at the exam again. "It's ironic that I ended up working in a field of science when it wasn't something I even liked back then."

"Really? What did you want to be?" I asked, surprised and curious. "Growing up, I thought I wanted to be an archeologist. You know, the Indiana Jones thing and all."

"No way!" Tracy exclaimed as if she'd had the same fantasy. She shook her head, grimacing. "You'd never find me digging in the dirt."

"Aren't you funny. So what was it?"

"An airline pilot. I always thought I'd fly one day and travel the world." She put the exam page in a blade of window light, asking, "The heart with initials M and G, that's what got your attention?"

I nodded, answering, "Might be nothing. Look at the date, it's recent."

Tracy took a picture of the exam paper too, commenting, "Late last week." She returned the exam paper and went to the laptop, adding, "I'll look for any names matching the same initials."

As we turned our attention to the laptop, I asked, "How long do you think it'll take to get on the laptop?"

"Not long." She held up a USB stick, showing it to me. It was the green one I'd seen before. "As long as I can cold-boot from this and the hard drive isn't encrypted, then we're good."

"Good," I said, watching the laptop screen flash briefly before turning black with a logo appearing in the middle. "I'll check the bed."

"Uh-huh," she mumbled, head down, fingers typing swiftly. "Good news, no encryption."

"Nothing on this side," I said, driving my hands beneath the mattress. I crawled around the bed, knees aching with a strike against the hard floor. "Nothing here, or here—"

"Casey," Tracy interrupted, the laptop's screen bright with photographs. "I mounted the main drive."

"Looks like some school pictures." I joined Tracy, thumbing the keyboard to turn up the brightness. "These would have been downloaded from her phone, right?"

"That's right, a cloud account," she answered, sweeping hair from her eyes. "If they were taken with her phone, they'd be shared with her parents' cloud account."

"Downloaded and then possibly deleted from her phone?" I asked, having seen photographs from my phone show up on my home computer, a cloud account synchronizing them. Nudging Tracy's shoulder, I commented, "Jill wanted privacy."

Tracy shook her head, questioning it. "Why though. They're just school pictures."

"Can you tile them?" I asked, kneeling, my eyes leveling with the laptop. "That'll let us seem more of them."

"Sure thing," she said, creating a page of thumbnails big enough to review.

"Click on that one." It was a classroom, the teacher sitting on the desk, a hundred pictures or more taped to the walls. There was lab equipment atop blacktop workbenches. "It's a science class."

"Why take a picture of it?" Tracy asked, panning and zooming in and out, searching the pixels as if one of them was a clue. "I'm not seeing anything."

"Seems to be centered on the teacher?" I questioned, the man sitting on the table looking studious with a soft-knit vest, white shirt, a thin beard and round glasses. "The focus is definitely on him."

"Like a student crush?" she asked.

"Possibly? Or maybe she was taking pictures for a school newspaper or something."

"That might not have been who Jill was taking a picture of," Tracy said, clicking on another. This one was in the hallway and centered on a boy standing in front of the lockers. He wore a denim jacket that matched torn jeans and had longish black hair that looked wet. Tracy flipped back to the other pictures, the same boy sitting in the classroom. "See, I think that's who she was photographing and the camera's autofocus framed the teacher."

"Good catch. The boy looks a couple years ahead of the victim," I said and checked my notes. "The victim's age is fifteen. A young fifteen. I think she must have skipped a grade."

"Look at the awards," Tracy said, and pointed to a shelf where there were plaques and ribbons. "Those are all academic."

"The victim is advanced academically, skipped a grade or two, which lands her in classes with senior students."

"She likes the bad boys," Tracy said, a smirk extinguishing when I shook my head. "From the looks of it, the boy never knew she was taking his picture."

"Might be something. And it might be nothing." I stood to check the shelves and drawers, an idea coming to mind. "Once you have access to the cloud account, report on what else the victim was taking pictures of."

"Copy that," Tracy said, finishing with the laptop. Closing the drawers we'd left open, I ran my hands through them in a second pass. "I searched them already."

"I know. Just answering a question that's bugging me." Tracy grunted and rolled her eyes, thinking I didn't notice. I did, but continued going through each drawer. When I was satisfied, I searched the shelves where the awards were. Tracy packed her things and waited at the bedroom door, content we'd searched enough to continue the investigation at the station. She stared hard, questioning. I finally told her, "It's not what's here. It's what's not here."

Her face softened, the impatience replaced. "What's not here?"

"Nail polish," I answered, recalling all the colors on the toenails and the remains of them on the victim's fingernails. "A house this big, she'd have her own bathroom?"

Tracy stepped into the hallway, turning to the right, and nodded. "Here."

"Whoa, that's strong." The smell of cleanser and bleach reached me the moment I entered the small bathroom. It'd been cleaned recently, the sink and tub and tiles glistening. There was a narrow closet for towels and other linens next to the doorway. "Check the closet, I'll look in here."

A few pill bottles lined the medicine cabinet behind the mirror, the medications over the counter. There were everyday items, a nail clipper and emery board, some cotton balls and face cleanser. But no nail polish. Tracy joined me, saying, "There's nothing in there."

"Nothing in here either," I replied, knees popping when searching beneath the sink. "She could have gotten them done at the strip mall we passed."

Tracy checked her watch, the hour inching near midday. "We could check, maybe grab something to eat while there?"

"I could eat," I replied, taking Tracy's hand to stand. "Afterward, we'll stop at the school. And put some names to the faces in those pictures."

NINE

This wasn't the first high school we'd been inside while investigating a murder. That was a sad fact, the students a popular target because of their youth. The school's principal, along with the district superintendent, met us outside to establish the ground rules. By now, the school's staff and students, as well as the parents, had been fully notified of Jill Carter's murder. They'd also been made aware of the possible outreach by the local authorities to aid in piecing together Jill's last hours. With permissions granted, we entered the school building and started our work.

High schools are one of those places where time doesn't stray. The tech might change and the clothes and hair styles too, sometimes dramatically, but the cliques stay the same. There are the jocks and the rebels. The stoners and goths. There are the overachievers and floaters, along with the loners and band students. Maybe it's the schools themselves that don't change? The funneling of a community full of adolescent and teen angst into one brick and mortar location day in and day out. Whatever it was, we'd come to rely on it, the profiles of each circle well understood.

Thinking back to my days, I was a floater in high school. I didn't have an inclination toward one clique or another. I had friends in the orchestra, and friends who played on the softball and field hockey teams. I'd also hung out with stoners on occasion and studied with the academics. They'd even talked me into participating in one of their math competitions. I didn't shine like they did, but I had enough game that we placed third in the final rounds.

Our footsteps echoed softly in the hallway, the warm smell of food coming from the nearby cafeteria. A distant yell bounced and was quickly followed by a laugh, sneakers screeching and a teacher yelling to slow down. Jill Carter's school was the same as any other I'd been inside. After the offices and cafeterias, there were lockers along the walls, narrow and painted a brownish-beige color, and edged in dark blue. Above them, posters were hung with pictures of Jill Carter, the count surprising. In them, I saw that she was a floater too. There was one where she was dressed in a marching band uniform and holding a clarinet. In another, she was at bat, the helmet big and her hands small as she choked up on the softball bat's neck. There were more too, schoolroom pictures and photographs with the teachers.

"Jill was popular," Tracy said. She stopped in front of a locker, the front of it dressed in hearts, some of them broken. Flowers and candles were set in front of it, flames doused. The number at the locker's top matched the one given to me by the principal. "This is her locker. They gave you the combination."

"Let's be quick," I said, noticing the students gathering at the end of the hall, a low chatter starting. As a precaution, we slipped on gloves, uncertain of what we'd find or if we'd want to gather evidence. I spun the lock and set the numbers, rolling the dial back and forth, the clicks felt in my fingertips. When I opened the locker, a brown bag tumbled to my feet, Tracy picking at it carefully. "What is it?"

She looked up, her face cramped. "Ugh! It's an old lunch. Tuna fish salad, I think."

"I think I saw a trash can back there," I instructed, shoving the bag to the side when the stink hit me. While Tracy tended to the old lunch, I inspected the top shelf, moving schoolbooks from side to side, opening them, turning them upside down, seeing if a note might have been left inside. I came up empty and moved on to the lower half where there was a thin jacket and a gym bag.

"Anything?" Tracy asked on her return. I followed her eyes to the crowd. "They sure are curious."

"Nothing stands out." I stepped back to look at the opened locker in its entirety and the cards and flowers. Kneeling to open one of the cards, I took a picture with my phone. A murmur reached us from the end of the hall. The chatter indistinguishable. Tracy followed, opening a card that came with flowers, the petals wilting. "Let's record all the names."

"This one doesn't have a name," she said, picking another. The card was simple, the inside blank, the outside with a charcoal drawing of a single broken heart. The flowers were fresher, none wilting. What struck me was the selection, a white rose with a red bow. "Pretty, but for sympathy?"

"I've seen roses at funerals. Red is common, it means love. A white color signifies innocence and purity." I lifted the end of the red bow, uncertain what, if anything, it would have meant. "Tracy, I don't think these are from one of the victim's friends."

"Could be the staff, a teacher?" she answered, not reading into it as much as I was. "They'd have given it more thought."

"The broken heart drawn in charcoal though?" I held the card, staring hard at the roses. "We're going to want to find out who brought these."

"All of them?" she asked.

"No, not all. Just the white rose." There was something about it that didn't sit right with me. Boyfriend or girlfriend, teenagers, even teachers. I'd think they would have brought other common types like carnations or tulips. Did the rose have a deeper meaning? "But get the names from all the cards. We'll reconcile them to the friends and staff we talk to."

"Casey?" Tracy's focus drifted past me to the group of students watching us. In the small gathering, I saw the nail polish, the colors matching what the victim was wearing. "I think that might be the friend Jill's parents mentioned."

"Shay?" I questioned, making note of her. She looked to be around the same age as the victim but was on the shorter side with dirty-blond hair that nearly touched her shoulders. With a round face and big eyes, she stared hard and had that look which said she had something to tell us. "Tracy, keep collecting—"

A buzzer sounded, alarming us both, the break between classes ending abruptly. Tracy jumped, saying, "Go."

I raised a hand, motioning to Shay, locking eyes with her. She turned to follow the other students, eagerness in her step, the curiosity of our hallway visit satisfied. "Shay?"

"Huh?" she answered, stopping. She couldn't have been more than thirteen or fourteen, a freshman perhaps. "I'm Shay?"

"I'd like to speak with you a moment?" I said, asking. A teacher nearby entered the hallway, a concerned look appearing. I recognized him from the victim's pictures on the laptop.

"Shay?" he began. When he saw my badge, the overhead lights catching it, he asked, "Is everything all right?"

"Yes, sir," I answered. "We'll be in the school today as part of an investigation."

"I understand," he replied, picking at his beard, fingers digging to scratch his chin. He was tall and slightly overweight, his middle pooching over his waistband. "Shay, would you feel more comfortable with your parents here?"

While it was the student's prerogative to have a parent

accompany them, there wasn't an obligation unless the discussion involved them being a suspect. "Sir, we're only asking general questions."

"Yes, that's understood," he replied, a hand raised as if to shush me. I'd need to speak with him and other teachers soon and didn't want to alienate him. When I backed away, he sighed with an apology, "I'm sorry. We're all a bit protective now. You understand."

"Yes, sir. I do." I didn't want to come off as disrespectful, but I knew our place and what we could and could not do. There was caution in Shay's eyes which I tried to satisfy with a smile. It softened as I extended my hand to her. "I'm Detective Casey White. You can call me Casey."

"Shay," she answered, nervously gripping my hand.

Without hesitating, I shook the teacher's hand next, putting him on the spot. He overcame the surprise, wiping his palm first, saying, "David Gantry. I'm the head of the science department." His grip was damp, his smile crooked. "Jill... she was one of my students."

"Mr. Gantry, you'll be around today?" I asked. Shay shifted impatiently. "I'll only need a few minutes of your time."

"Yes, certainly," he answered. He turned to Shay again, asking, "Would you like me to stay?"

"That's okay, Mr. Gantry," Shay answered, voice scratchy, chewing a fingernail, the one with the bright orange polish. She cleared her throat, nodding. "I'll be fine."

"Okay then," he answered, satisfied he'd been helpful. Leaning forward, the smell of antiperspirant reaching me, he hung a thumb over his shoulder. "I've got an open period. Classroom is empty. Feel free to stop in."

"I'll do that," I told him.

He began walking away, looking back once at Shay like a parent leaving their child on their first day at school. "Shay."

"Is this about the text?" she asked, the question unexpected.

Her eyes turned glassy as the chewing shifted to the turquoise-colored fingernail. Her voice rose enough to bounce, asking, "Is it... do you think it's related to what happened to Jill?"

The classroom across the hallway was empty, I motioned to it, inviting Shay inside. Her hands were trembling, and I thought she'd burst out in tears any moment. "It might be best if we speak in here?"

"Maybe I should have my parents?" she asked. And a moment later, she was crying.

"How about we start from the beginning," I said, handing her a tissue.

"What happened?" Tracy mouthed when entering the room, jaw dropping.

Shay took the tissue, blowing her nose, and watched Tracy take a seat.

"I'm Tracy Fields. Can I get you a water?"

Shaking her head, Shay answered, "I've got some."

"You and Jill were close?" I asked, motioning to her fingernails. "We saw that Jill had the same."

A grin. It was brief and sad, a little remorseful. "Last week," Shay answered, showing them to us. "I keep biting at them though."

Tracy leaned forward, nodding agreeably. "I do that too."

Shay swiped at her eyes, saying, "I didn't mean it, you know."

"Mean it?" Tracy asked, sitting back.

"That text I sent Jill," Shay answered, voice breaking.

"I'm sure you didn't." That seemed to settle Shay for the moment. "Tell us about the text."

Tracy caught on and opened her laptop, asking, "Would it help if we looked?"

"Uhm." A shrug, uncertainty waffling. "I guess that'd be okay."

Shay didn't wait for the laptop, swiping her phone. When

she reached what she was looking for, her lips thinned, the color on her face turning red.

"May I?"

She handed it to me, holding it a moment, reluctant to let go.

"We're here to help."

She let go, her gaze falling to the floor. "I really didn't mean it."

"'I wish you were dead,'" I said, reading the first line of the text. "'You know I liked him.'"

"You sent this that morning?" I asked, seeing the date and time. "During class?"

"I sent it after we got dismissed." The tears returned, her lower lip trembling. "It-it was the last thing I ever said to her."

Shay tucked her face into her hands, crying. The time on the text message held a truth Shay wasn't aware of. But I was and I told her. "Shay, Jill never read your text."

She looked up from her hands, face still cramped. "Huh? I don't understand."

"Jill never read it." I turned her phone around to show the time the text was sent, knowing that her friend was very likely to have already been dead. I dipped my head, asking, "Do you understand?"

"Oh God!" she replied, the words barely registering. "You mean, Jill was dead?"

"I'm sorry for your loss." She wiped her eyes, and I handed back her phone. "But about the text. Who is *him*?"

"His name is Michael," she replied, sliding the phone into her bag. "He's a boy we both like."

"Michael?" I dipped my chin, seeking a last name.

"Gibson," she said. "Michael Gibson."

A heart shape flashed in my thoughts, the initials M and G penned in the middle of it. "Michael Gibson," I said, verifying with a nod.

"Is this Michael?" Tracy asked, showing a picture from the victim's laptop. It was from the classroom, the teacher we'd met in the hallway sitting on a desk next to the boy who appeared in many of Jill's photographs. He had longish curly black hair and a narrow face with high cheekbones, deep brown eyes that said he didn't have a care in the world. "There were a couple like it on her laptop."

"She took pictures?" Shay asked, angered and hurt. She shook her head as if recalling her friend was dead and said, "Yeah, that's Michael. She knew I liked him."

"He's in your classes?" I asked, searching a list of Jill's classrooms the school principal supplied.

"Most of them, yeah," she replied, checking her phone and eyeing the door. "Is there anything else? I've really got to get back to class."

"A few more. I promise to keep it short." I held up my hand, insisting. "Was Jill in contact with anyone outside your school or friends?"

"Uh-uh. Nobody that I know of," Shay answered, shaking her head. Curling her fingers together, she stared at the picture on Tracy's laptop, adding, "We were close. She would've said something. Plus, I think it was Michael that she—" She stopped speaking, gaze darting past us toward the windows.

Instinctively, I turned to look outside but saw nothing. "What is it?"

"Jill told me she had a crush," she answered, her stare intensifying. "That's why I was mad at her. Coz she was with Michael in the hallway."

"You saw them together that morning?" Tracy asked, voice rising with surprise. A nod. Shay cautiously glanced at us, gauging if she'd said too much. "What can you tell us about the crush?"

"I mean, I just assumed," Shay began to answer, looking uncomfortable. "Maybe you should talk to Michael."

"Did something happen between them?" I asked, seeing that she was afraid.

"Are we done yet?" she asked, chewing on her lip. When I didn't reply, she stirred and went to get up while backpedaling. "You really should talk to him."

"We plan on it," Tracy answered, taking a note and shooting a look at me.

Shay was standing and heading for the door, moving fast as if there was a dark secret chasing her.

I followed carefully, asking, "Shay, if something happened?" She continued, moving faster. "Please. Jill was your friend."

Shay stopped, bracing the doorframe, and turned. "I don't know anything else. I like Michael and I don't want to see him get into any trouble."

Carefully, I approached and asked, "Shay? Are you afraid of Michael? Could he have hurt Jill?"

A hard frown. "Gosh no!" she rebuked. A smile bloomed and she went on to explain, "He's sweet and kind—"

"And you saw him with Jill last?" Tracy asked, seeking confirmation.

Hesitant, Shay nodded.

"They were exchanging words?"

Another nod.

"But I don't think, I mean he could never—" Shay didn't finish; Jill's friend exited without so much as a wave.

I looked at Tracy, confused by the reaction. "What was that about?"

"It's gotta be about Michael. Right?" Tracy questioned. "Maybe whatever she saw in the hallway scared her?"

"Possibly?" I questioned with a mumble.

"Want me to go after her?" Tracy asked, closing her laptop.

"I don't think we need to. Not yet anyway." Was it fear that had Jill's friend leaving? "Let's find Michael Gibson."

TEN

Finding Michael proved harder than expected. He wasn't in any of the classrooms. He wasn't in the cafeteria or the school's office. By the time we'd finished collecting the surveillance footage from the school's security system, the staff had declared that Michael Gibson was not on campus. That didn't come as too much of a surprise. There were a lot of students absent, the weather having been a significant interruption. It only meant that we'd take a trip to the house where he lived and ask our questions there.

The hour was deep into the afternoon, a nearby creek grabbing our attention. It was an idea Tracy had suggested, a review of a local map urging us to explore it. The creek was no more than a few feet wide, steeply banked with running freshwater. It was also in proximity to Jill's home, the junkyard, and the school. If there was a place the killer would have collected stones and pebbles, this might be it.

I knew better than to assume this was the place the stones would have come from. For all we knew, they might have been part of a bigger collection, the killer having broader plans. I hoped I was wrong about that but only the killer could tell us for sure. At a minimum, following Tracy's hunch would get us something we could use for comparison, samples that would show if we were on the right track or not.

I parked the car and heard water trickling beyond the bend of a hill. The day had warmed enough to thaw the ground, sinking our shoes into the soft earth. Sunlight filtered through the trees, the branches bare and clacking with a breeze. I grabbed Tracy's arm, and she clutched mine, the two of us navigating the walk like a pair of old biddies. But this wasn't a pleasant walk in the park, it was to identify a possible location that the killer had visited.

"We want to find stones or the smaller pebbles," she said, emphasizing pebbles. "I'll take them back and compare them to what was at the crime scene."

"I know they're different from rocks," I commented, squinting, sunlight shining on our faces. The ground sloped downward enough to strain my legs, a row of trees to our left, the running water to our right. "But stones or pebbles?"

"They're all rocks, but rocks aren't necessarily a stone or pebble," Tracy answered, letting go and jumping to the other side. She dipped her fingers in the water, eyes growing bright. "Wow that's cold."

"Pebbles would be considered smaller?" I asked, stopping suddenly. I froze, my shoes sinking subtly into mud. Mine weren't the only ones. There were other footsteps. A dozen at least, size elevens, maybe twelve. "Tracy, stop."

Tracy shook her head, face riddled with questions. "What's wrong?"

"Somebody was here recently. We've got footprints and what might be marks from kneeling next to the water."

She jumped back across, joining me, camera in hand. Pointing, she directed me, "Move your foot next to that one. It'll be good for scale."

"I mean, these could be from anyone." We'd never use the

footprints in court. Without a witness, a defense attorney would counter it easily. But for the investigation, it was a checkbox on a long list I'd use to confirm a suspect.

"They could literally be left over from before the storm," Tracy said while framing a picture. "But, I wouldn't want to know we passed on a possible clue that had been right under our feet."

"Exactly." After a few pictures, she made her way back to the other side, my asking, "About the pebbles? They're smaller, right?"

"I think so. As long as they're the same as what we found with the victim." Tracy plucked a stone from the creek and held it between her fingers. It was pale, water dripping from it, a shine glinting when she rolled it back and forth. "See the similarity?"

"I do," I answered, wondering if the killer had stood here like we were doing now. I took to a knee and dared the cold touch and picked up a few of my own. "Nothing with jagged edges, just pebbles that have been smoothed by the water."

"Exactly." There was a spark in her eyes while she fished a handful, rinsing the dirt like she was panning for gold. "This creek is the closest one to the victim's school and even closer to her home."

"That includes where she was murdered too." I washed a handful of the stones, the dirt clouding around my fingers which had turned red instantly in the near-freezing water. "We want to match the colors to make sure."

"That's what I was thinking. Seems most of these are different," she said, disappointed, emptying a handful, the stones plopping. "Any luck over there?"

I scoured a fistful, some black and white with a zebra pattern, others a dirty gray and specked with what could have been a green color. I shrugged. "None like that pale one you found." I dug in, driving my fingertips deep enough to feel sand scrape my nails. Sifting in the running water, shaking a chill, the pebbles did look familiar. "Got one."

"Lemme see?" she asked, jumping and missing the bank, her heels smacking the creek's edge with a splash. "Shit."

"Look," I said, handing it to her. She placed it next to the one she'd found, the two pearly colored ones a match. "I think we've got something similar to the collection at the junkyard."

I clutched another handful near her feet, the mud stirring as I rinsed them. "And this one here is kind of dark gray with brown spots. Those were near the bottom of the pile." I dropped the stones, turning upstream where the water foamed white as it raced over a rapid, the creek's drop like a small waterfall. "This creek is where the killer collected them. But it could have been anywhere along here. Miles up or downstream."

"Where would we even start? And what would we look for?" Tracy walked a few feet away, crossing back to the other side. I didn't say anything but stared beyond the rushing water, searching until as far as I could see. Tracy shielded her eyes, asking, "Do you see something?"

"I think I do," I answered, jumping back across with a stretching leap. When I was next to her, I pointed and said, "See the houses and that apartment building?"

"I see them," she answered. "It's walking distance too."

"You saw how long it took us to find just these couple of pebbles. The pile at the junkyard had at least a hundred or more." We began to work our way up the hill, holding one another upright against the incline. "I'm thinking they gathered the stones over time. Not all at once."

"Casey?" Tracy said, stopping abruptly. She clutched my arm hard enough to make me wince. "Look."

Ahead of us, standing next to my car, a teenage boy with curly black hair that reached his shoulders, the sunlight behind him, his face in silhouette. I squinted enough to recognize him from Jill's photographs. It was Michael Gibson. But how did he know that we'd be here?

"Ma'am, may I speak with you, please?" Michael was mannerly, a quiet tone, hair buffeting against a breeze. He held his hands together in front of him, a good sign. "It's about Jill Carter."

"You didn't go to school today?" I asked. I didn't wait for a response, suspicions already piqued. "How did you know to find us here?"

"I followed you," he answered, the honesty surprising. He ran his fingers up one arm, nervously scratching at his shoulder. "I was at school. Just not in any of my classes."

"I would've sworn we checked everywhere," Tracy commented.

"Well, there's lots of places they don't check," he said, sniggering. When I frowned, instant regret flashed, the smile doused. "Nothing bad, ma'am. There's a couple places we go to hang, you know."

"I was in high school once too," I told him, thinking to gain some trust. "What was it you wanted to tell us?"

"It's about Jill. I was with her... you know, before," he began to explain, hair falling in front of his face. He moved closer to us, stepping away from the car. His sneakers were tattered, old, the size close to the footprints found next to the creek. It was a checkmark on the long list of what would be used to confirm a suspect. Not that he was. Not yet. His clothes were in a sad state too, underdressed when considering the weather. "I think she was seeing someone."

"From what her friends said, the only person Jill was interested in, was you," Tracy countered.

He flinched and shook his head. "I mean, yeah, I liked her. I liked her a lot. But she didn't like me like that."

"Like that?" I asked. "What does that mean exactly?"

His mouth twisted with disappointment. "Jill liked someone else." Michael shook his head, his mouth turned down. "She didn't like me. Not the way I liked her."

"How about you tell us what happened in the hallway."

"The hallway?" he asked, surprised. "Uhm, we were talking and all. I asked Jill if she would go to a movie with me."

"Did she say yes?" Tracy asked, genuinely curious as if chatting with friends.

He shook his head, Jill having turned him down.

"Who was the other boy?" I asked.

"I don't know who she liked either," he answered. "But I don't think they were a student at our school."

"You're friends with Shay too?" Tracy asked, a hard breeze whipping hair around her head. "Were there problems since Shay was friends with Jill?"

"I don't think so. I'm friends with them both... I mean, was friends." He pegged the tip of his shoe into the dirt. "We hung out a lot."

"Was there anything else in the hallway that'd—" I stopped when I saw it. On the boy's right arm, above the wrist, a white gauzy bandage. There was a patch of blood at the center that had oozed dry. When he saw me noticing, he hurried to cover it. "The hallway. What happened after?"

"After?" he asked, voice changing like his throat was closing. He cleared it, saying, "I walked with Jill some more."

"Was Shay with you?" Tracy asked, the two of us moving closer.

"Uh-uh. It was just me and Jill." Michael backed away a step and raised the arm with the bandaging. "Jill fell. That's what happened."

"Fell?" I asked, the sudden admission a surprise. "What happened to your arm, Michael?"

"It's a scratch," he answered hesitantly. He must have realized how things looked from our perspective. There was a talk in the hallway. A rejection of his proposed date to go out together. And then a fall which resulted in injury. Michael spoke without words, stammering voiceless. When his voice came, he said, "Really, that's all that happened. She fell and I got a scratch."

"It might be infected," Tracy said, pivoting to entice conversation. It was a strategy to keep the questions flowing. "I've got a medical kit and can take a look for you."

"No thanks," he answered quick. "It's fine."

"Really, it'd only take a minute," Tracy insisted.

"How did she fall, Michael?" I asked, leaving no room for him to answer Tracy. "Help us figure out what happened? Can you do that?"

"Uh-huh." He stopped backing away and crossed his arms, the bandage tucked beneath. "Jill was walking me to my car and slipped on the ice. I reached out to help her and she grabbed my arm on the way down."

"She scratched you with her fingernails?" I asked, thinking about the cold and wearing gloves and jackets. There was also the school's security videos. Of the few minutes we watched, the student parking lot was blocked by a dozen long yellow buses. Anything he told us was his word alone, and without any supporting evidence. "She didn't have gloves on?"

"Not yet," he answered, rubbing the bandage. "It's a short walk and I didn't have my coat on yet either."

"It was awfully cold and stormy that morning," Tracy commented.

"I know how this must look," he snapped, anger in his voice. "Really, she slipped on the ice and I got scratched trying to help."

"With the early dismissal, did anyone else see what happened?" Tracy followed up, questioning Michael's story.

His lips were pencil thin, disappearing. "I-I don't think so."

"That's okay. We'll ask around." The boy looked like he was going to break out in a run any moment. I needed a few more questions answered before we lost him. "Was Jill Carter in your car, Michael?"

"Well, yeah. She's been in my car a lot," he answered, brow narrowing. He put up his hands in a whoa manner, saying, "Wait. Why are you asking me all these questions? I came here to tell you that there was someone else."

I didn't answer his question. The wind was picking up and I raised my voice over it, "Would you mind coming to the station with us? We can continue talking inside where it's warm."

He made like he was going to check the time, quickly answering, "I think I should get my mom to go with me."

"That'd be even better," Tracy said, encouraging him. "Bring your parents."

His face cramped. "There's just us. My mom and me and my little sister."

"She can come too," Tracy replied immediately. "If it will help."

"We'd really appreciate your help, Michael." I didn't want to think a fellow student could have done what we saw. However, his admitting to being one of the last with Jill, that she'd been in his car and that scratch which stood out like a neon sign... There wasn't enough to arrest him on the spot, leaving cooperation as a hopeful second. "You want to help us solve Jill's murder. Right?"

"Definitely, I want to help! That's why I'm here," he said, digging his fingers into his hair. He turned to leave, saying, "I just don't like that you think I could have had something to do with it though."

"What do we do?" Tracy asked, voice hushed so he couldn't hear.

"There's not much we can do," I answered, hands empty. "Not without a warrant."

"I'll think about it," he called back while continuing to walk away. When he was further, he glanced over his shoulder to see if we were following. We weren't, but I already had my phone in hand and a text message typed to the district attorney. It wasn't just the unanswered questions either. I wanted a search warrant for Michael Gibson's car.

ELEVEN

The sharp edge of cold air bit into Terri's skin as she dragged the trash bags across the pavement. Bits of blacktop broke the night's stillness, scraping like fingernails on a chalkboard. Her breath fogged in the February evening but the work had her sweating. She shook from the cold sweat, teeth chattering, the enclosure looming ahead. There were just a few security lights on the building where she worked, showing enough of the red brick, a stark contrast to the inky sky. She dragged the trash bags behind her, huffing another frosty puff when she reached the enclosure. The dumpster's lid belted a rusty screech. Instantly, the smell of decomposing food made her gag, her eyes watering as she leaned back and waved away the stench.

"This sucks," she said, talking to herself. She peered behind her at the fast-food restaurant, the smell of it deep in her hair and skin and clothes. "Why do I always get stuck with closing?"

"Jill," she said, fumbling, her thoughts wandering back to the funeral coming up. "Everyone's gonna be there."

She'd never attended one before, and the idea of it gave her pause. It was the company of death, of someone she'd known well, dead. It felt surreal. It felt heartbreakingly sad too. Jill was a friend. More than that, really. There'd been years of sleepovers and movie nights, and school lunches, and seeing her every day since the first grade. Terri lowered her head, plastic crinkling in her fist, she mouthed the words, "My sister from another mister."

Hoisting one of the trash bags, she spoke to the darkness, asking, "What do you wear to a funeral?" In her head, she sifted through her closet and realized she had nothing suitable, nothing formal enough to wear to such an occasion. The reality of her friend's murder struck her with shock, the strength draining from her arms, the trash bag plunking back to the gravelly pavement. This was the reality of life, the shock of it a violent jolt that left her reeling in the middle of the night behind a fast-food restaurant with garbage at her feet. Until now, the reality of it hadn't fully set in. It was now though, as she was forced to think about something as unimportant as what to wear to a funeral.

Footsteps approached. Soft but unmistakable. There was only Billy working with her this shift. He'd been eager to help with the closing, picking up some of the slack to win points. He wasn't exactly her type, but she could tell he liked her. "What do you want, Billy?"

No response. The footsteps grew louder; the thought of being alone at the dumpster made her heart thud heavily in her chest. She turned around, fear mingling with the icy air. It wasn't Billy, but the sight of a familiar face brought a wave of relief.

"Hey, what are you doing here?" she asked, her voice trembling.

Hands up in a whoa-motion, he replied, "Sorry. I didn't mean to scare you."

"You didn't scare me," she was quick to say, lying. Nudging a chin toward the fast-food restaurant, she continued. "Sorry, but we closed a half hour ago."

"Thanks. I'm not hungry. I saw an injured cat," he replied smoothly. "It came back here and went in there, behind the dumpster. I was trying to help it."

"A cat?" Terri's heart softened at the thought. "Poor thing. What happened to it?"

The edge of the spotlights drew a dark line across his face, leaving one half in black. "I don't know but it was limping terribly... and crying too."

"Crying? Oh no," she said, inside aching with compassion. Traffic sped back and forth just beyond the parking lot on Route 12. "Do you think it got hit?"

"More likely attacked. A fox or a dog," he answered, waving a finger. "Those cars would've killed it."

"Right," she agreed, nodding as he nodded. "What can I do to help?"

"Help? Yeah!" He smiled, an unsettling glint in his eyes. "How about you go behind the dumpster and try and get it to come out? I'll stay here and block the way so I can catch it."

"Sure, we can use one of the boxes stacked for recycling," she offered eagerly. "There's an animal hospital nearby. We can take it there."

"That's a good idea," he said, smile widening. "Go on, it's back there."

Terri quickly grabbed a cardboard box from next to the dumpster, her resolve strengthening despite the cold and the smell. She squeezed into the narrow space behind the dumpster, her eyes straining to see in the darkness, the spotlights not strong enough to reach.

"Do you see it?"

"Not yet?" she called out, her voice echoing. There were faint shadows falling ahead of her, motions in the dim light. But no cat. "Are you sure you saw a cat coming back here?"

"I know I saw something," he replied, his voice behind her, closer now. "It might be hiding. Try looking over in the corner."

"Okay." Terri moved deeper into the pit behind the dumpster, breathing in a shallow mix of cold and smelly air. She crouched down, scanning the ground. "What is that?"

"Is it the cat?" he replied, questioning.

Her eyes fell on a small collection of items, her fingers prodding gently. There were river stones, perfectly smooth, clearly handpicked, and stacked with meticulous care. Next to it was a collection of bottle caps that had been arranged in a pyramid, each one a different color to create a small mosaic of the discarded trash. Next to it, a pile of cattail leaves and wildflowers which seemed out of place, the blooms vibrant and fresh despite the winter chill. She'd been behind the dumpster a dozen or more times in the past week and never seen anything like this. Why would these be here? And the flowers? It's winter, there shouldn't be any flowers. "What is all this?" she asked, puzzled.

"They're just some things I found," he answered, his voice suddenly in her ear, the tone deceptively gentle. "Aren't they pretty? Now, see if you can find that cat. It's probably scared."

Terri hesitated, the odd collections making her uneasy. "I don't see a cat," she said, peering into the shadows.

"It's there," he insisted, his tone hardening slightly. "It's probably just hiding. You need to look closer. Maybe go in further."

Terri moved to the furthest corner where there was a small space that a cat could hide in if they wanted to. It was toward the darkest part of the enclosure, the side of the dumpster nearly flush with the wall. The air grew colder and damper as she crouched down, straining to see in the dark. "I still don't see anything," she muttered, more to herself than to him.

"It must be really scared. Go further if you can," he coaxed, his footsteps right behind her. "You don't want it to suffer, do you?"

His words tugged at her heart. She couldn't bear the

thought of an animal suffering. "No, of course not," she said, inching forward on her hands and knees.

One hand extended, feeling the pavement, the cold rifling into her fingers, she'd gone as far into the corner's space as she could and saw another small pile of items. This one was made up of broken seashells, their edges sharp, that glistened when the moon appeared from behind cloud cover. Terri's heart raced, a sense of dread washing over her. She turned back to look at him, her confusion evident. "Are you sure you saw a cat?" she asked, her voice trembling.

"I know I saw something," he replied, his face silhouetted by the moon's gray light. "Maybe we can try the other side?"

Terri's breath caught in her throat as she shifted to stand, cold pavement pressing against her palms. Her eyes scanned the dark corners, her focus falling onto the strange collections. "Those things over there, why did you bring them?" she murmured, confusion giving way to a growing sense of fear.

"Do you think they're beautiful?" he asked again, his voice almost hypnotic. "I brought them for you."

"For me? But—" Before she could continue, a sharp pain exploded in her head, white light blinding her. She felt the momentum of falling, her body tipping sideways until striking the hard pavement with a thud. Her senses dulled, the dumpster and the piles blurred. She tried to speak, to fight, and felt herself being rolled onto her back, his weight pressing down on her. Panic surged through her like a bolt of electricity, waking her mind to what had happened, but her movements remained weak, ineffective. "Wha—"

His hands wrapped around her neck, large fingers tightening like a vice. She had a scream in her, felt it rising like a volcano ready to erupt. But when she tried to let it out, no sound came. Strength came back enough to swing her arms and legs, kicking and batting, the attempts feeble and useless against his strength. Nightmarish fright consumed her when she heard her clothes tearing, the wintry air touching her bare skin. She tensed, muscles stiffening as his hands returned to her throat. He squeezed hard. Hard enough to pinch the life from her mind. The world began to fade, the shadowy face above her blending into the night's sky.

He's going to kill me, she thought sadly, his face in hers, an inch away. His stare was cold, emotionless. And just when she thought she'd black out forever, he released her. Falling backwards, she struck the ground again, air rushing into her lungs with a painful gasp that made her chest burn. She sucked in another breath and tried to scream but her voice was gone. Looking up, he sat on top of her, straddling, relishing the moment. When she swung at his face, his grip returned, fiercer this time, bringing her closer to the edge, the threat of death closer now.

She lost count. Was it two? Three? How many times did he let go just before her heart stopped? Did it matter? Each attempt took a little more of her until that last one. She had nothing left and welcomed the idea of stepping over to wherever it was we went after dying. As the light appeared and the soulful voices called her name, Terri's last thoughts were of Jill Carter and wondering if that's who she was listening to. She thought of the clothes that she was going to wear to Jill's funeral. Only now, in these last moments, she wondered what outfit she'd wear to her own funeral. The darkness closed in completely then and she felt her body go limp and the last drop of her life slip away.

TWELVE

Mattress springs creaked and Jericho's soft snores reached me from the other room. Tabitha and Thomas were asleep too, the hour almost three in the morning. I pressed the enter key to log in, and glimpsed a shadow racing across the floor, the swiftness leading me to think we had a mouse or that the late night was catching up to me. It was gone in a flash, my focus returning to the online sleuthing group and the case of the doctor's whereabouts. Beyond my desk, the wall with the clues and the colorful yarn hadn't changed. But tonight, on my screen, there was a change. A significant one. Someone was reaching out via the chat, saying they were the doctor.

The member's name was listed as *Doctor*. Nothing else. Just the name, Doctor. I didn't jump to dial the team of FBI and US Marshals working the Dr. P.W. Boécemo case. We get a lot of noise. I wanted to be certain. Most of the time, I'd ignore any chat invites anyway since they were usually reporters hunting down a quote. The popularity of the doctor's escape from prison had gone viral like it was a scene out of the movie, *The Fugitive*. The hunt for him stretched from the Atlantic to the Pacific and touched both the Canadian to Mexico borders. There'd even been sightings as far as England and Ireland, though I doubted those were valid. In my heart, I believed the doctor was still in the states. Nearby.

I hated that his case had garnered fame and attention. It wasn't deserving. The public didn't know the doctor like I knew him. They didn't know what he was capable of. But somehow, in the way online stories twist and morph and become something new, the mystery of how he escaped prison became hugely popular. It had also attracted a lot of attention to our corner of the online sleuthing world, enough for me to know to skip superfluous invites like the one beckoning me now. I moved the mouse cursor over the invitation, my finger hovering on the delete key. I hesitated, the question of *what if?* ringing in my head like a bell. Rather than send it to a digital trash bin, I clicked and opened it. While I didn't know what to expect exactly, I knew what to ask to weed out the junk.

"Detective, I trust you're doing well." It was the only sentence in the chat window, the timestamp showing the message was more than thirty minutes old.

"Doctor?" I typed in the reply, glancing at the blinking red dot in the corner. I'd enabled the chat session recording just in case this was legitimate. I also had a text message on the ready to go directly to my main point of contact at both the FBI and US Marshals offices. *"Doctor? Are you still online?"*

My heart jumped when the text dots appeared, each bouncing one at a time to indicate someone was typing.

"Good evening, Detective. Or should I say good morning where you are."

"It's late and I'm up," I replied, curious to the choice of words used, good morning where you are. A different time zone. The Midwest? Or maybe he was on the west coast? *"How did you find this forum?"* I asked. Silence. Was it a delay in the send and receive? If so, it could be the person was in a foreign coun-

try. Overseas perhaps? Maybe the foreign press running a story?
"Doctor?"

"Sorry, just opening a bottle of wine. A nice pinot noir," he replied.

Another interesting choice of words. It struck me as intentional. A rush of goosebumps rose on my arms and I readied my phone to send the text. When we'd arrested the doctor in Philadelphia, there was a well-established wine collection, including expensive bottles of cabernet sauvignon and a large selection of pinot noir.

"No need to explain how I found you. But it took some time."

"How can I be certain you are who you say you are?" I typed, asking directly. *"I get a lot of crackpots on here, all of them taking credit for this and that."*

"Do you still blame your daughter?" the doctor asked, the cursor blinking.

I stopped typing, my breath catching in my throat. Whoever this was, they'd brought up the one thing I'd never shared with anyone. That is, anyone except the doctor. I stared at the reply hard enough to think the screen's pixels would burn a hole in my eyes. Before the doctor's escape from prison, he'd been advising us on another case. Only, at the time, we didn't know if it was a ruse or his true involvement. There was a life at stake and I found myself on the other side of the questions, trading mine for his in a back and forth, tit for tat like I was one of his patients. I wasn't, of course, but progress on the case had to be made. Whether I liked it or not, the doctor was helping.

The questions he asked though! They weren't your run-of-the-mill office psychiatrist ones. Nothing about my childhood or my parents. The questions were about my daughter and her kidnapping. They cut to the bone, sharp with the intent of forcing me to look at what I refused to see. And in one of our last conversations, I revealed that a part of me blamed my daughter for her kidnapping. I'd never considered it before. How could I? It was the most ridiculous thought. Hannah was just a child. But I'd said it aloud. Blurted it actually, and there was no taking it back.

"Detective? Did I startle you?"

"I don't startle," I typed, lying, as I sent the text to the FBI and US Marshals. I thumped the *Enter* key, disturbed that his comment had actually shaken me, though I'd never admit it. The person online was the doctor and I had to remain calm. I had to tread cautiously if I was going to keep him online while the other officers did their thing. The longer, the better too. Whether by phone or email or this forum's chat, it was the doctor's ego that told me he would reach out sooner or later, his work with me unfinished. Perhaps it was his pride. Either way, he was full of himself, enough that I made certain to be prepared for such an encounter. Still, while this had turned into a sick game for the doctor, it was very real to me, and very dangerous too.

My ears began ringing, the tempo of my heartbeat racing. I opened a second window where there was a tool chest of networking commands ready. That's when I noticed I was trembling. That's when I noticed the metallic taste of adrenaline creeping up the back of my throat. The doctor began typing again, the text dots bouncing. It was a long reply and gave me a second to kick off a networking trace tool. Every forum member, anonymous or otherwise, comes from somewhere. And with their network connection, the underlying protocols deliver an address. While it wasn't the same as a physical street address, I could get an approximate location, a state, or maybe the city or the town where his connection was established. When the trace tool started, the doctor stopped typing. Shit, did I lose him? I hurriedly checked and saw his connection was still active.

"Are you trying to find me, Detective?" he replied, adding a smiley face at the end.

My heart jumped and I glimpsed the list of locations revealed so far, the trace busily working the route and dumping new network addresses with each hop. There were too many though. Even for the states, there shouldn't have been this many.

The doctor began typing again, adding, *"This pinot noir is very good. It tastes even better while I watch you work."*

"Watching me work?" I asked, my gaze pivoting to the webcam. It was off, the doctor referring to our chat, or simply trying to stir my nerves. Too late. They were already stirred, the network trace continuing to list new locations.

"Detective, I hope you understand that I've taken the liberty of retaining privacy for our discussion."

"Enjoy the wine while you can," I said, working to keep his attention. How could he know I was tracing him? It was impossible. I sat back, arms crossed. It wasn't that he knew. It was that he'd anticipated it. *"Care to tell me where you bought the wine? Maybe I'll pick up a bottle."*

"Tsk-tsk," he typed, followed by a laughter emoji.

It was a bit out of character for the doctor I'd met in prison, but when a chat window is all you've got... I glanced at the webcam again, wondering if he'd consider pivoting to an actual conversation.

"I'm doing you a courtesy, Detective. Don't take it for granted."

"A courtesy?" I asked, and enabled my webcam, the trace continuing to spit locations. Eager to see how long I could keep him online, I clicked the camera button, and showed my face. Would he reciprocate? I held my breath.

A window popped open, a hand covering the camera. I saw a palm and then fingers, an arm blurring before a face came into focus. It was the doctor, and it confirmed to me that he was alive. His face was gaunt with weight loss, but not in a bad way. His hair was longer and tied back in a bun, bleached blond with grays sprouting above his ears. With the warrants and APB since his escape, it was clear, the doctor was altering his appearance. He raised his glass of red wine, toasting the camera with a smile. *"Detective. Yes, a courtesy."* Shifting closer to the camera, he made like he was looking at the other windows on my screen. When he sat back, he waved his hand, saying, *"You can do away with those. There's no networking tools that will help."*

"What do you want, Doctor?" I asked, hands trembling as I discontinued the trace. It was stuck in a loop anyway, spitting up the same ten or so locations over and over. He was staring through the screen with an intensity that made me uncomfortable. The look would make anyone uncomfortable. Then again, he had a way of making his eyes soft and less off-putting. It was a part of his practice maybe, his being a psychiatrist and getting patients to open up to him. "Doctor? You contacted me. Why?"

"As a doctor, I never want to leave a discussion unfinished."

I leaned away from the screen, my chair back creaking. I wanted his location. Everyone involved did. But what did he want from me?

He sipped his wine, asking, *"Detective, you didn't answer the question."*

My hands grew clammy with an idea, fingertips hovering above the keys to work the trace. I looked over my shoulder out of habit and listened for Jericho's snore. When I heard it, I answered quietly, "I'll answer your question."

"Splendid," he said immediately, eyes widening with a broad smile. The background of his place was dark. There were no windows that I could see through to give me an idea of where he was. A bell rang out and sounded like church bells. I couldn't be sure though. The doctor didn't seem distracted by it while pouring another glass, the neck of the wine bottle lacking any distinguishing marks. Had he thought all of this through? I think he must have. He'd sanitized everything about this session so as not to give up any clues. He was as invisible as one could

be while being visible to me. The doctor looked into the camera, pausing a moment as though relishing it, and then asked, *"Do you still blame your daughter?"*

"How about I answer your question in person? Let's meet. Just you and me." My heart was beating hard and fast, my stare intense as the doctor pondered the question. I'd never go alone, but he didn't know that. I was certain he'd see past it and know that it was a setup to recapture him. When I opened my mouth to rephrase the proposal, the doctor was gone in a blink, the screen turning inky black. The online indicator showed that he was still online though, and I typed, *"Doctor?"*

"Sorry, but I must cut it short this evening," the doctor replied, the text dots dancing while he continued to type. *"Detective, please do think about my question, won't you? And say hello to your beautiful daughter for me."*

The doctor was gone, the chat's activity dead. I sat back and grunted a sigh, disappointed and annoyed that I'd pushed too fast. I checked my phone, a flurry of texts in the group chat with the FBI and US Marshals office. They had about as much luck as I did, the traces leading to a dead end.

Clicking through the session recording, I found a good picture of the doctor, brow raised, his toasting with the wine glass. In the lower left, the date and time were clearly visible and I composed an email, listing the FBI and US Marshals office, pasting the doctor's picture and the data from my own network trace. Maybe one of their analysts with steeper technical expertise could make sense of it. When the mattress springs creaked, Jericho grunting my name, I hit send.

"Babe?" Jericho asked, his groggy voice calling in a hoarse whisper. Footsteps approached, followed by a gentle hand. "What're you working on in here?"

I thumbed the screen's power button, turning off the monitor before he could read another sentence. "It's nothing. A cold case the group is reviewing."

"Casey, it's quarter past three in the morning." He pawed at his chin, fingernails digging through the gruff. "You should get some sleep."

I stood up and brushed my hand across his face and pillowy-hair, part of it sticking up. "Let's go to bed," I told him.

We entered our bedroom, my step feeling tired, my eyelids heavy. I snuggled close to Jericho, turning on my side, his arm draped around me. I clutched it, shifting close enough to feel his soft breath on the back of my neck. I began to hover in that place where the dreams waited, the doctor's case becoming a distant thought. One thought nagged though and kept the dreams at bay. The doctor was alive and contacted me. He was a free man. Why contact me? Why bother? Eyelids springing open, the night swirling outside our apartment window. In the fuzzy light, I saw the answer. The doctor wants to finish the session we started.

Headlights. They were like fire. Burning. It was a car. Not any car though. It was the car. The red car that took my daughter. It reared its monstrous head, its grill made of broken bones, its windshield a black glass that was void of reflection. I was terrified and then I wasn't. I'd battled this monster before, fighting it when it stole my baby. It was back again! And in my heart and every cell of my being, I knew my Hannah was still inside that car.

I was prepared this time with my badge slung around my neck, the chain made dense, made heavy, made to be a weapon. And on my belt, I had my gun, the first of two, with one ready in my hands, a full clip loaded with a hollow-point bullet in the chamber. But was it enough?

Black smoke spewed from the exhaust pipes and choked the air, the nearby trees instantly turning a dreadful gray and decomposing, crumbling into a pile of ash. It was poison. The car had come prepared to fight. I rolled across the ground as the acrid cloud hovered above, and then crawled around the bumper, hoping to crack the rear window, break through it and save my child.

The gassy exhaust touched my arm, searing my flesh, blisters forming into bulbous sacs. I stifled a scream as the skies opened, the white and blue peeling away to reveal a blood moon. I glanced up and down the road and dared a look at our home. It was gone. Every house, every mailbox, even the manicured lawns had disappeared. In their place was a stony desert, the sand piping hot, the rocks like smoldering coals, melting, forming streams that fed into a river of lava which ran wildly and burned everything in its path.

Pain ripped up my arm, another burn coming to my hand and fingers. I jerked my palm resting on the trunk of the car, the red paint on fire, the roof shooting sparks a hundred feet into the air.

"My baby," I screamed, my guts reeling with the thought of losing her again. "Give me back my baby!"

With no thought to the pain that would come, I batted at the windows. The black glass was lined with razors, each strike stealing a layer of skin, shredding my fingers and hands and arms to my elbows. I had one chance to find my daughter again and I was losing it.

The ground around me was swallowed by the river, the lava turning into a sea of fire, the flames crawling up my legs, dancing to a silent tune as though alive. The world began to burn. The driver's window opened, the woman's blue eyes appeared like a pair of jewels planted in the wall of a dark mine. They were like ice and instantly turned me cold.

"Casey, do you want your baby?" the woman asked, her voice like an old radio broadcasting a hissy sound, scratchy with static.

"I do!" I begged, pleading with a cry. Any thoughts I had about putting a bullet between her eyes turned distant. "Please. I won't tell anyone about what you did. Give me back my baby. Give me Hannah."

"Are you sure you want your baby?" the woman asked, her icy eyes throwing sparks like diamonds.

My teardrops exploded into steam as they struck the fire. "Oh yes!" I implored agreeably.

The car window rolled down, the skin on the woman's face dead below the eyes, stitched together in odd-shaped patches, a quilt made of human flesh. Her nose and chin were rotting stumps, bones jutting with sickening brightness. But I neither saw nor cared for any of it; my Hannah had suddenly appeared in the window, the woman's gnarled fingers holding my child.

"Catch," she said, letting go.

My reflexes were fast, and I jumped toward my falling child, reaching outward for her to land in my hands. But my arms were smoldering stumps, and Hannah fell into the fiery sea.

I heard my baby scream. I heard her voice as I remembered it, and I saw the horror of her skin burning, heard it sizzle and crackle. I dove into the river to save her and began to burn too. My girl's screams turned to laughter, the raucous tease coming from inside the car. I'd been fooled, tricked by the witch who kept my baby. There were cries then, mine, as my heart broke just as it had so many times already. Like the witch's face, my heart was a patchwork of flesh, made up of stitched wounds, the seams bursting with sorrow.

"Hannah!" I screamed, rifling upward, face slick and dripping.

"Wha!" Jericho asked, propping himself, a dazed and confused look on his face. "What is it, babe?"

"Hannah," I cried, the dream as real to me in that moment as the heat of our bodies. I blinked away the grogginess, the dreaminess too, and forced myself awake. "I'm sorry. It was a nightmare."

"The witchy one?" Jericho asked, joining me, sitting up with his face near mine. I nodded with a whimper. "You haven't had that one in a while."

"I know," I replied, lying down, pulling on his arm. He joined me and within a few minutes, his breathing deepened. I was wide awake though, the dream remaining fresh. I think it was a warning, the doctor playing a game. What if it was vengeance? What if he was coming after my daughter?

THIRTEEN

The early morning light in the Outer Banks held a haunting beauty. The sun casting long, eerie shadows across the deserted parking lot of the fast-food restaurant, its colors golden like butter. The air remained cold and nipped at my skin while making my breath smoky. We were a few blocks from the beach, the ocean's salty tang mingling horribly with the acrid smell of rotting food.

The restaurant was a stark, cold landscape compared to the commotion seen with the summer tourists filling the seats to get a breakfast bite and drink coffee. I stood just outside the dumpster enclosure behind the red-brick restaurant, trying to steady my nerves for what lay ahead. The young manager who'd called in about the body was visibly shaken, enough to have me worrying for him.

He couldn't have been more than a year out of high school. A bad rash of pimples covered his cheeks, his greasy hair thin and longish, wispy strays drifting errantly around the edges of a paper cap. His face was pale and his eyes wide with the shock of what he'd seen. The smell of fried food clung to him, a scent that now seemed grotesquely out of place when considering the morbid reality of our morning.

"I just... I just can't believe it," he stammered, his voice quivering. "Terri was a good person. A really good worker too, you know? Always showed up on time, did her job and didn't complain. I didn't even have to tell her to get off her phone. Not ever. Why would anyone do that to her?"

I said nothing as he droned on. Sometimes witnesses needed to do that as if they were purging their systems of the horror so they could tell me what I needed to hear. I forced myself to focus on him, to listen to every word, every flicker of emotion in case there was something that rang like a bell. When he started to repeat himself, I asked, "Tell me about last night. Anything unusual happen during Terri's shift?"

He shook his head, his Adam's apple bobbing as he swallowed hard. "No, nothing out of the ordinary. It was just another closing shift. It wasn't busy like it is in the summer. We had a few customers, locals only, but it was mostly quiet. Terri was in charge of taking out the trash, like always."

"Did she mention anything else to you? Something that might have happened before?" I'd already glimpsed the body and knew it was the same person who'd killed Jill Carter. But I had to ask the questions. "Anyone bothering her, any strange occurrences?"

Again, he shook his head. "No, she didn't say anything like that. She was just, you know, like normal." The manager gulped again, pawing at his throat. He'd seen the body too and saw how she'd died. "The last time I saw Terri, she was dragging the trash bags out here. She'd already clocked out and I thought she went home after."

"How about those?" I asked, pointing to the security cameras. They were perched like seabirds at the corners of the roofline. Only, these didn't move, their eyes fixed on the parking lot. "We'll want to review the footage."

The manager began shaking his head. When I frowned, he replied, "I didn't see anything on the video footage." He pointed at the dumpster, adding, "It's out of range. You can see Terri taking the trash to it though. But that's all."

"Still," I nodded. "We'll need to review it."

"Is-is that it?" he asked, continuing to clutch his throat as if guarding it.

I nodded, processing all the information. "Thank you. We'll take it from here. If you remember anything else, no matter how small the detail, you'll let us know?"

He agreed vigorously, grateful to be dismissed, and hurried back inside the restaurant. I turned my attention to the dumpster enclosure. It loomed ahead, a metal behemoth casting an oblong shadow onto the pavement. I took a deep breath and walked toward the crime scene, the smell hitting me. The rusty screech of the enclosure's door echoed in my ears as I pushed it open and walked to the back, revealing a nightmare behind the dumpster.

Terri Rond's body lay crumpled on the gravelly ground, naked and lifeless. Her skin was already a shade of blue from death, her eyes staring blankly toward the sky. Her neck bore the unmistakable marks of strangulation, more than a dozen bruises and welts, and deep indentations from where the killer had squeezed the life out of her multiple times. It was the same as we'd seen before, my heart aching for her and her family.

"Samantha, Derek, over here," I called out, my voice steady despite the revulsion churning in my stomach. Samantha and Derek hurried over, their expressions grim. Tracy was already beside the body, her camera clicking as she documented the scene. "Let's get started."

Blowing bangs from her eyes, Samantha exclaimed, "Time of death was confirmed to be late evening." She looked up, asking, "That aligns with what the restaurant manager said?"

"It does. We've also got video surveillance footage showing when the victim exited the building and came back here."

Derek nudged two black trash bags, the bottoms scarred with scrape marks. "She was dragging these?"

"Taking out the trash," I answered. At the front of the dumpster, I went through what was believed to be the victim's final moments. "She brings the trash bags to the dumpster, but then doesn't put them inside."

Waving the stench away, Tracy photographed the bags, adding, "She was attacked outside the enclosure and dragged behind the dumpster?"

Shaking my head, I made my way back to the victim's body, the path to the murder scene undisturbed. I paused when seeing the body in full, seeing it was another young woman about the same age as Jill Carter. The hair was different, shorter and dark. The victim was heavier but not overweight, her face small and round, her arms and legs muscled, leading me to think she was into sports. She looked strong, capable of putting up a fight, my focus shifting around the immediate area. "There's no signs of a struggle... not until we get back here behind the dumpster."

"Those collections," Tracy said, pivoting and kneeling in front of them. She froze them in time with a series of flashes, recording them as they were. "They're the same as Jill Carter's crime scene."

"We need to document every detail about them," I said, my eyes scanning the area for more. "Those piles have got a meaning of some kind."

Samantha knelt beside Terri's body, her gloved hands moving with practiced precision. "The bruising patterns suggest a prolonged struggle." Tilting the victim's head, the neck popping and cracking from the rigor mortis, Samantha put on a sad frown, shaking her head. "She's been strangled multiple times too."

"It's brutal," Derek said, holding a powerful light to illuminate the marks. "Why? Is the killer making sure they suffer?"

"We're still working on that," I answered as I crouched down, examining the strange collections around the dumpster. River stones, bottle caps arranged in a pyramid, cattail leaves, and wildflowers. All had been carefully selected and collected and then were meticulously placed here. "These collections... they're not random."

Tracy snapped a few more photos before speaking, camera clacking mechanically. "They look like they were placed in a way to be seen, like the killer meant for us to find them."

I nodded, hating the idea of the intentions. "It's a signature, that's for certain. Our killer is leaving a mark, creating a pattern. And Terri... she's part of that pattern now."

Samantha's voice broke through my thoughts. "Casey, take a look at this."

I moved closer, peering at where she was pointing. "What is it?" Tracy followed, camera lens nosing over my shoulder, the shutter clacking in my ear.

"The victim's fingertips," Samantha said, her voice tinged with curiosity. "There's dirt under her nails. And look at the abrasions on her palms. She was trying to fight back, maybe crawl away."

Derek added, "There're also some marks on her knees and feet. She was on the ground, struggling."

Anger and sadness surged in me, seeing that the victim had fought hard, the injuries evidence of a struggle to survive. But it hadn't been enough. "She was out here alone. It's winter, there's little to no tourists, nobody was around to hear her scream."

Tracy stepped closer, her camera still in hand. "What about the collections? Do you think she saw them?"

I felt my expression drain, an idea sparking in my brain. "Yeah. It's very possible. Even probable." I got up and went to the enclosure's east-facing wall, the ocean a short distance away.

The walls were eight feet high and made to hide the ugliness of a waste dumpster. The killer knew this and used the walls, the enclosure. "What if the collections were for her, the victim. She might have seen them and been lured back here. The killer knew this spot would be secluded enough."

"You mean the killer staged the crime scene for the victim?" Derek asked while lifting the body onto its side, Samantha shoving her hands beneath. "Sick."

I looked around the enclosure, my mind piecing together the scene. "He planned this. The collections, the secluded spot, the timing—he knew exactly what he was doing."

Tracy's camera flashes struck out of the corner of my eye, illuminating more of the strange collections. "If the killer brought them here, I'd think it would have taken a considerable amount of time to put them in place."

"I'm sure it did. But look around," I said, waving at the walls and how the dumpster blocked the front. "The killer could have been back here all day and nobody would have known."

"Sick," Derek repeated, his thin hair standing on end with a breeze racing over us.

Tracy's camera clicked again. "So what now?"

I turned back around to face the victim's body, my eyes scanning the area one last time. "All we can do is follow the evidence. Let's marry up these collections with what we found at Jill Carter's crime scene. Maybe we'll see a pattern in them?"

"What about Michael Gibson?" Tracy asked. The question got the attention of Derek and Samantha. "We should find out if the victim knew him or if he knew her."

I didn't answer immediately. It bothered me a little that she mentioned his name. Samantha and Derek knew to be discreet, but any of the patrol edging the crime scene could have overheard it, leaking the name as if Michael Gibson were one of the FBI's most wanted. Nodding my head, brow raised, I answered, "I expect we'll find out when we interview him."

"Understood," Tracy said, focusing on the injuries around the victim's middle.

Samantha continued with her assessment, saying, "The strangulation marks are consistent with someone using their hands. The killer is strong, methodical."

"Sexual assault?" I asked, suspecting.

"Likely," Samantha answered, her gaze falling to the victim's naked body. "I'll confirm it for the preliminary report."

Samantha and Derek began the process of carefully bagging and tagging the evidence. Tracy continued to document everything, her camera capturing the smallest details. I took a deep breath, trying to steady my thoughts. The wind picked up, rustling the leaves and loose trash, a chill shooting through me, a mix of cold and disgust mounting. I looked at Terri's lifeless body, her face a mask of frozen terror, my breath hot with determination. From my pocket, I produced my own collection, plastic evidence bags and a black marker for labeling. It was time to collect the findings and clear the crime scene to return it to the custody of the fast-food restaurant.

Tracy packed her camera, having taken enough pictures to document every inch of the crime scene. She helped secure the evidence left by the murderer, my mind returning to each collection with new and renewed questions. River stones, bottle caps, flowers—each item meticulously placed, a part of some twisted tableau. The killer was more than just a murderer; he was a collector, someone who found meaning in these macabre displays. And now, the killer had added Terri to his collection.

By the time we finished processing the scene, the sun had fully risen, casting a cold, pale light over the parking lot. The manager returned, standing at a distance, his face still pale and drawn. He waved me over eagerly, grasping his hands, clutching them nervously. I approached him, slipping the pair of nylon gloves off, fingers sweaty and instantly made cold. When I reached him, he handed me a thumb drive.

"It's the video surveillance from yesterday," he said, handing it to me, the drive pinched between two fingers. Perching a thumb over his shoulder, he added, "I... um, I also added surveillance footage from inside? Thought it might help?"

"It does," I answered. "Did you watch it?"

"Some, but I had to fast-forward, we're open now with a few customers seated." He glanced back at the restaurant. "We still gotta work, ya know."

"Did you see Terri talking to anyone? Was there anything unusual? Anyone following her, watching her?"

He shook his head. "No, nothing like that. Last night was quiet. On the video, you can see her cleaning mostly. She kept to herself too, talked to a couple kids at one point, a few friends maybe, but nothing out of the ordinary."

"Beyond last night, has there ever been any problems with customers? Anyone who might have had a grudge?"

Again, he shook his head. "No, we don't get much trouble. Especially this time of year."

I nodded, knowing this wasn't going anywhere but had to ask. Handing him my card, I said, "Thank you for the surveillance video. And like I said, if you think of anything, anything at all, call me."

He nodded, his eyes flicking once more to the dumpster enclosure. "I will, Detective. I promise."

I left the fast-food manager and rejoined my team. We loaded the evidence into the van, the weight of the case heavy in our hands as I helped Derek secure Terri Rond's remains. We'd turn left on the adjacent road and head to the station. Derek and Samantha would go in the opposite direction, to the morgue, where the formal cause of death would be documented.

The drive back was silent, Tracy working one of the cameras while I remained lost in thought about the macabre collections. The Outer Banks stretched out around us, the beaches opening to the ocean with sandy flats and stilted homes passing on the opposite side. It was a stark contrast to the darkness of the crime scene.

Finally, I broke the silence. "Any thoughts?"

"Well, there's Michael Gibson. But I already commented about him," Tracy answered, shutter clacking as she took my picture. She looked at the back of the camera, thumbed through the image before deleting it. "This is the second murder. Same M.O. Whoever it is, they're going to do it again."

"Yeah," I acknowledged, focusing on the road. "If we could find something in those collections, or whatever they're supposed to be, or even get some understanding of them, then maybe—"

Tracy interrupted, "Yeah, I mean, what's with those piles? There's nothing meaningful about them."

I agreed, suggesting, "It could be that the killer is showing off how he's collecting victims?"

We entered the station, the bags slung over our shoulders. The conference room table was already prepared with the evidence from Jill Carter's murder and I carefully placed the new collections side by side with them. They were the same. The river stones and bottle caps. But it was the wildflowers which were new.

"I'll get started with the bottle caps," Tracy said, joining me. She held a coffee, its steam curling around the lip of the cup. "If there was any hope of the killer getting sloppy, they'd be the best in holding a partial print."

"We should get so lucky?" I said with a faint thread of hope. An ache squeezed my insides as I looked over the conference room table. In most cases, we'd barely cover a tenth of the area. But in this case, we'd covered nearly half of the table. "Looking at these, I feel like anything we find would be grasping at straws."

"It's missing," Tracy said. She motioned to the table. "Look, there's no white rose or flower petals?"

"I noticed," I said, thinking of the makeshift memorial outside Jill Carter's locker. A sigh, chest rising and falling with an emotional breath, blood racing with rage and disgust. Regardless of how sad and tragic the circumstance, I had to understand the evidence we had. It was the only voice of the victims who could no longer speak.

Tracy tapped her laptop keyboard, Jill Carter and Terri Rond pictures showing on the room's large screens. There were two now. Two victims that we knew of. Young women. Senseless murders. Lives snuffed out in a similarly brutal manner. The likenesses and parallels were undeniable. How many more were in the killer's morbid collection?

FOURTEEN

Terri Rond. A second victim found earlier today. My head was still spinning with thoughts of a serial killer while I made my way back to the station from my apartment. We were far from done and I couldn't get back fast enough. This was a killer who'd targeted two victims in as many days, the pattern like a spree killing. Was there going to be a third. Tomorrow perhaps? Three in three, the killer's M.O. continuing with a vague hint of alliteration. The thought stopped me cold. We had ample evidence and none of it was showing me a direction to follow.

The morning warmed since working Terri Rond's crime scene at daybreak. I carefully hopped over a puddle, drops of hot coffee stinging my fingers. The pavement was wet again, the air foggy with wispy steam rising off the heaps of snow piled along the sidewalk. I couldn't see the beach or ocean but smelled them and heard the distant waves. A Marine Patrol boat raced by too, its motor revving while traveling south en route to a nearby fishing pier. Jericho was home with Thomas and Tabitha. Home and safe. I'd give him an extra hug later, selfishly thankful he wasn't on the water working the oceanside patrol anymore.

"Morning, Alice," I said, eyeing the station doors. Rock salt crunched with each step, my feet clumsy against it. I took hold of the railing while our station manager waved for me to be careful. Alice stood on the second step from the top, her round face blotchy with a sheen glistening. She panted heavily and struck the step with the end of a broom handle, forcing a smile and kicking at the clumps of ice.

"It's messy dear," she replied, sweeping briskly, the chunks clinging. I reached the landing and smelled the dark English tea Alice liked to drink. "Someone's apt to break a neck if we don't clear it."

"Isn't Karl around to do that?" I asked, expecting to see him. At one point, I'd thought his name was Charles and called him by the wrong name for a week before someone finally told me. He'd never corrected me, which I thought oddly funny, his being so polite. I peered through the front glass but didn't see him.

"Died," Alice answered coldly with a sad frown.

"What?" I dipped my head in shock, recalling the last time I'd spoken with Karl. Was it the day before the storm? It had to be, right? He was fixing the station's heater and had helped with a faulty outlet near my desk. That's when he'd jokingly scolded, telling me to stop plugging in a floor heater for my cold feet. "What-what happened to him?"

"It was a heart attack." She leaned hard against the stair's railing and clasped the broom handle tight against her chest. Her eyes glistened wet like the sweat on her brow. The two were close, which wasn't a surprise, both having worked at our station for nearly two decades. She motioned to the sidewalk, saying, "It hit him right over there the other day while he was shoveling the snow."

"Oh, Alice, I'm so sorry." I gripped her arm with a light squeeze, my balance tipping when she hugged me unexpectedly. "I know you two were close."

"Thank you, dear," she replied, holding me steady. "He always liked you guys."

"Well, we really liked him too," I commented, emotions stealing my words. In my job, I'd grown callous to delivering the most terrible news. It wasn't that I was cold or emotionally stunted. Nothing like that. It was a reverence all law enforcement has for death. Particularly when the crimes are heinous. Otherwise, it'd be too much and would make for a very short career.

But Karl was different. He was someone we knew, and his passing came with an entirely different kind of hurt. If only there was comfort in knowing another angel was watching over us. There wasn't though. Karl's death was just bitterly sad. "We'll miss him."

"Here," Alice said, a pen appearing from her hair. I had no idea where she kept them, but learned where there was one, there were two more of them nesting close by. She wrote down a name and number, along with a time and handed it to me. "It's his viewing and the funeral. You'll come?"

"Yes, certainly. I'll get a sitter too. Jericho and Karl go back—"

"Those two go way back, since before Jericho was elected sheriff," she finished for me, grinning fondly. "Karl would have wanted him there."

"We'll be there." I hugged her this time, initiating it.

A knock came from inside the station, the clamor breaking Alice's hold. We turned to see Tracy rapping a knuckle on the glass. Alice tapped the side of her head, eyes widening, "Oh my. Right, yes. Casey, the district attorney is here for you."

"Already?" I asked, the DA's arrival early. I hadn't expected to see her until this afternoon. With every murder, there was the pressure for answers. We had two that were similar and close together, questions mounting. It wouldn't be long before news crews were parked and press conferences held. "I wonder what changed?"

"Changed?" Alice asked, confused. She didn't wait for me to reply and continued sweeping.

I nudged my chin toward the door, asking, "You'll be okay, Alice?"

"Thank you," she said. "I'll be fine."

The door swung open, heat lifting my hair. Tracy fanned herself, saying, "It's the thermostat. Damn thing is stuck again."

"No kidding." I followed her inside, the station hot and muggy like a sauna. I peered over at the thermostat where we'd seen Karl working. "You heard about Karl?"

"I know. Isn't that terrible," Tracy replied. She looked at me briefly and then at the main conference room. "The DA is here already."

"Yeah, she's early." I glanced at the front of the station out of habit, an officer behind the counter in place of where Alice usually stood. He dabbed his balding, shiny head with a handkerchief and gave us an approving nod, recognizing me. "Did she say anything?"

"Talk to me?" Tracy scoffed. When I didn't laugh, she shook her head, turning serious. "Nothing other than to ask if the coffee was fresh."

"Is it?"

"She didn't complain," Tracy said, walking ahead.

In the quiet, our footsteps rang out and air pumped steadily from the vents, the morning early. Tracy opened a small gate which separated the public side of the station from our offices and the conference rooms. The wood clapped shut behind us, the air turning still and thicker. She ducked into her cubicle across from mine while eyeing the empty desk next to us. I sighed with understanding. The cubicle was empty due to the recent resignation of a coworker. It left us shorthanded which had frustrated Tracy. It frustrated both of us, though she seemed resigned to the idea that all the slack was falling on her shoulders. It wasn't.

"We're doing the best we can," I commented civilly, anxiety itching like a rash. "The applicants just aren't what I'm expecting."

"Would you mind if I took a look?" she asked, hand out. I plopped my bag and coat down without care, thankful to shed the layers, and eagerly grabbed a stack of applications and résumés.

"Be my guest," I replied, surprised by the initiative. Handing them over, I warned, "They're a bit all over the place."

"Really?" she said, eyes growing. "I get to help out?"

"Tracy, you are a part of the team," I answered, relieved to hand off the duty.

"This is gonna be awesome," she said, sifting through the top folders. "I'll set aside the ones I think we should interview."

"Have at it." I fished my laptop from my bag, the district attorney waiting patiently. I glanced over, questioning if it was patience I saw. I could have been wrong. She'd seen me, her gaze drifting above her phone briefly, one brow cocked. When I turned back, Tracy had already returned to her desk. I pointed at the conference room, saying, "Let's get started, what do you say?"

She didn't look up. It was quiet, save for the sound of keyboard keys. I poked my head into her cubicle, the stack of résumés sitting next to a litter of computer parts. Bright green headphones the size of coffee mugs hugged her ears, a yellow light blinking.

I'd expected her to join the meeting but from the looks of it, she must have stayed late last night to work on Jill Carter's computer, the laptop cracked open and gutted like a clam. I recognized it immediately, the colorful stickers placed on the front by the victim. Cables snaked through the parts, connecting some of them to a computer in the corner which was setup for forensic analysis.

"Huh?" she asked, glancing up a moment.

"What's going on?" The screen that had her attention was filling with numbers, a mountain of them scrolling fast from the bottom to the top. The other monitors were deep into what looked to be more diagnostics. "What is all this?"

"There was an extra disk partition that I found on Jill Carter's laptop," she replied, focus returning. "I think it was left over from whoever she got the computer from."

"Do you think it's relevant to the case?" I asked, thinking of Terri Rond's murder. Jill Carter's laptop could've come from several places and didn't seem related at all. When she didn't answer, I faced the conference room, adding, "It could be anything."

"Or it could be something?" she challenged. I wanted to get her some face time in front of the district attorney. A part of this career was managing up which meant working with attorneys and politicians. It would be good for her. "If you don't need me, I thought I'd work this?"

"I'll take the meeting," I said reluctantly. A flash of relief appeared. Could I blame her. Sometimes it was the hands-on we needed. "But if you discover this is a dead end, then you'll join us."

"Immediately," she replied, turning back to the screen without another word.

I opened my mouth to say something but didn't. Or maybe couldn't was the right word. It wasn't like Tracy to be so short. Not ever. Not with me or anyone. It wasn't just that. Tracy hadn't kept me informed on her progress, the laptop pieces adding up to a significant amount of work. I dismissed it, choosing to see it as her taking the initiative which was good.

I opened the door to the conference room, heavy glass passing with a woosh. "Ma'am," I said cordially, the back of my neck stinging with nervous sweat. The district attorney stood to shake my hand, diamond studs in her earlobes bouncing the light. Her hand in mine, I added, "Sorry for the wait, but I wasn't expecting you until this afternoon."

"It's Pauline, please," she insisted. She wore short, auburn hair that covered her ears, the color matching her golden-brown eyes and year-round tan. A narrow face and small nose, there was a pinkish lip gloss that did well to cover what the cold, wintry weather had been doing to her skin. Her handshake was firm, ending with a squeeze as she kiddingly warned, "If you call me ma'am again, I'll have to reciprocate and start calling you ma'am too."

"Pauline," I said, not wanting to feel older than I was. A New York Assistant District Attorney for the last five years, Pauline Pool was born and raised in the Outer Banks, the barrier islands remaining her family's home. She'd returned home recently to get married and decided to continue her career of civil service by throwing her hat into the ring of recent elections, including the one for a new district attorney.

She won, and we'd already butted heads a few times which was enough to put me on my toes around her. Terri Rond's and Jill Carter's sexual assaults and murders were the biggest case we'd worked together, which meant we had to both tread carefully and ensure nothing compromised it. Plugging in the video cable to my laptop, I'd received a text from Pauline earlier, telling me that Michael Gibson was the subject of our meeting. "Give me a second while I pull this up."

"I'm early because there's been a development... that is, in addition to this morning's crime scene," she said, blowing the steam from the top of her coffee. She cringed at it and put it back down. "It's really too hot in here. Even for coffee."

"That it is. I'm sure Alice is working on a fix." The case appeared on the large monitors, Terri Rond's crime scene pictures from this morning on one screen and Jill Carter's autopsy photos on the other. Mentioning the heat got me up from the table and opening one of the windows a crack, the sea air blowing over my arms. "Additional developments?"

"It's about Michael Gibson, the student you notified me about." She gripped her arm. "In the email, there was mention of a scratch, and that it looked suspicious?"

"Yes. The timing of it was suspicious," I replied, clarifying while opening my notes. "The injury was on his right arm, between the elbow and wrist, closer to the hand."

"Did he know the second victim?" she asked, attempting another sip of her coffee. It was met with the same cringy look and she put the cup down.

"It's possible that they were all friends."

"Hmm," was all she said, pondering. When she was ready, she asked, "And there was also a recovery of tissue from beneath the first victim's fingernails?"

I nodded, saying, "On Jill Carter's left hand, but we'll need more time for any DNA recovery." The district attorney drummed her fingers on the table. "What's this about? Can you share what the development is?"

"I believe we have enough for an arrest warrant," she replied, focus shifting to her laptop, fingers racing as if she were typing the warrant herself.

"An arrest warrant?" I asked, the evidence lacking any clear direction to me. Like the old disk partition Tracy discovered on the victim's laptop, the scratch on Michael Gibson's arm could have been from anything. Yes, of course I wanted to question him more, believing he may have been the last schoolmate to see Jill Carter alive. That didn't mean we should jump direct to an arrest and leapfrog to a warrant. Doing so wrongly could seriously jeopardize the boy's life.

Maybe the new DA was being too ambitious? I counted to ten in my head while watching her type, her lips moving as she dictated an email to herself. She was the district attorney and had final say, but I had to speak up. "I don't want to step on any toes, but isn't an arrest warrant premature? I'm planning to question Michael Gibson officially here at the station, including the scratch, and about Terri Rond too. His parents will be there, a lawyer too, if they're more comfortable having one."

She finished typing, hands raised like a conductor over a great symphony. "The affidavit is written and submitted and has sufficient factual information to establish probable cause. Now we wait on a judge to sign-off." She looked up from the laptop and saw my concern. "Trust me. I know what I'm doing."

"Maybe let me in on what you know?" I asked, heat rising on my chest and neck. "We have my initial interview, tissue beneath the victim's fingernail, a scratch on the arm. But we don't have a connection yet to either victim other than high school friendships."

"We'll collect his DNA when he's brought in," the district attorney answered in a nonchalant way that annoyed me more than the legal authority she was flinging around so carelessly. When she saw that I wasn't convinced, she tilted her face and spun her laptop around.

The name of another school edged the top of her screen, East OBX High School letters clipped but still legible. I knew the school, having worked a case involving both West and East OBX high schools. Michael Gibson's attendance and grades were listed beneath it and showing he'd been doing well academically. Confused why the DA was showing me this, I read on. There was a transfer out of East OBX earlier in the year, the transfer dates showing, but without a reason. I looked up, feeling more confused.

"Michael Gibson was removed from East OBX after allegations of a sexual assault taking place in the girl's bathroom."

"Sexual assault? What happened?"

"From the victim's statement, it was forced sodomy." The DA swung the laptop back around, tapping the keyboard before returning it to face me. On the screen, a copy of a handwritten statement, the penmanship big and swirly and uncannily precise. I scanned the single page, the victim from the girl's bathroom describing how her classmate, Michael Gibson, had followed her into the bathroom and threatened physical harm if she didn't do as he told her. A teacher had walked in on them. When I looked up, the DA said, "She was fifteen."

"No charges were filed? What about an investigation?" I asked, understanding the crime, and also believing I would have heard about it since the jurisdiction was local to the station. "I don't understand why Michael would have been transferred to another school?"

"The investigation for the bathroom sexual assault is still ongoing. The investigator chose to delay it," the DA answered. From the look on her face, she didn't know why there was a delay. "There were questions about the charges. Michael Gibson was adamant that he'd been invited into the bathroom, and that what happened in there was consensual, that the victim had initiated the activities."

"Consensual? And then the victim made the claim of sexual assault afterward?" I asked, needing more of the details. "Regardless, Michael Gibson would have been arrested?"

The DA acknowledged the question with a nod. "That's what one would have expected, especially since a teacher found them and reported it. The claim of sexual assault came later from the girl's parents when the school notified them of the incident and that a suspension was issued to both for skipping class."

"Skipping class, together?" As a detective, I don't want to feel doubt when building a case. However, I'd come to rely on it as a kind of scoring rubric in vetting all aspects of a crime. "Let me get this right... the victim's parents made a claim of sexual assault after their daughter was reprimanded with a detention.

The school board opened their own investigation and made the decision to transfer Michael Gibson while it was in progress?"

A slow nod. "The parents of the fifteen-year-old were threatening to sue if an action wasn't taken immediately." Pauline cocked her head, adding, "I know, it's a case of she-said, he-said."

"You think!" I belted. The next look I got told me instantly why she was issuing the arrest warrant. "You don't want to take any chances of it being true. That Michael Gibson did sexually assault that girl in the bathroom and now there are two dead students at the school he was transferred to."

"Imagine the press running stories with what you just said," she replied, closing her laptop, blowing out a long breath. She made a face at the cup and then looked me square in the eyes. I saw that she'd made up her mind about the warrant, regardless of any doubts. "We have to go with what we have. And at the moment, that's Michael Gibson."

FIFTEEN

When the district attorney left the conference room, she commented that a judge was already reviewing the affidavit. Support for an arrest warrant was expected to be issued shortly. When she reached the wooden gate and knocked it with her knee, she asked, "You'll handle the warrant once it's been issued?"

"I'll take care of it," I assured her, my stomach doing turns. The decision felt rushed. Even if the result got us an interview with Michael Gibson, an arrest was premature. She nodded slowly, looking at me again as if knowing there was doubt. I couldn't stop it if I tried anyway. Not with the affidavit issued. The machine had been started and it would take much more than doubt to shut it down. "We'll bring Michael Gibson in when the warrant is finalized."

"Soonest," she answered, the gate latching between us. Soonest wasn't in my control. It wasn't in anyone's control, but I held back the eye roll that was pressing in my head. "We don't have time to let it go beyond this afternoon."

"Soonest," I repeated, understanding a deeper motive. It was her position and the pressure from the school districts.

Their mismanaging of the first sexual assault reported. "We'll get it done."

I didn't look back when I returned to my desk. Questions circled my mind like buzzards over a dying animal, its fate known. Only, Michael's fate wasn't known yet, and that meant finding the truth. When I reached my desk, I glanced over at Tracy. The bright green headset was gone from her ears, and she was bent forward, her nose close to the screen.

"There's a warrant being issued for Michael Gibson's arrest." I made room behind her and perched my bum against the edge of the desk. Arms crossed, I continued. "It turns out, there was an incident at his school last year."

"There are incidents at schools all the time," she said casually while staring hard at the screen. She was being dismissive again, busy with her own work. Whatever she was looking at firmly had her attention.

"Well, this particular incident occurred at a different school, East OBX High School. It was a sexual assault in the girl's bathroom. The victim was fifteen."

Tracy sat up, chair spinning to face me. "That was Michael Gibson?"

"You knew about the case?"

She shrugged, answering, "It wasn't a case that came through here." A frown, questioning. "Actually, it wasn't a case at all, just a report in the news with some rumors about what actually happened."

"Beyond the rumors, someone knows the truth of what really happened," I commented, thinking we should interview the girl from the bathroom. A screen caught my attention the way a spark in the darkness draws your focus. It was filled with text, mostly computer gibberish, a raw data dump from the partition she'd found. "The girl's parents made some threats and that's how Michael Gibson ended up at Jill Carter's school."

"Now both Jill Carter and Terri Rond are dead," Tracy exclaimed, brow furrowing. "And there's a sexual assault claim."

"I know, it looks bad for Michael." I moved to the other side of the cubicle, to where parts of Jill Carter's laptop were, the pieces scattered, a cable plugging in the hard drive. "I'm not convinced about what happened in the school bathroom. Not like the DA is."

"Do you have the name of the first victim?" Tracy asked. She looked up, wary of how that might have sounded. "I mean, we could interview her after and compare their stories if you're doubting what happened."

"It's not that." The subject was making me feel restless, squirmy. "I never want to be that person casting doubt over a victim's claims. I'd think if there was something substantial then the investigation would have been completed."

"Why are they sitting on it?" Tracy asked, filtering the data on the screen, removing the unintelligible stuff. She faced me, adding, "There's got to be a reason."

"From what the DA said, it's a she-said and he-said argument. The victim claimed it happened and Michael claimed there was consent."

"And without any hard evidence," Tracy began, reading the scowl on my face, "it's impossibly difficult to prove a sex crime occurred."

"Beyond reasonable doubt," I added. "I think the delay in the investigation is on purpose."

We traded looks, Tracy scowling, confused. "Why would they do that?"

"What's apt to change between the date of the incident and a few weeks, maybe months later?"

She shrugged. "The victims will be older," she answered without giving it any thought.

"Think about it," I said, hands perched on my hips. "Michael claims it was innocent. There's lack of medical proof.

Lack of any witness to the incident. It was only reported after the parents were notified. What might change between then and now?"

"Their stories," Tracy answered. "You think the investigator is going to look for any discrepancies?"

"It's one way to figure out who is telling the truth," I answered.

"But, Casey, Jill Carter's murder and the sexual assault?" Tracy argued. "There's a pattern that can't be ignored."

"I know it," I answered short. There was a name on the screen. A familiar name. I moved closer, finishing my thoughts, "With the issuance of an arrest warrant, I'm sure the investigator of the sexual assault will be in touch with us."

Tracy saw me reading the screen, a grin appearing. "I knew there was something on that old partition."

"That's Jill Carter's mother. Right?"

"Janine Carter," Tracy answered, jotting it down. "I think this is from a bank statement. Check out the address."

"Cayman Islands?" I asked, curious why a foreign account was used. "I barely know the local banks let alone any offshore ones."

She tapped the screen, the money listed in US currency, the figures high, one of them near a million dollars. "If I'm reading this right, a lot of money passed through the account in a short period."

"Is it still there?" I asked, speaking aloud, and then realized we were looking at old data. "It's a disk partition that was deleted. That laptop is a hand-me-down."

"That could be," Tracy commented. "But that doesn't mean there weren't large sums of money being passed through a foreign account."

"It's a few million dollars? Is that enough to be suspicious?" I asked, growing curious. "We know Jill's parents are lawyers and they work in real estate. What if it's a foreign investment in the Outer Banks?"

Tracy regarded the possibility, answering, "Might be investments. But why only in her name? Jill's mother?" A pause, Tracy sat up, wanting to ask something but held back.

"What is it?"

"You could be right and I'm seeing something that isn't suspicious at all," she commented with a frown. "Any objections if I want to investigate it further?"

I looked for any relevance to the case, relevance to Jill's murder. There might have been a strong suspicion in Michael Gibson, but that didn't close the case automatically. Everything was relevant. "Keep looking," I told her. But then warned, "It's probably nothing. Just a hand-me-down laptop with old business records."

The corner of her mouth rose. "I'm probably just being nosey."

"All ideas are good ideas until proven otherwise," I said, reminding her. "We're investigating a brutal murder of a young woman. You wouldn't have gotten this far with her laptop if you didn't have something in mind."

"Or I was just being nosey," she countered.

"In our line of work, nosey is a good thing." I had the warrant covered when it got issued. "Dig into it. If there's something there that strikes you as odd, let me know."

"You're going after Michael Gibson?" she asked.

"We are," I confirmed.

SIXTEEN

We needed some answers. I could feel the heat from the DA's office which was no doubt a redirected heat from the mayor's office. I lowered the sun visor, turning left onto the last road adjacent to the beach, Terri Rond's home less than a few miles from the station. Tracy bit into a cream cheese bagel, her eyes half-lidded while she let out a small moan. She ate like her father, every bite a joy.

"What?" she asked, catching a look. "It tastes good."

"Sounds like it." I laughed. My smile faded when I reached the home address on my phone, car tires scraping the curb when I pulled in close. Ducking my head to look up to the front door, the house stilted, our medical examiner was there, Samantha shaking hands with Terri Rond's parents. "We're here."

"Coming," Tracy said, mouth full while shoving the remains of her late breakfast in a bag and wiping her mouth.

I opened the car door, the sea air crisp, and draped my badge around my neck. The sun was high in the sky as Tracy exited the other side, staring up at the Rond family home. It was a modest beachfront house on the Outer Banks, painted in a soft blue that seemed to blend with the clearing bright sky above.

The ocean's rhythmic roar served as a constant backdrop, the home sitting on the beach. The setting was a sad contrast, its serene beauty in the face of the tragedy the Rond family were facing.

The salty breeze carried a sense of foreboding, a weight that settled in the pit of my stomach while I ascended the front stairs. This part of the job was the hardest, facing the loved ones of the victims. Samantha gave us a nod, saying nothing as she passed us on the steps. We'd meet later and trade any notes, remaining quiet for now while in hearing distance of Terri's family.

Tracy adjusted her bag, glancing at me with a look that conveyed both readiness and empathy. Together, we finished walking up the wooden steps to the front door.

Mrs. Rond stood in the doorway, her silhouette outlined by the bright light of the hallway behind her. Her face was a map of grief, her eyes red and swollen, her husband close behind, sniffling and wearing the same grief. She forced a small, weary smile, one that couldn't mask the depth of her anguish.

"Detective White, Investigator Fields," she greeted us, her voice wavering. "Thank you for coming."

"Thank you for taking the time for us," I replied gently, surprised she knew our names. Samantha must have provided them, knowing we'd be arriving soon after she was done. "We are deeply sorry for your loss."

They didn't speak or couldn't speak, the moment catching up to them when their eyes found my badge. The sight of it triggered another wave, the woman's face disappearing in the crook of her husband's arm and chest, the sobs muted. I hated that I was the face of a parent's worst nightmare—a morning where the familiar sounds of children are replaced with a knock at the door, law officers telling you that your child has been brutally raped and murdered. Tracy shifted uncomfortably as we waited, the couple exchanging consoling whispers.

A moment later, they turned and led us into the living room, where Mrs. Rond dropped onto the sofa, her head down, a box of tissues next to her, crumpled remains strewn across the seat cushion. Mr. Rond sat in an armchair, a photograph of Terri clutched in his fingers. His hands shook slightly as he held the frame.

"I'm so sorry for your loss," Tracy said, her voice soft.

"Terri was a bright young woman," Terri's mother began. She corrected herself then, brow jumping, "Barely a woman. It's not fair!"

"She was our light," Mr. Rond replied, his voice breaking. "It just doesn't seem real."

We spent a few minutes offering more condolences, asking about Terri's interests and her friends, piecing together her life from their memories. It was clear she had been the center of their world, full of dreams and plans for the future. None of the answers spoke to me. None of them stood out. I thought of the earlier meeting with the DA. "Jill Carter. She was a friend of your daughter?"

A fading grin. "Uh-huh." Terri's mother glanced at her husband, bracing his knee with a squeeze. She shuddered, sniffing back a cry. "They grew up together but drifted apart some with high school."

"Kids do," Tracy said, commenting. "But they remained cordial?"

"Yes... just found different crowds," Terri's mother answered.

"Was your daughter also friends with a Michael Gibson?" I asked.

"Michael Gibson?" Terri's father said, questioning. When his wife began to shake her head, he did the same and asked, "Why? Who is he?"

"He's a student at the same school—"

"Did he do this?" Terri's mother suddenly sat up straight as if jolted by a bolt of electricity, her interruption accusatory. "Is he a suspect?"

"Not a suspect," I answered quickly. "We're gathering names of Terri's friends and anyone who might have also been friends with Jill Carter."

"You mean, he was friends with Jill Carter?" Terri's father asked, nodding.

"That's correct." I had to ask about Michael Gibson but wanted to be careful not to be leading. "Was there a group that Terri may have hung around with? Any other names of other close friends?"

"There were a few from her work," Terri's mother replied. Shaking her head, she added, "Jill wouldn't have known them though? Do you think my daughter's murderer is someone the girls knew?"

"We don't know that yet," Tracy answered, picking a staple response.

"I see," Terri's mother mumbled, the anguish finding her again. The woman braced her heart, her body folding, crushed with sadness. "Who would do such a thing?"

"That's what we're going to find out, ma'am." It was another staple response, the promises Terri's parents wanted to hear remaining unspoken.

The questions ended with a list of names and the victim's work and school schedules, the main purpose of our visit quickly approaching. Tracy stood slowly, asking, "May we see your daughter's bedroom?"

A hesitant nod, the process unfamiliar to them. Terri's parents traded glances, nodding to one another. I explained, "It would also mean moving things, possibly taking anything we believe could be related to her murder."

"Yes, of course—" Terri's father began.

"Anything you need to take," her mother continued. "Please take it."

"Thank you," I said, joining Tracy.

Mr. Rond pointed toward a hallway. "It's the last room on the left."

"I can show them," Mrs. Rond said, standing. She hesitated, her pain palpable in the silence that followed. A moment later, she mouthed, "Sorry," and led us down the hallway.

The room was at the end of the hall, the door slightly ajar. As we stepped inside, I measured up decor, much of it typical for a teenager. There were posters of a few boy bands and other pop stars draped along the walls. There were also photos of Terri with her friends, a few of them taken inside the school. One of the pictures showed her at the beach with Jill Carter, both of them years younger and smiling brightly, carefree and full of life. I don't know if it was the sudden sadness that hit me, but I found myself staring hard, unable to break away.

"Oh wow," Tracy said, camera in hand and taking a picture. "That's sad."

"Terribly sad," I said, voice stuck in my throat. "This is more than a friendship broken."

"How do you mean?"

"I've got to believe that both Jill Carter and Terri knew the killer," I said. There was no signs of a struggle outside the dumpster. The trash bags had been left outside as well, the work-task incomplete. "Terri was taking out the trash and something, or someone had interrupted her. Someone she knew. That Jill knew too."

Tracy motioned behind me where I saw Terri's mother in the doorway. Did she hear me?

"Find anything?" she asked, looking into the bedroom, sighing heavily.

"We'll let you know," I told her while Tracy moved quietly to Terri's desk, opening drawers and examining their contents with a practiced touch. I approached the nightstand, noticing a stack of romance novels, paperbacks, one of them on the bed, well-thumbed and unfinished. "She liked to read?"

"Terri loved to read," her mother replied. A smile. "She gets... got that from me."

"Anything in them," Tracy asked, her voice a hushed whisper, fanning the novels. She opened the romance book on the bed, lifting it close enough to read. "Maybe something in the margins?"

"Anything?" I asked. Tracy shook her head. "I thought most everyone was reading digitally these days."

"eBooks," Tracy corrected me. "Blogs too."

I scanned the room, my eyes landing on a slender green vase by the window, its glassy neck long and thin. Inside it was a long-stemmed white rose, the petals wilted, the edges browning. It seemed out of place among the vibrant chaos of a teenager's room. I slipped on a pair of latex gloves and picked up the vase carefully, noting the way the dried petals fell loosely at the slightest touch.

"Tracy, take a look at this," I told her, holding the vase in the window's light.

She joined me, her brow furrowing as she examined the rose. "A white rose," she murmured. "It looks like the one outside Jill Carter's high school locker."

Mrs. Rond, who had been standing silently in the doorway, stepped forward. Her expression filling with a mix of sorrow and curiosity. "I asked Terri about that rose," she said, her voice tinged with a mother's worry. "She wouldn't tell me who gave it to her. She just smiled and said it was a secret."

"A secret," Tracy echoed, glancing at me meaningfully. We both knew secrets could be pivotal in understanding what had happened to Terri and Jill. "Did she mention anyone specific recently, Mrs. Rond? Someone new? Maybe a friend, or someone she was spending time with?"

Mrs. Rond shook her head slowly. "Sometimes she was

private about her friends. Especially lately. But I just thought it was part of her being a teen." The woman stopped as if a memory had struck her. "She did mention someone once or twice. She only called him 'M.' I never got a last name though."

Tracy and I exchanged a glance, the kind that communicated both realization and urgency. It was a lead, something we could pursue. "Thank you, Mrs. Rond," I said. "This could be very helpful."

We continued our search, methodically examining every corner of the room. Tracy found a small notebook under the bed, its pages filled with doodles and notes. She paused at a page where Terri had scribbled a poem. It was about the ocean, longing, and secrets whispered by the waves. There was something hauntingly beautiful about it, and my gut told me it held more meaning than met the eye. "Get a picture of it," I told her.

"I got it," Tracy answered, paging through the notebook, photographing anything that might be pertinent. "I think I've seen enough."

"Yeah," I said, finishing up.

We met the Ronds outside their daughter's bedroom. "Ma'am, sir. We're going to do everything we can to find justice for your daughter." Inside I was cringing. I was hating the canned responses, but they were staples for a reason, rehearsed so as not to give any false hope. "Thank you for your time."

"Please, anything else you need," they said, speaking together, voices thick with emotion while walking us to the front door.

Outside, we paused on the porch for a moment, the late morning sun casting long shadows across the wooden planks. The ocean was a deep blue expanse under the bright sky, its waves crashing rhythmically onto the shore. Despite the beauty, there was a somberness to the scene, as if nature itself mourned the loss of the girls too.

Tracy broke the silence, her voice thoughtful. "Two roses,

two girls, both murdered. There's no questioning the connection here, Casey."

"I agree," I replied, feeling the weight of the case pressing down on me. We had more than the collections. "Whoever this 'M' is, Terri may have accepted the rose from them."

We walked back to the car, the wooden steps creaking softly beneath our feet. As we drove away, I looked back at the house, where the Ronds appeared in the doorway, clinging to each other for comfort and strength. Their lives had been shattered in a way that could never be mended. As we sped along the coastline, the road stretching out before us, bright and winding, my mind raced with possibilities. The white rose, the mysterious "M", and the secrets Terri had kept—all were pieces of a larger puzzle. We needed to fit them together quickly before more lives were lost.

SEVENTEEN

The sun had finally returned to the Outer Banks, the beaches and ocean surface gilded and bright. It was like something out of a painting. That is, if paintings were alive with sounds and smells. Only, this wasn't artwork hanging in a famous museum, and it didn't have an artist's name scrawled along the bottom. This was my backyard, our apartment a beachfront bliss. Jericho had brought up the need for us to find a new home. A house that was big enough for the four of us. Bigger was better, he'd said, but I liked the cozy cottage feel, the touch of sand and beach grass on my bare feet only yards from our patio door. Maybe he was right though. Thomas was growing like a weed and Tabitha would catch up soon, both sharing a single room.

I turned my face into the sunlight, an orange glow bleeding through my eyelids. The snows were gone from the beaches for what I'd hoped was the remainder of the year. A nearby bird chirped and seagulls flew overhead, their voices mixing with the crashing waves. If I was closer, I'd be able to feel the ocean thundering into my feet and legs, the tide high and the surf rough. It was also a reminder of how powerfully beautiful and dangerous the shoreline of the barrier islands could be.

It was already after the noon hour and my stomach ached for food while my soul hungered for the company of my family. There was urgency in this case, two dead girls and a killer on the loose. As much as I wanted to keep going with the investigation, I had to eat and rest and fill up my tanks both physically and emotionally if I was going to be any good to anyone, especially the victims and their families.

I came home, leaving Tracy to work the bits and bytes of the data puzzle she'd found; that's where she'd find her fuel, filling up for the next round of investigations. She had a drawer full of protein bars and powdered shakes to nibble and drink. I'd send a text in a few, reminding her to eat, her suspicions of the foreign bank activities consuming every ounce of her attention. There was also the white rose from Terri Rond's room. That was occupying thoughts in my mind. Tracy's attention was in the tech. She could be onto something too. It might have been nothing at all, but until she came back with more information, it was worth exploring.

"We got grilled cheeses waiting," Jericho called. The window to the apartment shut before I could reply. I came to eat and see them, but my thoughts were on Jill Carter. This was the part of an investigation I disliked most. It was about waiting. I was waiting on an arrest warrant to be issued, and on Tracy's report. There was also Jill Carter's full autopsy report and Terri Rond's preliminary too. Though I didn't believe anything new would come of them. Samantha was always thorough, even in the findings from the crime scene. Metal sliding on metal, the window opened again with a giggle. It was Tabitha this time. "And mato soups. Jericho say hurry up."

"Mato soup sounds wonderful," I told her, returning to the apartment. She grunted trying to close the window, metal screeching. "Careful, girl—"

"There's tomato soup and grilled cheeses," Thomas announced when I entered. His voice whistled these days, a front baby tooth knocked out recently, the sight that late afternoon making for its own crime scene. Tabitha stood amidst the mayhem with a plastic toy gripped in her hands, the end of it bloodied while Thomas covered his mouth, blood running through his fingers. Two stitches later, the inconsolable cries finally quieted, a pediatric doctor explained how the adult teeth might migrate given Thomas's age. It was a wait and see, and it was a very minor thing to worry about. "Casey, are you hungry?"

"I'm famished," I answered, kissing the top of his head.

"Me me me," Tabitha yelled, rushing to clutch my leg, her big, round, hazel eyes fixed on mine. I combed my fingers through her whitish hair, its touch like silk. She put on a frown. "Me?"

"Yes, of course," I answered, kissing the top of her head too. She was racing around the other side of the table before I could finish and climbed onto her booster seat, the plastic clapping against the wood.

"And me?" Jericho asked, insisting while putting on the same pout the children guilted me with. "Don't forget me."

"Never," I told him, wrapping my arms around his middle, squeezing. I planted a longer kiss on his lips, surprising him with a touch of romance. I thought of the marine patrol boat from this morning, its motor revving high while it raced along the shoreline. Though he hadn't said anything, deep down, I couldn't help but wonder if Jericho was missing it, missing his career. I'd dared to pester with a question now and again, his forfeiting nothing to indicate he was. While he didn't say it outright, I found his replies hard to believe. He'd been a cop like me, a sheriff, and a major in North Carolina's Marine Patrol. He'd even run for mayor once. He returned the kiss with a playful moan and looked at me soulfully, mouthing the words I love you. "I love you too."

"What's on your mind?" he asked, noticing.

"Do you miss work?" I dared to ask. I didn't wear a good poker face and was never able to hide my feelings from him.

He shrugged and returned to the stove and piled grilled-cheese sandwiches on a plate. As he dished each, he asked, "Would you be disappointed in me if I said every day?"

"Shit, really?" I hated being right. "A lot?"

"Ohhhhhhhh," Thomas sang, his gaze locked on his sister until she joined in, their chorus gaining. Together they announced, "Quarter for the swear jar."

By now, half my paycheck was in that damn jar. "Do you?"

"It's a different kind of feeling though," he said, clarifying. "The rush of it maybe?"

"It's like a drug." I knew exactly what he was talking about. He was talking about fight or flee, how we'd been trained to resist the urge to flee. When the body gets flooded with adrenaline, we experience a high. I took his hand and the pan of sandwiches to help, my fingers brushing over one of the scars that his career had given him. He'd been torn apart and put back together more than a few times, wearing his career like a map. In my heart, I selfishly believed he'd survived his career for us. For me and for our family. I searched for the right words. But what do you tell a man who is missing the dangers you fear most? "Are you thinking about returning?"

He took in a deep breath, lips pinched. My heart sank at once and I suddenly couldn't breathe. The room was suffocatingly small, and I stirred, wanting to be back outside. I could see he'd been considering it. Jericho didn't need to answer me. He didn't need to say another word. He saw that I knew and asked, "Are you mad?"

"I can't be mad at something like that," I replied, lying to him. Inside, I was beyond disappointed. Troubled was a better explanation of how I felt. I faced the children, Thomas busily dunking a corner of his sandwich into the tomato soup. He glanced at us, soupy drops puddling onto the table. Tabitha held her sandwich with two hands, the triangle bread looking massive in her tiny fingers. She stared blankly at the television in the other room where the cartoon characters were in a race, legs spinning in a blur, white smoke trailing. "What about the adoption."

"I know," Jericho answered guiltily, biting his lip, regret on his face. Concern edged the disappointment. We'd almost lost our chance to adopt Thomas and Tabitha, child services having deemed our work lifestyles as being high risk. That's when Jericho made the decision to step back from his career and become a stay-at-home father. "I've been thinking about that a lot."

"Jericho, I don't know what to say." It felt like a stone had lodged in my throat, my voice breaking. I didn't want him to be unhappy, but I didn't want to change what we had either. I draped my arms across the kids, kneeling between them. They were oblivious to what we were talking about, both stuffing their faces and craning their necks to watch the television. I peered up at Jericho, adding, "Thank you for doing all this. But maybe it was too much to ask for it to have fallen all on you."

"Casey, it's what we agreed to," he said and pulled my chair for me to sit. He sat down, motioning to my plate, my phone dinging with a text message. "Let's eat before you get pulled away."

"We'll have to talk about this?" I told him, setting the expectation of tonight's conversation.

"Yeah," he answered gruffly, soup spoon plunking a bowl. It got the kids' attention, silence descending between us. For a long moment, there was only clamoring cartoon noises. "Look, to be clear, I haven't committed to anything. You only asked if I missed it."

"No, I know," I replied, stammering, I put the sandwich down, my appetite bitten by the conversation. It wasn't just his welfare I was afraid for, it was the home we made for Thomas and Tabitha. Could we lose them? The adoption was contingent on one of us leaving our career. None of these questions could be answered. Not yet. Not now. I attempted a smile but felt the awkwardness. My phone buzzed again. "We'll talk later."

The truth was, I think in my gut, I'd wondered if Jericho could stay at home with the kids. Even when he'd made the offer, there was a reservation about it, a seed of doubt. I couldn't fault him for it or be mad at him. Jericho was a cop like me. And once a cop, always a cop. But now we had a family together and I didn't know where that left things if he went back to the Marine Patrol. I couldn't lose Thomas and Tabitha. I couldn't lose Jericho either.

EIGHTEEN

Michael Gibson's car had been spotted near his high school, but the officer couldn't confirm seeing him inside it. Twenty minutes had passed since then, the search radius expanding fast like a murky puddle. I punched the accelerator, eyeing my speedometer while passing a speed limit sign, barely stopping at the intersection while I craned my neck to search up and down the streets. My car's rear tire struck the curb with a thud when I steered hard into a right turn and almost plastered the back of a parked car. Michael had to be in the vicinity, possibly right under our noses. We just hadn't seen him yet.

Take a breath, I warned, adrenaline coursing through me like a drug, throat swelling with a rapid heartbeat that I could feel pulsing in my head. When the school came up on the left side, I cranked the steering wheel, speeding into the parking lot where Michael had mentioned seeing Jill Carter before her death. Around and around, I covered every inch of asphalt, hoping Michael had parked his car in plain sight amongst his peers and the school's faculty. There were hundreds of cars and with each row of them covered, I felt time slipping.

Jill Carter's home was next, passing by it to my left, the

windows shaded, a steady stream of visitors entering and exiting. They were dressed drably, their faces downcast and sullen. The girl's body remained in the morgue, its release coming later today. The same was likely occurring at Terri Rond's place too, two sets of parents, their futures suddenly blighted by the loss of a child. Losing a child isn't something you feel once. From the moment they're gone, the pain of it is with you every day.

I spun the steering wheel when reaching the end of the street, the junkyard coming up next. Where else would Michael Gibson go if he was seen near the school? Was he on his way to the crime scene? Murderers did that when it was possible. Sometimes they'd take a token of the murder too. Not sure why, but they were like arsonists revisiting the scenes of a fire to relish in the mayhem and violence of what they'd done. What it satisfied exactly was something I'd never understand. I only knew that it was a behavior we could rely on.

The car tires kicked the stones of the gravel path to the mouth of the junkyard, the parking lot widening. The gates were closed and guarding the entry, a couple working them, chains clanking. They were middle-aged and on the heavier side, both arguing loud enough to hear them through the windows. The man wore black and red flannel with a brass-colored zipper which he jerked down, opening his front to reveal a faded green T-shirt with a clown's picture on it. His cheeks were ruddy, his thinning hair slicked back. When he saw me, he dropped the chains and nodded in my direction. "Can I help you?"

"I'm Detective Casey White," I answered, pressing the brake pedal and showing my badge through the open window, the sun catching the tin. The woman gave a short wave, pressing her hair in place which was stiff with hairspray. Her face was blotchy red, but it was makeup that had become messy in the heat, both sweating. "I'm following up on the murder—"

"They cleared it out," the woman answered before I could

finish. "Took anything to do with what happened in there. Nothing left to see."

"Yes, ma'am, I understand," I replied, throwing the car in park. I holstered my gun and slipped the badge around my neck, the lanyard finding a place between my collar and neck. The chain was cool and gave me a shiver. When I opened the car door, there were tire tracks leading inside the junkyard. They were fresh, the ground muddy-soft from the fast-melting snow. A warm breeze rushed over me, the temperature feeling like early spring. I approached the couple and saw a resemblance. They must be the son and daughter of the late owner, the family Jericho had mentioned. My hand extended, I repeated, "Detective Casey White."

"Ma'am. My name is Tina, and this here is my brother, Gary," the woman said, wiping her brow of a light sweat. Her hand was damp, but I didn't take it as being from nerves; there was eye contact and an eagerness to speak. "We called ahead to make sure it was okay to reopen."

"The yard's been closed a few days now and we got customers waiting, their trucks sitting with full loads," Gary answered, speaking from the side of his mouth. "They need to empty so they can fill 'em again."

"We get paid by the pound," Tina added, motioning to a concrete pad next to the office. Her brow narrowed. "Not a lot of money in junk but that don't stop the taxes on the property."

"I understand, ma'am. I'm not here to close your place." It was the ground I was interested in, the tire tracks fresh. I took a picture with my phone, noting there was only one pair leading inside. There were two trucks parked next to their office. I photographed them as well, asking, "Your vehicles?"

"Uh-huh," Gary answered while working a handkerchief across his face. He frowned again, asking, "Why? You need to search 'em too?"

"No, not at all," I answered, pitching my toe near the

deepest part of the tire tracks. "It's the tread and wheelbase. I'll use the pictures to eliminate your vehicles from the vehicle that made those tracks."

"I didn't see them," Tina said, speaking to her brother. He pawed his chin, a frown deepening. "Gary?"

"Those aren't from one of ours," Gary commented, tipping the end of his workbook near the track. He glanced at the chains, saying, "Gate was open when we got here."

"Unlocked?" I asked, pointing at the padlock.

"Been unlocked since the murder," Tina replied, fingernails scratching her scalp. "But the gates were supposed to be shut."

"Maybe they're old?" her brother asked. He looked up at me, hands on his hips. "One of yours?"

"The ground was frozen yesterday," I began, and joined them. "The warm front came in earlier today."

"Ya know, she's right," Tina said, staring hard at the ground. "You got here first. Was those gates closed?"

Gravel crunching beneath his shoes, Gary turned to look at the chains and gates, studying them. "Gate was closed."

My hand twitched, rising to instinctively cradle my gun. The timing of the warm front and the rapid snow melt told me a car had driven past this spot at some point earlier this morning. There was only one set of tracks too, which meant they were still inside. "Sir? Ma'am? I'm going to ask you to step inside your office."

"Who you think is in there?" Tina asked, putting on a scowl and crossing her arms. "This is private property. Nobody allowed to just park inside there."

"I'll find out for you," I answered, motioning to the office. "If you could step inside your office for me."

"Come on," Gary said, voice low and brusque. Before turning away, he asked, "You'll clear this up? We got trucks waiting."

"Yes, sir," I answered, phone in hand, the station on speed dial.

Alice answered with the same greeting I'd heard her use a hundred times. I didn't wait for her to finish, interrupting, "Alice, it's Casey. Detective White."

"Detective?" she replied. "What do you need?"

"Radio one of the patrols near my location, have them join me."

"Jill Carter's crime scene?" she asked.

"That's right, thank you," I answered, hanging up. Before the brother and sister were inside, I asked, "Is there an exit on the property?"

"Nope. This is the only way in or out of there," Tina answered.

"Our pops walled the property with old cars," Gary added.

A wall could be climbed. "What's on the other side?"

"Some woods and marsh land," the woman said, office door letting out a rusty screech. She turned back, asking, "You'll be quick about it. We've got some dump trucks coming in an hour."

"We'll be quick," I told her without knowing anything about the other side of their gate. It all depended on whether or not it was Michael who'd driven inside. The brother and sister disappeared behind the office door, shutting it quietly as if not to scare off their trespasser. A moment later, yellowing blinds opened slightly, the shape of a round face appearing. The windows were covered in grime, making it impossible to tell who was watching. But when another face appeared, I knew it was both of them.

A patrol car arrived while I texted Tracy, blue lights flashing silently. Tracy replied with a thumbs-up emoji. The patrol exited their car, one of them stepping into a puddle and grimacing. I warned, "I'm afraid we'll see a lot of that."

"Ma'am," she said, scraping her shoe. "Was there a break-in?"

"Not quite. Likely a trespasser." The patrol exchanged a look, sharing disappointment, the call a minor offense. "It's the warrant for Michael Gibson."

"Oh, he's inside?" the taller of the two said, more interested. He sleeved a concealable baton, firming the grip first. "Do you think he's hiding?"

"I don't even know it is him," I answered, waving a whoa-motion, the officer too eager. "He was sighted a few miles from here and the timing of the trespassing worked."

"Well, whoever it is, we'll take care of it," the other officer said, walking past me, one foot crossing the tire marks.

"I'll lead," I instructed, taking hold of the gate, the metal sweaty, the damp air clinging. Before swinging it open, I told them, "Listen, I met with Michael Gibson briefly and didn't get the impression he was dangerous. He's just a kid. Probably scared."

"Had my jaw broken last year answering a call about a runaway," one of the officers said. She turned her head to show a small scar beneath her cheek. "The runaway was twelve."

"Precautions are fine," I commented, the gate bigger than I first estimated, muscles straining. The officers were past me before I could say another word, trudging forward like a pair of hunting dogs sniffing out game birds. I made my way around them, eyes set on where the crime scene was, explaining, "Around the corner."

"What is this place?" she asked, searching the tall walls made thick with cars, the carcasses flattened and stacked. We turned left, the path winding around. "It's like a junkyard version of a corn maze."

"Children of the Junk," the other officer quipped.

"Yeah, something like that," she said with a chuckle.

"This way," I said, turning left, my foot slipping in squishy mud. An old Chevy Impala sat before the clearing where Jill Carter had been murdered. I raised a hand to halt the officers and peered around the car's headlight to see Michael Gibson kneeling on the ground. He was positioned where Jill's body had been discovered, the remains of our forensic investigation barely visible. Whispering over my shoulder, I told them, "He's over there."

"Easy pickings," one of them said.

"Hold," I demanded, wanting to assess the situation. His long black hair hung limp in front of his face. I could see that his hands were clasped together. My breath caught in my throat when noticing a rose in Michael's hands. It was pale white. The stem short and flower bud slightly different than the one found at Jill Carter's locker and Terri Rond's bedroom. But it was a rose. Leather creaked behind me with a telltale metal snap of a gun holster. I breathed slow and steady, whispering, "Easy. The suspect appears unarmed."

"What are we waiting for?" the other officer said eagerly.

"He's not." Pointing up, I added, "He's not going anywhere."

"Just the backseat of our squad car," one of them commented as I stepped out from behind the Chevy.

"Michael?" I asked, carefully moving closer, keeping my gaze on his hands. I stood between the tire tracks that led from outside the gate, Michael's car close if I needed to duck behind it. "What are you doing here?"

"Huh?" he asked, the flower dropping from his hands. His eyes were red-rimmed and round, the whites of them pink. He wiped the tip of his nose, saying, "I just wanted to be where she was."

"How about we go somewhere and talk about it?"

The officers joined me, metal chinking, a pair of handcuffs made ready. When we were close enough, Michael saw them and stood abruptly, pants soaked where he'd been kneeling. I waved off the patrol officers like I was ignoring them, and said, "It'd be just you and me?"

"Go where?" Michael asked, his eyes more alive, chin trembling. "You-you think I did this. Don't you?"

"That's what I'd like to talk to you about."

Michael began to back away, his eyes darting around wildly.

My words weren't helping, and I tried to reason. "Michael. Listen. It was you who came to me at the creek. You wanted to talk to us about Jill."

He shook his head eagerly, locks swinging limp. "That was because I knew you were looking for me."

"We were talking to everyone," I replied.

The officers were getting anxious and close enough that I could hear them breathing fast. If I wasn't standing between them, they would have tackled Michael by now. I didn't want that to happen. It didn't have to happen. I waved Michael toward the exit, insisting we leave together. "Let's go talk. Just you and me."

By now, his eyes were fixed on the officers, and he shook his face defiantly. "Uh-uh. You're going to blame me for this. I know it."

"That's not true," I insisted. And it wasn't true. A suspect is only a suspect until proven guilty. "We'll get your parents and make sure you have a lawyer if you want one."

But my words weren't helping, and Michael spun around whimpering, his shoes in motion to run. There was nowhere to go though, and the move had me staring in wonder. Though his back was turned, I heard him cry out as he raced clumsily toward the east side wall, the shoreline and ocean beyond it. A radio squawked, an officer calling for backup from their handset. While Michael wasn't the best runner, he could climb and tackled the clunky metal carcasses, ascending like it was the side of a cliff. I was close behind, staying within a couple yards but out of reach while the officers split left and right of us. "I didn't do this," Michael yelled, glancing over his shoulder. For a second, our eyes locked and I thought he was going to throw loose chunks of junk. He didn't though, turning back and continuing the climb.

"Where you going?" one of the officers shouted.

I clutched an old side mirror and dug a foot against the headrest of a Volkswagen bug. "Michael," I pleaded. "Don't make this difficult."

"There's nowhere to go," the other officer yelled. She slipped, her foot crashing through a windshield. The three of us stopped dead, staring until she waved. "I'm good."

"I saw that, Michael," I yelled.

He'd stopped with concern. He was on the move again, ascending the wall like a spider. He didn't look back, climbing faster, surprising us all. I followed as best I could, grabbing anything that jutted from the pile. And from deep inside the wall of rusting metal and glass and tires, the discarded cars groaned against our weight. The makeshift wall was never meant to be climbed, and for the first time, I saw how they'd been piled, some teetering precariously. "Michael, this is dangerous and there's nowhere to go."

"I didn't do this," the boy continued. He'd made it three-quarters of the way when a piece of bumper in his hand ripped loose. A flash of pitted chrome was suddenly in front of me, the corner of it striking my arm. Blood oozed from a rip in my shirt, the injury scalding like a burn immediately with a soundless throb. Michael looked mortified, maybe even a little green. "Oh God! I'm so sorry."

"Michael, help me out, would you?" I asked, playing it up, knowing that he cared. I offered my hand, my feet balancing on the ledge of a car door, a nineteen sixties Ford Mustang. I made like I was impaired and struggling, arm hanging limp, blood pulsing and running toward my fingertips. "Take my hand and help me get down."

"Yeah, of course," he said, agreeing without thinking. When his hand neared mine, the officers were closing around him.

When he noticed, the matter of my injury was forgotten and the look of fright returned, his face turning ghostly white. He leveled his eyes with mine, a look in them that had me pitying him. "Detective, I didn't do this."

The bigger officer's hands grabbed Michael's leg, but the young man was a swift climber and worked across the wall in the opposite direction. My hand was sticky with blood, and I wasn't sure if I could continue. Not that I had to. He couldn't escape the second officer, nearly running into her as the first moved faster. Michael didn't fight them, his face dripping with sweat, the climb tiring him. I dropped to the ground and braced my arm, sunlight gleaming on it. It'd need a stitch or maybe it'd hold with just a butterfly, but my shirt was ruined.

"Ma'am?" the officer asked. She was breathing heavy, beads of sweat on her upper lip. "Do you need an ambulance?"

"I'll be fine. Thank you."

"We have a medical kit," the other officer said, holding Michael's arm, fingernails white with pressure. "I'll wrap it."

"That'll work," I replied appreciatively. I faced our suspect. "Michael."

"I didn't do this," he said, continuing to chant the words quietly as if in prayer.

"Cuff him," I said, giving the officers instruction, following procedure. Michael stared at the ground, at the faint outline of where Jill took her last breath. His cheeks were flushed and tearstained. "Michael Gibson, you have the right to remain silent. You have..."

And as I mirandized him, he never stopped pleading his innocence. I didn't know what we'd ask him first but texted ahead to Alice and the district attorney, making certain we had an interview room at the station waiting.

When I finished reciting the Miranda rights, Michael looked me squarely, his eyes wet. "Detective, you have the wrong person."

On our return to the gate, the owners of the junkyard were waiting. A second patrol was waiting as well. Michael was placed in the back of the squad car while one of the officers retrieved a medical kit and the owners peppered us with questions about Michael's trespassing and the boy's car. I did my best to answer, the antiseptic spitting foam and stinging more than the initial injury. And all the while, images of the collections next to Jill's and Terri's bodies flashed in my mind. I saw nothing similar in Michael's car. We'd looked in his school locker too, finding it resembled every other locker we'd searched. A troubling thought stirred in the back of my mind. If we did have the wrong person, was the killer looking to add to their collection of victims?

NINETEEN

Tracy's face glowed with the colors of the screen, bright green pixels racing from the bottom to the top, the data a blurry reflection in her eyes. She'd printed what she thought to be important, the high dollar amounts and dates of money transactions, the transfers to and from overseas accounts. On her whiteboard, there was an elaborate diagram with more than a dozen bubbles, all of them connected with crisscrossed lines, along with names circled and underlined, the biggest name being the first victim's mother.

"I think we have to take this to the district attorney," she said without looking at me.

I didn't reply and searched the screen instead. I glanced through the printed documents next, assessing how any of this might correlate to the odd little collections discovered at each victim's crime scene. Try as I might, I couldn't make the connection. I decided to say nothing, washing my face of any disappointment and to listen instead.

Tracy spun her chair and moved to the whiteboard. "Janine Carter was involved in something. Casey, it's big and I think it might be why her daughter was murdered."

"Is it possible that whatever you found here was actually legal?" I questioned carefully, not wanting to dismiss it outright. Tracy cocked her head. I looked to the screen, the streams of data like gibberish. "Tracy, what I mean is that we're not accountants. Let alone forensic accountants."

"You're right!" Her eyes bloomed, the whites in them shiny. "That's what we need. A forensic accountant."

I hung a thumb over my shoulder, hoping to steer her back to the present. "Tracy, we've got Michael Gibson in custody and the DA will be here soon."

"Who would we call for that?" she asked, phone in hand, ignoring my comment. It wasn't a familiar question since we'd never had anything in past cases that dealt with financial crimes, if that's what this was. When I didn't answer, Tracy looked at me, brow raised with a grin appearing. "Really, no answer? That's a first for you."

"What? I don't know everything," I replied, shrugging. "Who do I look like? Jericho?"

"Yes! That's who we call," she answered. "He'll know."

"Ask Alice too," I added, playing along, seeing that I wouldn't be able to persuade her to do anything else. "I'm sure there's been a case in the history of this station where a forensic accountant was needed."

"Speaking of Michael Gibson, you might want to see this," Tracy said. She'd heard me after all. Tracy tapped the keyboard, the screen flicking on and filling with a social networking site, a picture showing hands and feet with the same nail polish as Jill Carter's. Across the top, the profile listed the name *Shay Parker*. Tracy scrolled to the newest post with more of the same. "Jill's friend has been busy posting about Michael with some mentions of Jill too."

"Anything about Terri Rond?" I asked, scrolling through them. I stopped when I reached a post with condolences, asking, "Just that?"

"Uh-huh. From the social media, I'm thinking Shay knew Terri but was closer to Jill and Michael."

"Must have been if she was posting about them. What else is there? Anything about the crime scenes, like the collections?"

The light near the holding cells dimmed with the shapes of the DA and Alice, the two talking. The DA glanced over, urging me to join her. I held up a finger, eager to read the post. I waved to scroll up. A picture of Jill Carter and Michael Gibson came into view, the two pictures sitting side by side, the text beneath reading like a news article. It was about Michael's arrest and showed a third picture of the junkyard and Michael being handcuffed. That last picture shouldn't have existed. "What the... but we were alone."

"Not entirely," Tracy said, stretching out the first word. She took a long breath. "Who else was with you?"

"The owners," I said, recalling their round faces in the window, dingy blinds draped around them. "How many have seen the post?"

"It's getting around but there's no exact numbers," Tracy shrugged. "I wouldn't consider it viral. Not yet. I'm sure the press will be coming soon though."

"I was expecting they'd be here anyway. We can't issue a warrant without them finding out about it."

"Casey, it's the rest of what she posted that you need to read," Tracy said, pushing hair back from her eyes while driving the laptop. She opened the post, clicking on the word *more* and scrolled further. "Shay Parker posted pictures from the school and about how Michael was a sexual predator and that he'd done this before."

"Shit. She must have found out about the transfer from the first school. How?" I asked, reading faster, seeing that Shay had a knack for vocabulary and didn't mince words or censor details. It was the action behind the post that surprised me. "I think everyone in the area is going to know about this. And of course,

Shay tagged her school in the post, as well as Michael's previous school, the teachers, the administration, and the press." I just about fell over, the rush of anger making me light-headed. I grabbed a corner of Tracy's desk and leaned heavily against it, the cubicle walls rattling.

"Casey, check out the responses," Tracy said, the sentences moving faster. The replies were filled with burning faces and weepy emojis, even a few death threats. "From public opinion, Michael Gibson is already guilty."

"Whether they like it or not, it's not up to the public to decide," I said, glancing toward the station's front, imagining a mob parading toward us, feet stomping in a march, carrying pitchforks and all the necessary ingredients for a public execution. "There's reasons we have a judicial system in place."

Tracy lowered her voice and rushed her words. "It looks like your judicial system is walking over here." She sat down, spinning the chair around to work the data from Jill Carter's laptop.

"Detective? Are you coming?" The district attorney asked, the faint smell of hairspray following her. She was red-faced and breathing fast and clutching her phone. "I've got half the school board and the superintendent on with me. We're not sure what happened but this is turning into a real shit-show!"

"Social media, ma'am," Tracy said. The DA stopped what she was doing, cupping the phone. Tracy clarified. "One of the students posted online about Michael Gibson's transfer. Just about everyone was tagged and was notified."

"Does it mention what happened at the other school?" The DA asked, color slipping from her face. Tracy nodded. The DA returned the phone to her ear, saying, "I'll have to call you back. For now, the answer to use for any press inquiries is... there is no response during an active investigation."

"We'll get to the truth," I said, trying to assure her. She didn't look confident. In fact, she looked downright frazzled. "Pauline, it was bound to get out."

"This is bad," Pauline said, the words soft like a whisper. Her focus floated to the station's televisions before returning to Tracy's desks and the torn apart laptop. "There's going to be lawsuits and reprimands. There'll be at least a handful of resignations too."

"Was there fault?" I asked, a knot in my gut sitting like a cold stone. The DA cringed and shook her head, her focus remaining on the computer parts like it was a disemboweled body. "I'm asking from a parent's perspective, they'll view it as a sexual assault that was reprimanded with a school transfer."

Pauline glanced around to see if we were alone. "With what was known at the time, it was the only thing the school board thought to do. Even then, there was a risk of Michael Gibson's family suing too."

"Do you think he did it?" Tracy asked, interest sparked. There was controversy with this case and it was growing. "I mean, what if he was telling the truth about what happened in that bathroom?"

"I don't know. All I know is we have two dead students who were sexually assaulted and both of them knew Michael Gibson. Add the fact that he'd been involved in another sexual assault. It's bad." The DA slowly closed her eyelids and spoke slowly. "Detective, I need you to find the truth. We need to know the truth. The people need to know it too."

"I'll do that," I replied. "It might mean interviewing the girl from the other school."

"That's what I'm expecting." I didn't know Pauline well enough to assume any next steps but could see how this case was troubling her enough to rely on us. "If this goes to trial, I'll have to use the bathroom assault. That means putting the first victim from Michael's other school on the stand as a witness."

"A witness?" Tracy asked, a flash of confusion showing.

"On the stand, the victim would account for what happened in that bathroom with Michael," the DA explained.

"It would establish a pattern for the jury to connect to Jill Carter and Terri Rond."

Tracy looked at me, saying, "I'll get the student's name and contact information."

The DA frowned when looking past me to the whiteboard. When her focus returned with questions about it, I answered, "Tracy is investigating another angle to Jill Carter's murder."

"I don't understand. We've already got a case around Michael Gibson," she said, annoyed. "Detective, this is your area. I'd expect you to pool efforts on one line of enquiry, okay?"

"Ma'am—" I insisted, but the DA's phone interrupted. I continued anyway. "I don't believe the case against Michael Gibson is clear cut. The evidence is lack—"

"We got his DNA," she said, phone near her ear. "His DNA matches the tissues found beneath Jill Carter's fingernails."

"His DNA?" I asked, shocked. It was the first I'd heard about it. I felt my phone buzz, guessing it was Samantha with the results, texting them while speaking with the DA. The questions flowed without a breath. "When was his DNA collected? Did we have a warrant to collect it?"

"Detective!" the DA said with insistence. "When we processed him, it included a mouth swab, a collection of his DNA."

"Mouth swab? DNA?" I asked, my throat closing and feeling hot. We hadn't even interviewed Michael yet. "Who authorized—"

"The law authorized it, Detective," the DA barked, suddenly frustrated with my questions. Her gaze was piercing as she recited the law. "Arrestees with any history of sexual assault are eligible to have their DNA collected."

"Eligible?" I asked, unconvinced. "But he's a minor. Seventeen years old. And he wasn't convicted of sexual assault. He wasn't even arrested, only transferred to another school."

"He's seventeen years old and will be eighteen in a couple weeks. And with the accusation of sexual assault, he'll be tried as an adult."

"Is that admissible? I mean, if this goes to trial?" I continued to challenge. I wasn't a lawyer and couldn't argue the legalities, but I knew enough to ask the questions.

With a subtle smirk, Pauline replied, "You're right, it can be argued, and there's the risk that the judge might strike it from the record. However, that doesn't mean the jury will forget what they heard."

My heart dropped with what Pauline planned. It was one of the oldest legal tactics. As the DA, she was going to say whatever was needed to build a case against Michael for the jury. Even though the judge would instruct the jury to disregard what was heard, they wouldn't. How could they?

"What is it, Detective?"

"Do you still want the victim from the sexual assault interviewed?"

"DNA evidence is substantial in any case." The DA pondered the question, her long fingernails drumming atop the desk. She was working out a game plan for the court if a plea deal wasn't met. Talking to herself, she said, "I can introduce the school transfer in my opening and closing statements. That way it can't be challenged. I might still need the bathroom victim as a witness—"

"Ma'am, with all due respect," I said, interrupting. She leveled her eyes with mine. "We owe it to Terri Rond, Jill Carter, as well as to Michael Gibson too. We owe it to the court to determine the truth."

But the DA was losing interest in my argument, the case against Michael strong. She'd lost interest in the data mining that Tracy was working as well. Glancing at the screens once more, saying, "Do the interview. Michael Gibson might surprise us all with a sudden confession and end this thing once and for all." That didn't answer my question, but it did give me time to work with Michael. "Detective, I'll delay submitting Michael Gibson's DNA to CODIS."

"Combined DNA Index System," Tracy said, spelling out the meaning of CODIS. "Will the submission be used to search unsolved cases or to list Michael Gibson as a sex offender?"

"It wouldn't be the latter. Not yet." The DA grimaced, my answer countering whatever she had in mind. "We can't submit Michael Gibson to CODIS as a sex offender until a conviction is reached first."

"Fair enough. So, as the detective, it'll be up to you to finish this," the DA replied coldly, and motioned to the investigation room. There was a witness who saw Michael Gibson with both Jill Carter and Terri Rond. The DA now had hard evidence in a DNA match which would make it nearly impossible to dispute if this went to trial. From the eagerness in the DA's eyes and the sound of it in her voice, I could tell she didn't want to go to trial at all. She was looking for a deal. She put her phone away, a ridge forming above her eyes. "Are you coming?"

"I'll be there in a minute."

There was the chance Michael Gibson did do this. I just wasn't convinced yet and when the DA was out of earshot, I told Tracy, "Get everything you can about what happened in that school bathroom. The school administration handled it without the DA or our station's involvement. I want to know why."

"I'm already on it," Tracy said, the screen refreshed with listings of names and dates. She warned, "There might be some pushback since they were both minors."

"Ask everyone at the school who was involved with Michael's transfer. One of them will talk to you. The idea of losing a job has a way of motivating people." I turned to leave, adding, "Regardless of what actually happened in that bathroom, there's nothing right about how it was handled. I want to know why."

TWENTY

An interview room is an interview room regardless of what city or station it resides. Other than the wall color, white and plain as vanilla, our station's interview room was near identical to the ones in Philly. When I'd first walked the city beat and wore the uniform, we called the rooms what they really were—interrogation rooms. But the vocabulary had been considered too harsh, too politically incorrect, as though it were a reflection of a torture room from the Middle Ages or something. And perhaps it was like that at times. Thankfully, I'd never been witness to any of it. The interview room became the new normal, and the word interrogation was scrubbed from the station's vernacular.

When I entered the room, Michael Gibson's face was pale and damp. The look of him was everything the word interrogation was meant to instill. Fear. Black curls hung above his eyes, limp like a mop. His left knee bounced, the heel of his shoe clapping against the tiled floor. There were dark circles beneath bloodshot eyes and his stare jumped around feverishly at every sound. I took a step, pulling out the chair across from him, scraping the metal feet with a grating sound.

There were two young women. Dead. Raped. And I didn't

know if it was their killer across from me. Should I treat this like an interrogation, bringing into it every coarse word and harsh tone I could use that sounded accusatory? It was a tactic that sometimes worked. Or should I play this like I was Michael's friend? That I was here to help guide him through the judicial process like a chaperone? I wanted the latter, unconvinced he could have done this. But the DA and everyone else involved would demand the former. They wanted certainty the killer of two innocent lives was in custody.

When I sat down, the sour smell of sweat hit me. Michael's face was slick, and beneath the layers of junkyard dirt and grime, I saw a glimpse of the high school boy who'd followed us to the creek. Next to him was a woman I'd met a few times at the courthouse. I'd seen her here at the station too. She was a public defender. Court appointed for those who did not have the means to get an attorney. Jacquie Walker was her name. She wore hair that was pinned back tight enough to put a strain on her eyebrows. Thick round glasses covered her face, the weight leaving deep red marks on the sides of her nose. She glanced up, courteously nodding. I did the same, the exchange beginning.

"Michael," I began, taking care to keep my voice steady. It didn't matter though. He flinched. Picking at the bandage that covered the scratch, I thought to start there. "Michael, tell me about the scratch on your arm. Tell me about when you last saw Jill Carter."

"Relevance?" the public defender questioned abruptly, immediately setting a tone for this meeting.

I blinked it away, feeling instantly annoyed. "You are aware of the case against your client?" I asked, stating the obvious, a touch of snark in my voice.

She tugged on a locket around her neck, sliding it back and forth without replying. She wanted me to state it aloud and I understood why. A camera was mounted in the corner where the walls and ceiling met. It was our proverbial fly on the wall, recording every move, every sound, everything that occurred in this exchange. Like the district attorney, the public defender was building her own case. Only, hers would be a case to dismiss the charges. She didn't have anything yet but I felt my cheeks warm with respect. Later, my words were going to be analyzed just like every piece of evidence we collected and used in bringing this case to trial.

It meant she cared and that meant she'd do right by Michael Gibson. I still wasn't convinced if Michael was guilty or innocent, but maybe with her perspective and questioning, it would get us some answers. I opened two folders, the first containing pictures of the crime scene, Tracy's photographic touch becoming more recognizable with each new case. The second folder was from Samantha, released by the medical examiner's officer, and containing the first victim's autopsy photographs along with Terri Rond's crime-scene pictures. Maybe I should have warned Michael. I didn't, and when the first picture slid across the table, his color turned green, and his cheeks ballooned. It was only a picture of Jill's hand and arm, but it showed significant discoloration, pink and dark purplish where gravity had driven the blood.

"This is your relevance. Michael, tissue with your DNA was found beneath Jill Carter's fingernails."

"Tissue?" he asked, voice hollow, throat opening with the threat of a heave. He held it in, eyes swimming a moment before focus returned to me. "I-I don't know what that means."

"Michael, it was your skin that we found beneath Jill's fingernails," I explained, frowning some. The public defender already had this information and would have had a meeting with him to explain the charges. She didn't and that annoyed me. I paused, waiting for her to say something else, possibly rebut my questioning. She said nothing, leading me to wonder if he was fully aware of the charges brought against him. I looked at the public defender and then back to Michael, asking in a softer voice, "Michael, do you understand the charges and why you are here today?"

"He's been fully briefed of the charges against him," Michael's lawyer replied, brow rigid. She pinched her glasses, repositioning them. "The pictures though. Were they a necessary part of your question?"

"Sometimes they are," I replied. I'd selected to take the path of a more rigid interview and had to stick with it. The crime scene and autopsy pictures scared Michael and that was part of the strategy. It was his reaction I was gauging, having been in the room with ruthless killers before and having seen how they relished reviewing their work. Some of them grinned evilly as if they'd just found the prize at the bottom of a Cracker Jack box. Michael's reaction wasn't like that. The pictures mortified him. He could have been acting though. I'd had that happen before but saw through it. I redirected my attention, asking him again, "Michael, help me understand how your DNA got there? Why did Jill scratch you?"

His gaze drifted to the other photos. His breathing quickened to the point I thought he'd start hyperventilating. I slid some of the other pictures away, forcing his concentration only on Jill's hand, the nail polish removed. He settled some, answering, "It's like I told you before. It happened in the school parking lot." He stopped to look at his lawyer. She nodded for him to proceed. "We were walking to my car, and she slipped on some ice."

"Slipped?" I asked trying to see it in my head. There'd been the storm. It was unusually cold. Windy and wintry weather. There was ice and snow everywhere and if you were outdoors, you were dressed for it. I pointed at the gauzy bandage and asked, "Were you wearing a coat? Was Jill wearing gloves?"

Michael's brow dipped, his answering quickly, "She wasn't wearing her gloves because they were still in her school bag."

"What about a coat?" I asked, not letting him off that easily. "If you were wearing a coat, how did you get scratched?"

"I took it off already and put it in the backseat of my car along with my book bag." He turned to his lawyer who said nothing. "You believe me, right?"

His attorney motioned to me, directing his question. Whether she believed him or not was irrelevant. She was there to defend him and countered, "Plausible. Jill Carter exited the school in a hurry, pair of gloves still in her bag. Michael was at his car, the motor running, the heat on, and his coat and book bag in the backseat."

"Who grabbed who first?" I asked, his lawyer making a reasonable argument. Michael shook his head. I reframed the question. "You said that Jill slipped. That resulted in the scratch. Who reached for who?"

He thought about it and shook his head again. "I think we both reached at the same time. I had my hand on the door handle coz I remember pulling hard to hold her."

I sat motionless a moment, eyes fixed. Was Michael lying? Beneath my glare, he stirred uncomfortably, his lawyer too which was unexpected. But she was newer and carried a touch of inexperience. Her explanation was credible though and could help sway a jury's decision-making. "Michael, here's where I need you to help me out with something."

"Sure, yeah," he replied eagerly while I shuffled the photographs enough for him to see the crime-scene pictures of Terri Rond as she'd been found. He swallowed dryly, asking, "Could I maybe get something to drink?"

"I can do that," I answered. But I didn't get up. Not yet. The public defender was staring at the crime-scene photographs too. Part of her job was to act as an investigator. She was Michael's advocate. His only advocate from the looks of it. She was also the one person who was going to champion his innocence. A public defender can only do so much when the case is stacked with evidence. This was one of those cases, the DNA a sharp nail in the coffin of a jury's verdict. If Michael lied to her about anything, then she was going to lose. "You said that Jill walked with you to your car. Before that, you'd been seen exchanging words in the hallway. Were you arguing?"

"Uh-uh. It wasn't like that," he said, swallowing hard, dark curls draped in front of his eyes. He shoved the hair out of his face. "It's like I told you at the creek."

I repeated myself. "Jill followed you into the parking lot. But she didn't get into your car?" He shook his head. "Even with the weather? As bad as it was? Were you still arguing?"

He hesitated. It was brief like a sharp breath, and most wouldn't have noticed. But I noticed. There was more that he wasn't saying. Something happened between them. "Jill wanted to talk," he replied. His answer wasn't enough, and he saw my dissatisfaction. He leaned in as if it would help. When his gaze dropped to one of the pictures, he caught himself, palms bracing the table. "We didn't finish talking in the hallway because I walked away from her."

"Why? What happened?" My question floated alone and without a response. His attorney grew curious too, brow rising. "Did it have anything to do with Terri Rond?"

"Terri? Gosh, no!"

"What was it?" I insisted.

"I didn't like what she said. So, I left." Michael crossed his arms defensively. And for the first time, I saw more than fear. I saw anger and hurt. His reply also stirred his lawyer into motion. She sat up and whispered something to him, cupping his ear. I couldn't tell what was said, but Michael immediately added, "What I mean is that I was okay with what Jill said to me. It just hurt my feelings is all."

"Hurt your feelings?" His attempt to rephrase what was said didn't help. There was motive slipping from his mouth like sweat from his pores. He just didn't know but I did. So did his lawyer.

The public defender spoke up, "That's already been established."

"Yes, it's established," I agreed. I had to explore it and reworded. "You exchanged words with Jill in the hallway. She said something that made you angry. You were mad at her. Furious?"

Michael caught on immediately. He'd missed whatever warning his lawyer had given him but heard what I was implying. "Uh-uh! It wasn't like that."

"Then tell me how it was?"

"You're trying to twist my words." He was rattled. I held back, silence filling the room and making him more restless. I sensed it'd bother him enough that he'd say more. I was right. "I got mad because I asked her out and told her how much I liked her. She said she really liked me. But that she only liked me as a friend."

"That's when you left?"

"Uh-huh," he replied. "I didn't even know Shay was in the hallway watching us. Not until later."

"Did you know Jill had followed you to the parking lot?"

"I saw her when I'd already gotten to my car." His expression shifted. There was sadness in his eyes. "I said something mean to her."

"What did you say to her?"

"I..." His lower lip trembled as if the words were too painful to speak. "I told her that I couldn't be her friend. It was the last thing I ever said to her."

"What happened when you said that to her?" The sadness turned to guilt and Michael wore it on his face like a cancer.

"I could have offered Jill a ride to her house." He hung his head low. "Then maybe she'd still be alive."

"It wasn't your fault," his attorney said, consoling. I wanted to be convinced of his innocence but wasn't. Not yet. Not with the stakes of this case so high. I had more questions.

"She lived close to the school, and you didn't offer her a ride home," I stated the obvious. The defense attorney glanced up at me, questioning. It was a tactic, a ploy to get Michael to tell me more. "What was the thinking? Did you want to hurt her?"

"Well—" A hot flush climbed his neck. "Yeah. I mean, I was mad. But I only wanted to hurt her feelings."

"You said that Jill liked someone else. Did that make you mad too?" I asked, staging the accusation. "Mad enough to kill her?"

"Gosh, no!" he said, revolted, eyes glistening. He swiped at them, annoyed. "I could never—"

"The junkyard was nearby. Did you offer her a drive home and then changed your mind?"

"Where is this going, Detective?" the attorney asked.

I hated pressing like I was but had to do it. I had to drive out the truth like a demon if it was there to get. I ignored the lawyer and continued. "Is that when you turned into the junkyard?"

The public defender stirred with that question. She should have stirred. I was fishing for a confession, and she knew it. Michael glanced at his lawyer and then back to me and shook his head. "Uh-uh. Jill never got in my car," he answered calmly.

"It's understandable to be upset. Even angry when someone doesn't respond to your affections."

"It wasn't like that," he answered, voice raised.

I leaned into the table, spreading the photographs some more, revealing most of the horror that ended Jill Carter's and Terri Rond's lives. "Then tell me what it was?"

His eyes bulged and he shoved at the table, his chair sliding back with a screech. "Not that!"

"My client has already established innocence. You're attempting to coerce a confession that'd be used as admissible evidence to support a conviction—"

"I'm just asking a question," I said, interrupting. She was right though. Michael admitting to being angry could be conveyed to a jury as motive. It would be used by the district attorney to squash any reasonable doubt the public defender could raise. A confession would seal Michael's fate. I circled back to my earlier question. "If Jill told you she just wanted to be friends, then what did she say when she followed you?"

"That she was sorry," he answered, voice breaking. "That's all."

"That's all?" I said, questioning dismissively. That couldn't have been all it was. I went silent again, sensing there was more.

"It's okay to tell her," Michael's lawyer finally said. Michael looked reluctant and I motioned him to continue. At this point, he'd said nothing yet that'd help his case. Anything else would have been better. "It's okay."

"There was another reason I didn't offer her a ride," Michael said, voice scratchy.

A guard opened the door, a cup of water in his hand. I'd thank Tracy later for helping. I spied the camera in the corner of the ceiling, she was watching and listening while working the laptop.

Michael sipped eagerly, his nerves had drained every drop of spit from his mouth. He cleared his throat, adding, "Jill told me that she was hoping to get a ride with someone else."

"When you approached us at the creek, you said there was someone else." A nod. "Who was it?"

"I don't know," he answered, drinking again. "That's all Jill said. She liked someone else."

"Jill liked someone else. And it had nothing to do about Terri Rond?" I asked, trying to establish exactly how Michael knew both victims. "When was the last time you saw Terri?"

"The hallway?" he answered quickly, eyes darting around. "I saw her behind Shay Parker when Shay was taking pictures."

"Nothing afterward?" I continued. He shook his head. "How about after Jill's murder?"

"Uh-uh," Michael said. "I don't remember seeing her since the hallway."

"Tell me about the bathroom?" I asked, shifting to Michael's history. Alone, it wasn't enough for an arrest warrant—the DNA had solidified that. However, to a jury, just the mention of sexual assault in his past would become more powerful than any other evidence presented. "You have a history of sexual assault."

"There was no arrest, only a transfer to another school," the public defender reminded me, brow cocked. She had to know it would be used in the case. Hesitating, she motioned for Michael to answer. "It's okay."

"Claire wanted to," he said, struggling. His face was as red as I thought it could get. It was embarrassment. "I-I said that we shouldn't, but she told me that it'd be okay. She said she'd done it before and wanted to do it again, with me."

"Claire? She was in the bathroom with you?"

He nodded and sipped water, swallowing loudly.

"She invited you into the girls' bathroom?"

"I was just standing there, you know. That's when Mrs. Stacks walked in on us."

I wasn't following, and asked, "You were standing in the girls' bathroom and one of your teachers walked in. That's all?"

His eyes rolled and he looked away. "I mean, my pants were down. You know, down around my ankles."

I got the idea.

"She said she wanted to do that. I-I never did... I mean, had that done to me—"

"It's fine." I motioned for Michael to stop while texting the first name of the girl to Tracy. "I understand."

"It was the girl's parents who made a stink to the school board when they were suspended," the public defender offered.

From her bag, she handed me a form, the school's name and date of the incident printed across the top. "It's the email they sent to Michael's mother, explaining the suspension."

"'Skipping class,'" I read, gleaning the page. I held it up. "The transfer to the other school was because of skipping class?"

"Uh-uh. It was Claire's mom and dad. They made it sound like I'd forced myself on her or something." He was shaking his head fast, curly hair swinging. "They said those things so Claire wouldn't get in any trouble."

"A case of he-said, she-said," I mumbled, recalling what the district attorney had said.

"I don't know what else to tell you," Michael said, a plea in his voice for the questions to end.

"Did you do this?" I said, asking again, dipping my head to lock eyes with his.

"No!" he answered adamantly, tearing up. His whole body was shaking like he was going to have a fit. "You have to believe me. I could never hurt Jill or Terri—"

"Michael, one more question?"

"What," he said, weepy.

"The rose?" I asked. "The white rose?"

"I knew Jill liked them," he answered softly. "I'd seen her in the hallway with one before."

"And Terri?" I asked, thinking of the one I'd seen in her room.

He shook his head slowly. "I-I don't remember if I saw her with one or not—"

He broke down, unable to finish.

I sat back in the chair, his attorney consoling our only suspect. Deep down, I wanted answers and for this case to be over. We had a suspect in custody. A district attorney with a solid case. I just didn't believe we had the truth.

TWENTY-ONE

The low rumble of waves crashing joined my typing, the time growing deep into the night while everyone slept. The tide was high, and I'd opened the window just enough to let the sea air billow behind the curtain. I was restless. I'd been irritable too, the first glass of wine doing little to arrest my discontent. Jericho felt it and gave me space while we went through the motions of the evening. I wore the faces the children expected though. The playful one. The parenting one. All of them through dinner and its cleanup and into homework and bath time, and finally when putting them down for sleep. As a cop, I'd learned how to wear many faces. If I could have put my finger on exactly what was bothering me, I would have. It just felt like everything was wrong.

There was Jericho's career, his considering a return. I still had no idea how we'd navigate both of our careers and raise the kids. Actually, I did have one thought which had started to take root like a sapling. I stopped typing and stared at the window, the curtain dancing in a salty breeze. A text from Tracy jolted me. It was a reply about the victim's laptop and the findings, a few words. She'd tell me more tomorrow.

There was impatience in her text, a response to some earlier questions. I know that's not a thing that can be picked up via text, but my instincts were running hot, a maternal instinct if you wanted to call it that. There was distance growing between us, her choosing to stay back in meetings and other ceremonies of the job. She was still pulling her weight, just choosing to do it alone. Tracy would never come out and say it, but I felt that she wasn't happy, that she was seeking a change. Like I said, nothing felt right.

I tapped the keyboard, refreshing the list I'd been working on which showed the points the district attorney would use in the case against Michael Gibson. Somewhere in the Outer Banks, I imagined Michael's public defender was staring at her laptop too, trying to decide how best to proceed for her client. I poured another glass, playfully mocking the screen. I wouldn't want to be in the public defender's seat. She had a tough case ahead. The DA had a great case. There was going to be an arraignment in the morning for Michael Gibson. The simple process which was governed by the state and included a judge who was required to notify the suspect of the state's charges. The arraignment was also going to be used to establish any penalties Michael was facing, as well as the trial date or possibly a preliminary hearing as well as his right to an attorney.

I sat up abruptly, would the public defender offer a deal this soon? Deep down, I hoped she wouldn't throw in the towel just yet. While the DA was convinced that the case against Michael was complete, I wasn't on the same page. In the arraignment, innocence or guilt wouldn't be established yet. Not until the conclusion of a trial. However, with a public arraignment, the damage was done. Regardless of any trial outcome, the arrest and arraignment proceedings were forever. From this point forward, Michael would have a criminal record that listed the arrest, even if he wasn't prosecuted or acquitted. That thought made my gut flip. I couldn't commit to the idea of Michael being the killer of those two girls, and shut my eyes. In the gray darkness, I saw the boy's face grimacing in shocked panic.

I needed more evidence. Not necessarily to help the DA's case but to tell me Michael's claims of innocence were real. It was those collections. With two victims from the same high school, the killer had targeted them. The killer had put a lot of time into elaborately designing a crime scene. How long did it take to collect all those bottle caps? Those river stones? Did Michael have that kind of time?

Time?

I texted Tracy an idea: We'd get Michael's school and work schedules. We couldn't use anything from his home life since we'd learned he was mostly home alone, his mother working. But his school and part-time jobs would have recorded his hours. Tracy replied with a question mark and asked why. I didn't reply right away, dots bouncing on the screen while she continued to type. Her next text said that she'd collect them and build a timeline for the week leading up to the murders. It could be something. Or it might be nothing. We wouldn't know until we saw it.

We did a search for additional evidence tying Michael to Jill and Terri. It was more of a formality, and it was required. After Michael's interview, and with a fresh search warrant in hand, we'd torn through his car with the help of our station's mechanics. From prying the car's ceiling open to removing the seats and everything else, there were plenty of fibers found. Long hairs that matched Michael's curly mop and some strands the same color as Jill Carter's. These only helped the DA's case. The public defender would argue Jill had been in Michael's car before. More than a few times. We found no evidence that Terri had ever been in Michael's car.

We tore into his bedroom next. Blankets and sheets stripped, a discarded bundle on the floor. The bed mattress was tossed too. Every drawer in the dresser was dumped, the contents piled inside the bed frame, each piece closely inspected for any secrets. The furniture was inspected too, having seen compartments built into the backs and bottoms of drawers as well as above the inside lip of closet doors. The killer I suspected we were dealing with was apt to have kept something from each victim. After all, this wasn't a random act. It had been planned, orchestrated and then executed. The details mattered.

In both murders, the victim's clothes were gone. Every stitch of them. Most likely burned, turned to soot and ash, evidence of the killer's interactions irretrievable. But did they keep a piece? A single article? A swatch of a shirt or pants? We pulled the carpet from the corners, the old shag stapled wall to wall. There was only the carpet padding beneath, the spongey material brittle and deteriorating. When we were through, standing at the doorway, sweaty with hair pasted against my forehead, the bedroom looked like a tornado had touched down inside it. There wasn't a single piece of physical evidence that was directly from Jill's or Terri's murder.

Per proper procedure, the results of the search were forwarded to Michael's defense attorney. Our finding nothing in Michael's car or bedroom helped her case if this went to trial. I could almost see her standing in front of the jury and delivering her closing argument, explaining how there'd been nothing in Michael's vehicle or his home to link him to the murders. All we had was the DNA, and I wasn't sure just how compelling the argument would be if the DA spun up a tale of defensive wounds vs. Michael's claim Jill Carter slipped on the ice.

I couldn't get the collections out of my mind. The existence of them told me we had a horror show in the making, a killer with predatory traits. The collections were the killer's props, and the pain and suffering of the victims turned the killer on. If I was right about the killer, they suffered from a disease of more.

If it made them feel good then they'd want more. They'd want another victim.

I needed to see similar in Michael's car or bedroom. Anything that had the same semblance of hoarding. Baseball cards. Beach shells. Old coins or antique pocket watches. I would have even entertained drawings. Sketches that demonstrated a form of collecting. We'd worked cases in the past where booklets were discovered, pages and pages of drawings and outlines detailing what they'd done or what they were planning to do. If we found something like that, I could get on board with the district attorney and testify knowing we had the killer in custody.

But the only collection we'd found was a mess of crumpled paper with sappy poetry that had been written in long-hand cursive. Two of the poems were written for Jill, her name used over and over. Terri Rond was absent from Michael's life outside of a contact on his phone. He knew Terri Rond but didn't pine for her like he did Jill Carter. I wrestled with the obligation of turning the poetry over to the DA. What might have only been the infatuation of young love presented in poetic prose, would get spun into the DA's explanation of motive—the rage of a jilted love that carried forward over to a second murder.

Sleep continued to escape me, the case would certainly be there tomorrow. For now, I continued to venture online, exploring the dark web and other seedier places my team of online sleuths had recently discovered. It was the doctor's case I decided to work on while waiting for the wine to make my eyelids heavy. We were down to two online sleuths helping me from what had been a team of five. When a case doesn't get any movement, sleuths get bored and move on to something else.

"Detective Casey White."

The doctor appeared on my screen, surprising me. I checked the network status, seeing he'd re-engaged the earlier session. I'd purposely left it open, hoping he'd choose to continue. Only this time, I added security and additional trace capabilities to improve identifying his location. Fumbling gracefully, if that's a thing, his eyes stayed on mine while I pinged my FBI contacts to let them know what was happening. In turn, they'd contact the US Marshals in charge of the doctor's recapture. Nobody could do anything yet, but they'd put their own techs in place to help determine the doctor's whereabouts.

"Doctor," I replied, grinning slightly, the wine warming my confidence while the network activity spat numbers like an algorithm on steroids. He surprised me then, making like he was peering through the screen at the same numbers. My grin faded. When his focus returned, he cocked his head and did a little shake. Snidely, I remarked, "What do you think you're looking at?"

"Tsk Tsk. Trust me, Detective, you can use every tool at your disposal, and you won't know if I'm a thousand miles away or around the corner in a little beach bungalow." He lifted a brandy snifter and swirled it before tucking it beneath his nose. The doctor gave it a good sniff and sipped. *"Now, Detective, as to why I've reached out to you."*

"Why indeed?" I questioned point-blank, my FBI contact hinting that the team was struggling. "You do know that you're a fugitive with charges of first-degree murder to answer for. The district attorney is recommending life without the possibility of parole. No death penalty. Not here in the state of North Carolina."

"Lucky for me. Isn't it?" He stared back, face still, the screen pixels like jigsaw pieces, some twinkling in his eyes as the video feed went in and out. For a moment, I thought I'd lost him altogether.

"Doctor?"

"I'm still here," he replied, finally moving. I breathed and

drank my wine to cover the relief. *"If it's all the same to you and your district attorney, I'll keep my freedom. It suits me well."*

"Not if we have anything to do about it," I challenged, hating that he held himself in a regard that was above the law.

"To freedom." He drank his brandy as if we were enjoying a toast together. It sickened me. When he finished, he commented, *"I've earned it."*

"Earned it!" I nearly yelled, voice carrying in the stillness of the night. "You arranged the murder of an innocent girl. You surely earned something, Doctor, but it wasn't freedom."

I swiped stray hair from my eyes, anger roiling in my chest that hitched my breath.

"I guess that all depends on perspective."

The screen froze again, my heartbeat skipping as the list of network addresses paused. Was it the extra tooling installed by the FBI? Maybe just a network hiccup. When the screen flashed, showing the doctor had moved, I asked, "Doctor, what is it you want?"

"I called to ask about your daughter. How is she?" He leaned back, turning his head like a psychiatrist ready for a therapy session. He was dressed like one too, a wintry sweater made of thick wool, the kind you'd see in a catalog from Ireland or Scotland perhaps. An orange glow of a fireplace flickered on a wall behind him, a mantel emerging in the dark, carrying knick-knacks and candles. His silver hair was slicked back, and a pair of horn-rimmed glasses were perched on his nose.

In the doctor's glasses, I saw a reflection of his screen. Two of them sitting side by side. While the reflection was small, I could make out my warped image of our online chat session. But in the other screen, I saw what might have been a map, the pixelation too chunky to provide any details. Before answering, I grabbed a screenshot. I didn't have a lot of hope of being able to do much with it but would give it a try.

On television, the detective shows could find usable images

in the warped reflections from a doorknob or a headlight, that sort of thing. You'd see them working on the computer, images rolling up the screen like an old film strip, the killer's face slowly revealed to them. That's just television magic. It doesn't happen like that in real life. There's no amount of technology, AI or otherwise, that's going to create something from nothing. I saved the screenshot anyway, knowing there was always a chance of recognizing something in the image once I magnified it. It was that map. A bit of basic image manipulations and we might pull a city name from it or identify the shape of a lake or river?

"Detective White? Did I lose you?"

"I'm still here," I answered, hurrying to save the file and send it to Tracy.

The doctor figured out what I was doing and snatched off his glasses abruptly, turning them around to look at the lenses as if the screen images were burned in. He folded them neatly and set them down.

"My daughter is fine. Let's talk about something else."

"How about the case you're working? The one about the young woman in the junkyard and the other found behind a dumpster." He returned to the psychiatric pose, showing only the profile of his face. *"Jill Carter was her name. And Terri Rond? They were friends?"*

"I see that you're keeping up with the local news," I replied. It was another red flag. The news stories were carried locally. But there was also Shay's posts online. It was possible the doctor saw them? That he knew more than he was letting on? Nothing had been published at a national level yet which meant the doctor would have had to go out of his way to learn about it. "Home sick?"

"Philadelphia is my home," he sneered. *"Just as I know it will always be yours too."*

"True," I commented, felling odd about connecting with

him on anything. "The Outer Banks is home now. Which paper did you read? Or did you talk to one of the local reporters?"

"Tsk tsk tsk," he answered with a laugh, the smile sinister. *"You won't win any points that way."*

I leaned closer, narrowing my eyes. "Doctor, there's only one outcome. You know that."

"The boy in custody, Michael Gibson. You've made an arrest."

Sitting back, I texted in the other chat window, telling Tracy the doctor must be discussing our case with someone here, someone possibly at the station. "Who have you been talking to?"

He cocked his head. *"Detective, it's late and I'm bored. I'm only looking for some conversation. Tell me about this Michael Gibson."* His eyelids peeled back slightly, brow rising, his voice turning husky. *"Tell me, Detective, did Michael Gibson do it?"*

"He's been arrested, hasn't he?"

"Arrested yes," he commented. *"I was arrested too. I was arrested for a crime that hadn't been committed."*

I was wondering if he'd mention that. We'd saved a girl named Allison and that's all that mattered to me. That, and getting the doctor back behind bars. "Yet," I quickly added to his words. We had evidence of what he'd planned for Allison. We arrested him for other charges, child pornography, and nothing related to Allison. I reminded him of that. "Doctor, you were convicted on charges fitting the crimes committed which is why you were eligible for parole within five years."

His face was suddenly filling the screen, anger pooling in his eyes. *"Do you know what they did to me in there!"* A moment later he composed himself and eased away, returning to the prior conversation. *"Michael Gibson, he murdered those girls?"*

"Hmm." I grunted, hesitating. It was just long enough for the doctor to pick up on, curiosity returning to his face like a playful riddle.

"You don't think so!" he said, delighted. Before I could answer, he asked, *"What about the crime scenes? Was there anything about them that stood out?"*

"Collections," I told him. It was privileged information, but the doctor was a psychiatrist and had no stake in the case. Wait, I thought, biting my lower lip. That wasn't true. The doctor did have a stake. It was in me. He'd been trying to get into my head since the day we first met. I bit down until wanting to wince. It was a warning to myself about how much I could, or should, share with this man. Relaxing with a sigh, it was a chance to take and it spurred hope when I saw his mouth move to speak, the word collections formed in silence. Understanding changed the look of him as though that one word told him more about the case than everything else we knew. "They were small collections."

"Like a child might collect? Stamps and rocks, that type?"

I nodded but didn't confirm what was collected.

"I trust you've done your work to search the suspect's house and vehicle. Did you find the same?"

"We didn't find anything like it," I answered, the subject a sticking point in the case.

"But you expected to find some collections he'd started as a child. Toy cars or Legos." I nodded again, his eyes leveling with mine. *"Michael Gibson is not your killer."*

"How can you say that?" I asked, needing more.

"Detective," he said softly. Chair creaking, he shifted forward, perching his elbows and cradling his chin. *"Casey, you already know why."*

"But I don't," I said, suddenly feeling like this was a therapy session and I was on the brink of some horrific discovery. I sat back, my thoughts coming together, the elements of the case suddenly brighter. "Or maybe I..."

"Go on. Who is the killer?" the doctor encouraged. *"Give me a profile of who they are."*

"A profile?" I asked, chewing on my lip again. His brow rose with a shade of disappointment. "The killer is someone who takes great pride in presenting a collection as a form of attraction. I believe... I think they do it as a type of courtship behavior." I stopped, the sound of what I was saying too abstract.

"That's good," the doctor said, validating. *"What else, Detective?"*

"The killer is the man who buys a house and presents it to a potential spouse. It's part of their courtship, like a ritual or ceremony."

"What else do you know about rituals and ceremonies?" he asked.

"That they are repeated." With the profile, I sat back and felt the weight of another murder coming.

The doctor toasted the screen, saying, *"It's a conduct that was old when the earth was still new. Think of the man bringing flowers to a potential spouse. Those are your collections."*

"The roses," I commented. "The killer is meticulous about ceremony, about planning—"

The doctor sat back and made a steeple with his fingers, pressing it against his mouth. *"Go on."*

"And the killer is very likely already collecting again with another murder planned." I shot up, back straightening. "It's not just about attracting a mate. The killer is collecting victims."

"Your killer is collecting victims," the doctor said, repeating my words. *"He attracts them first in a courtship behavior and then murders them."*

"This isn't Michael—"

"Your daughter is a pretty little thing," the doctor interrupted, discussing Tracy again. He wasn't letting up. This time he spoke in a low growl that made me uneasy, the hairs on my neck standing on end. As mannerly as he could be, there was no forgetting that this was a very dangerous child predator. There'd been conversations with him already about Tracy and her

kidnapping, his seeming fixated on her, our relationship and what happened to our family.

"Why do you want to discuss Tracy?" I asked, growing annoyed. "The kidnapping happened a long time ago. She's an adult now and we're both doing well."

"Yes, Detective, you've done well to rebuild your life just as I'm attempting to rebuild mine," he commented, lifting a book from a nearby table. He looked into the camera, his gaze directed behind me. *"She is a very pretty thing."*

"Tracy is a grown woman," I said, confused.

"That's not the daughter I'm referring to," he replied, nudging his chin.

I turned around to find Tabitha standing close by, a small blanket she called her binky, her light hair sticking up, pink mouth circled around her thumb. There was curiosity in her hazel eyes, along with sleepiness, her tendency to wander at night becoming a common occurrence.

"Hi there, little one. What's your name?"

"Tabitha," she replied, thumb shiny with spit when she waved.

I hit the screen and camera in a single motion, knocking them sideways and out of her sight. More importantly, I blinded the doctor, all the while cursing to myself.

"Who that?"

"Shh, baby."

I hoisted her into the air. Her clothes were damp, her skin clammy. But she wasn't feverish. It was probably a bad dream, our girl suffering from them since her parents' murder. My heart was stuck in my throat, the doctor seeing Tabitha. He did well to keep up with our lives, including Tracy's, and must have known about the adoption.

"Let's get you back to bed."

"I'm tired," she grumbled and shoved her thumb back into her mouth. She was in that sleepy dream state and wouldn't remember any of this. Her eyes were closed before I got a blanket over her to cover her.

"Night, baby."

I planted a kiss on her forehead and got back to my computer, righting the camera and screen. The chat session remained open, the doctor reading his book, flipping the pages, an index finger running from the top to the bottom of each as if speed-reading.

"Doctor."

He closed the book, his stare returning. *"Maybe I'll be seeing you soon,"* he said, his words stealing the breath from my body. *"You and that pretty little daughter of yours."*

"Don't you threaten—" I replied, heated, a finger crooked at him. He was gone in a blink, the screen where his face had been turned black. I sat back, shaky, and raised my empty wine glass, tilting it to get the last drops. I don't rattle easily, but tonight I did. The doctor had made a threat, and until now, I'd never felt concerned about him or the dangers he posed. I should have though. There's a level of reverence needed with criminals like him. It wasn't respect, nothing like that. Instead, it was a healthy fear of them. I'd gotten complacent with the doctor. Not any more though.

TWENTY-TWO

It was the urgency in Tracy's voice that had me pressing hard on the gas pedal. The excitement spilled from my phone's speaker loud enough to rouse me awake. When I got to the station, I passed the front where Alice nodded toward the large conference room. She didn't say anything but from the look of her, she was telling me to hurry. I shed my gloves, coat, and a scarf at my desk, leaving them piled in my chair, keeping only my laptop. The lights in the conference room were dimmed, the faces of those seated glowing blue and orange from the bright screens. Tracy stood at the front, driving a presentation, all three screens filled edge to edge with spreadsheets and bubble charts. At the center, she navigated a timeline with detailed dates and what appeared to be account numbers, Janine Carter's name listed again and again next to big dollar numbers. Stunned, I stood a moment. I was outside and staring in at what was a meeting to go over the laptop findings. Only, I hadn't scheduled one yet.

The glass door clinked softly when I opened it, my chest heavy when I saw who was in attendance, the small gathering seated at the table and drinking in every pixel on the screens.

Without me, Tracy had called the district attorney and the sheriff direct. He was seated at the opposite end of the table and might have been attending as a courtesy to the DA. There was a third in attendance, a woman with her head down, typing fast like a scribe recording everything. She was driving the screens, moving spreadsheets in and out of view. I'd seen her around the station a few times and knew her to have something to do with financials.

I walked quietly to the rear of the conference room, Tracy catching my eyes once. Maybe she saw the look on my face, the sight giving her pause while she continued to present. I didn't motion or nod or anything, and turned away to lean against the back wall, reading what was on the screens in a hope of catching up fast. To say I was disappointed would be an understatement. It was more than disappointment or annoyance or even embarrassment. I think I felt a little hurt. I felt heat rise on my chest and face when the DA glanced over with a dismissive look on her face.

It wasn't that I was late to the meeting. This just wasn't how we did things. Why would Tracy schedule a meeting without me or go over my head? Normally, any findings presented at this level would be done with reviews first. Meaning, Tracy would have presented it to me, and then I would decide if the DA should see it. Instead, Tracy broke protocol. She not only broke protocol but jumped ahead without giving me the courtesy of a timely invite.

While I wanted to know why, this wasn't the first time I'd experienced something like this with someone on my team. She'd grown so much in the last couple years, flying through the work, gaining experiences that few are apt to ever see. Tracy wasn't one to settle into the daily grind of one job and it was becoming a struggle to keep the fires stoked. She needed more. And more meant she might have to find a new role. One that I could not give her.

This behavior had a name too, soil the nest, or something like that. While it was meant for teens when leaving their homes, it applied to employees too, especially those early in their careers. By soiling the nest, it made decisions about moving on easier for Tracy. I clapped my eyelids shut and staved a soft whimper. That's what Tracy was doing, soiling the nest. Tracy was getting ready to move on.

"Detective, thoughts?" the district attorney asked, putting me on the spot. Like me, the DA worked through the ranks and knew the chain of command. Sitting there, the light of the screens reflecting in her eyes, long fingernails drumming against the table's glass surface, she expected that I would have been fully briefed already. I wasn't. I'd only had that short review in the few minutes before the interview with Michael Gibson. "Detective?"

"Well—" A light sweat ticked beneath my arms while consuming every pixel in one big swallow, the screens filled with too many numbers and dates, threatening to choke me. I was looking for a pattern or a sequence. That's how you present to someone like the district attorney. You show them the story that had supported a crime. That's how I would have done this. Only, I couldn't find it. I couldn't find anything other than Tracy's face, her eyes wide, seeking my support. I only had what Tracy said yesterday and went with that. "My apologies for the tardiness—"

I stopped when the DA stood, her attention gone in a flash. Tracy's face filled with disappointment. The DA raised her phone, swiping it and said, "I've got a meeting with the mayor."

"If you give us a minute—" I offered, trying to salvage the meeting. It wasn't easy to get the DA's time. Exactly how did Tracy convince the DA to come to the station? I was about to find the answer to that question too as she made her way toward me, the newly elected sheriff close behind. As a courtesy, she took my hand and shook it. "I'll reschedule when we've ironed out the kinks."

"Kinks?" she scoffed quietly. "Michael Gibson's case is strong. I didn't see anything here that would dissuade this morning's decision."

"Decision?" I asked. The clock on the wall told me we had two hours before Michael's arraignment. "What decision?"

"I'm recommending no bail," she answered with a nod, brow raised. "I'm also moving him out of here. He'll be processed at the prison holding cells."

"What?" I heard myself ask. But the DA had to do it. Our station's holding cells were temporary. They weren't made to keep someone in custody for extended periods. Without bail, there was no knowing how long Michael would wait behind bars for a trial date. "Is he a flight risk?"

"They're always a flight risk." I needed more and dipped my chin, insisting. The DA saw and elaborated, "It's his history coupled with the heinousness of the murders. Nobody will allow bail."

"Understood," I said, the conference room door clinking as the sheriff left the room. He didn't contribute a single word. That rubbed me the wrong way, but he was still new and apt to follow the DA's lead. Could her decision have been swayed if Tracy's findings offered more? It was too late to make a difference this morning. Or was it? Tracy made herself busy cleaning up, her eyes averting away as we exited the conference room. My concerns shifted to Michael Gibson and where he was going to be held. It wasn't the same as the prison's general population, but it could get rough. "Will he be in protected custody?"

A frown. "I'd need a reason to recommend it?"

"I don't think he did it." My words were soft and unconvincing. The DA looked at me then like I had three heads. I pressed a fist against my heart, pleading, "Call it a gut feeling or intuition! Call it whatever you want! Pauline, I believe Michael

Gibson is a victim of circumstances and poor timing. He did not commit these murders."

"Casey," she began, calling me by my first name, dropping the formalities. That meant I'd reached her with my plea. She sighed. Deep and long. "What about his DNA? It was found beneath the victim's fingernails."

"True—" I began and was suddenly shutdown when the sheriff appeared with two other uniformed officers. Michael Gibson's lawyer was with them too, along with Michael, chains slapping the floor as he stumbled, his arms held. The young man was as white as a sheet, the blood drained from his face, shocked panic in his eyes. He looked over at me and then beyond to where Tracy was approaching, the time on the wall clock indicating the arraignment was going to take place soon.

"It's time for his arraignment?" Tracy asked, passing by to go to her desk.

"It is, and it's time for me to leave," the DA replied.

"Wait." I'd never gone out on a limb for anyone in custody before. Not like this. Not when there was this much evidence supporting a case against them. I could walk away, let the DA do what she was elected to do. It wasn't in me to turn a cheek against what I believed though, and I dared a touch, lightly pressing a hand against her arm. She glanced hard at the sleeve of her blouse and my fingers. I let go, asking, "Pauline, after Michael Gibson's arraignment, bring him back to the holding cell? Give us another day."

She leaned in, whispering, "Detective, I don't think you understand the full scope of what's happening here. Michael Gibson has to be arraigned, no bail, and jailed until trial. There are too many things in motion already." When she straightened, her focus shifted to where the press met Michael Gibson's entourage, the sheriff giving them a few words. "There's too much at stake."

"The school board? The mayor too?" I asked, miffed at the thought that this was about politics and not justice. She didn't nod or shake her head but there were multiple elections coming up, including her position. "Pauline! This is his life!"

"What about the victims, Terri Rond and Jill Carter? Who's going to champion their lives?!" I'd struck a nerve and was glad to have done so. Tracy ducked behind her cubicle wall, steering clear of the exchange. "From where I'm standing, it isn't you or your team advocating for them. It's me."

"One day. If Michael Gibson did this, we'll have more evidence for you to use. But if he's innocent, we'll present the findings as they should have been presented."

The tension leveled, silence descending between us. When Pauline searched my face, I mouthed, *one day*.

"I guess one more day here isn't going to ruffle anyone's feathers." Her brow narrowed and she turned her back to the press so they couldn't see us. "Casey, do you really believe he's innocent?"

I thought on her question before answering, glancing at the top of Tracy's head, hearing her keyboard rattling. It was the evidence we found at the crime scenes and could not find anywhere else. This wasn't about teen angst or a jilted lovestruck boy who wrote sappy poetry and had murdered his classmates because he'd been shoved into the friend zone. It was about a killer with different intentions. "It's the river stones and the bottle caps and feathers. It's those collections the killer made. We didn't find a single piece of evidence indicating Michael Gibson had made them or that he had anything similar to them."

"I'm glad you mentioned that." The DA's mouth twisted, responding, "I'm sure it'll come up at trial."

"All the difference?" I asked, heart lifting. "So, you see where I'm coming from about this case?"

"Nonsense." She shook her head sternly, answering, "It's to bolster my case."

"I'm sorry, I don't understand."

She hung a thumb over her shoulder, exclaiming, "The defense attorney is sure to bring up the same thing and use it to seed doubt on the jury." And just like that, my heart hit the floor. Once again, I was helping the DA while failing to help Michael Gibson or get closer to finding who'd killed these girls. She saw the disappointment, her brow rising, she offered some encouraging words. "I know you have some doubts about this one. That's okay. It happens. You'll get your day. I'll personally make sure that after the arraignment, Michael Gibson is brought back here and given his own holding cell."

"Thank you."

She was leaning again, her face close to mine. "Listen, Casey. I've been meaning to ask you something. If you ever think of leaving here, my office is searching for a new investigator. I think we could work well together."

I was stunned by the suggestion. "Really? A job offer? I've been on the other side of your opinions on multiple cases now."

"Which is exactly why I'd want you on my team."

"I didn't know you had a team?" I said. The DA's office was on the smaller side compared to what we had in Philadelphia. In the city, the DA's office had large teams that worked full time, salaried and with benefits. "I need more than just relying on you and Alice and the sheriff."

"I'm flattered," I said, unsure how to reply and picking words I knew were appropriate for the response. "I'll give it a thought, after this case. If that's okay?"

"Certainly." She forced a grin and turned to leave, reminding me as she walked away. "You've got one day."

My gaze stayed on the DA until she was out of sight, walking out of the station behind Michael Gibson. I went to Tracy immediately and stood at the entrance to her cubicle. She didn't look up, my shadow thrown across her keyboard. I cleared my throat, asking, "What happened in there?"

A shrug. "I presented my findings."

"Tracy, there's a reason we follow protocol. It would have given me an opportunity to—"

"To do what?" she snapped, her neck and face flush. "It wasn't an angle on this case that you were interested in following so I took the initiative."

"Initiative?" I was at a loss and growing confused by the dissension. "Tracy, I'm open to every lead. You heard the conversation with the DA. I'm fighting to find the killer."

"And I'm not?" she asked, chair rolling backwards, arms crossed.

"Tracy, that's not what I said or meant. You know that." Heads were turning and the exchange was getting uncomfortable. I'd never felt this way with her before. "And don't ever put words in my mouth."

"Sorry," she answered, lips pressed white. "Casey, I just wanted to impress her."

"You've always impressed her," I said, pivoting. Tracy was aware of the break in our protocol and was slipping from the defensive. "Tracy, you've always impressed me too."

"How bad?" she asked, one of her dimples appeared while she nervously chewed on her lower lip. "How bad did I make things for Michael Gibson?"

"It's not like that," I assured her, grabbing a chair. "If I'm reading between the lines, this has more to do with the elections coming up; their constituency is hot about how the sexual assault was handled. They want someone's head for transferring Michael Gibson instead of filing charges."

Her eyes grew. "That's why I jumped to show the DA and sheriff what I found."

I had to be constructive here, doing so in a manner that wouldn't trample any feelings. "The data you found looks compelling. But I-I think it was the way it was presented."

"Really?" she asked, tapping the keyboard, her desktop screens turning bright with what I'd seen in the conference room. "I thought it was good."

"Did you include a motive?" It was the one point I knew the DA would have needed to hear to add any doubt about Michael. "Did you give her anything to doubt Michael's guilt?"

"I thought I did." Tracy sat back again, knee bouncing as her focus jumped from screen to screen. "It's a lot of data that shows something potentially illegal was going on with Jill Carter's mother."

"I can see that," I replied, the screens filled with transactions and account numbers. "The DA needs a solid motive to consider anything else. Unfortunately, it's going to take some hard evidence to sway her."

"The DNA?" Tracy asked, already knowing. "What I showed her, you think she ignored it?"

"I don't believe she ignored it at all," I answered, thinking of how the DA was going to prepare to address the collections and lack of other supporting evidence. "If anything, she'll make sure to have an answer about it if Michael Gibson's attorney enters it as part of her defense."

"You mean we have to turn it over?" Tracy asked, a look of concern flashing. Her brow lifted and she added, "Wait! That could be a good thing. If Michael is innocent and his attorney introduces what I found, then it might give a juror some doubt."

It was a good point. I'd been involved in more criminal trials than I could remember. However, I couldn't be sure a defense attorney was allowed to introduce alternative theories as evidence. "Right now, what you have is a theory. We need more for it to be admissible."

"But there's so much already," Tracy defended. She tapped keyboards, screens flashing. "If I did the math right, at least a million dollars was routed to offshore accounts."

"Why though? How does what you found on an old hard drive connect to Jill Carter's murder? And then there's Terri Rond's murder too. How are they connected?" Tracy listened but kept working. I feared it was a rabbit hole, the kind of investigative hook that had her caught, making it impossible for her to see that it wasn't helping to further the investigation at all. I waved at the screens, saying, "There needs to be new evidence somewhere in there that directly ties to both murders."

"I'll find it," she said defiantly, turning busy again, focus locked straight ahead.

All I could do was shake my head, the feel of tension returning. If she were any other of my subordinates, I wouldn't have been walking on eggshells. I would have cut them off and filled that rabbit hole to get them back on track with the investigation. But this was Tracy, my daughter, and I realized I was too afraid of anything coming between us again that I was bending to let her work her angle if it kept her close.

I got up and dragged my chair back to my desk, keyboard clacks and mouse clicks filling the air. Alice waved from the front of the station, catching my attention, her hair pinned tall in a crooked bun. Next to her was a finely dressed handsome couple. They wore nice clothes, expensive, their faces fixed in a sour expression. They didn't want to be here. That was clear. A third man was next to them and instantly I could tell he was a lawyer by the way he doled out business cards and constantly primped his three-piece suit.

Between them was a young woman, college age. High school perhaps. Her face was a pale blue from the light of her phone's screen. I was confused who they were to me, and then Alice mouthed the name, *Michael Gibson*. The girl seemed to hear Alice, looking up briefly before her attention returned to her phone. Claire Reynolds. She was the girl in the bathroom with Michael that resulted in his being accused of a sexual assault. She was at my station, and she'd brought her parents.

TWENTY-THREE

Like their daughter, the Reynolds didn't come alone to the station either. They'd brought a lawyer. That had me wondering what they knew. Did they doubt what their daughter had claimed about Michael Gibson? It occurred to me then that they had to have passed the district attorney and sheriff, and Michael too. If they had, you'd never know it to look at them. They might as well have been embarking on a cruise ship.

"Detective Casey White," I offered, my card in hand.

Mr. Reynolds reached to take it, their lawyer intervening.

"Yes, Detective, thank you," the lawyer said and reciprocated with a card of his own. "Jeff Sommer to represent Claire Reynolds."

"Representation wasn't expected," I said, speaking to Claire directly.

"Ma'am, I'll be fielding the questions," the lawyer replied, stepping between us while clearing his throat.

"Was there a question?" I asked, feeling snarky and immediately annoyed by his presence.

As a courtesy, I offered my hand to Claire. She accepted, her grip soft, barely noticeable. I did the same with her father and mother who offered a firmer touch, a squeeze held by Mr. Reynolds, acknowledging me with a courteous nod. He held my fingers a moment more, saying, "We wanted to clear up any questions about the-the incident."

"The incident. Yes, we've got a few questions too, and appreciate your taking the time to address them," Tracy said, surprising me. She'd joined the discussion, appearing from behind her desk with a laptop in hand. She made the rounds of handshakes while I introduced her, "This is Tracy Fields, she's helping with the investigation."

"Wow, you have the prettiest blue eyes," Claire gushed, taking Tracy's hand.

"Thanks," Tracy answered, smiling. It was nervous banter, Claire's nerves showing. They hadn't at first, but I could see them now. Tracy leaned in and said, "We'll try to get this done quickly."

"If you'll follow me," I said, leading them to the conference room. One by one, chairs were selected, the commotion settling. I remained standing at the front of the table and was about to begin when Claire's mother spoke up.

"Will my daughter be asked to take the stand?" she said, voice shaky. Her nerves were showing a little too.

"It'll likely be a subpoena," Tracy replied.

"Sub-poena?" Claire asked their lawyer, repeating the word slowly.

"It's a written order that would require an individual to appear before a court." His answer was textbook and did nothing to answer Claire's question.

"It's when the court needs to hear something from you, in your words," Tracy told her, rephrasing the response.

Claire shook her head. "They'll ask me what happened with Michael? In the bathroom?"

"Amongst other things," I replied. "It's why we've asked you here."

"But in court?" Claire asked, her voice shaking with uncertainty. Tracy nodded, Claire continuing. "So, like, how does it work? I just go there and tell them the stuff that happened?"

"When you testify, you'll take the stand and get sworn in. Once under oath, the prosecuting attorney will ask questions." I stopped answering when seeing fright cast over her face like a dark shadow. She glanced at her father and mother. "When the prosecuting attorney finishes their questioning, Michael's lawyer, his defense attorney, will want to ask you questions too. That's when I'd expect the questions will get tough."

"Tough? Sworn in?" Claire asked, hands shaking. "I don't know what that means?"

"Hon, it'll be okay," her father consoled. "Before the appearance, we'll tell you what to say."

The Reynolds' lawyer grimaced instantly. As he should. When he looked at me, I cocked a brow, the tone set. As an officer of the court, I couldn't let it go. "Claire, when you appear in court, only the truth can be spoken. It's against the law to lie under oath."

"Against the law?" she asked, voice cracking. Her eyes widened, flicking from her mother to her father and her lawyer. The idea of being sworn in and providing a truthful testimony bothered her deeply. She clapped her hand to her chest, asking, "So what can happen? Like, you mean, they could say I'm lying and then I'd be the one to go to jail?"

"Claire?" Her mother raised a brow the way mothers do, an understanding between them, silent words spoken.

Claire settled and said, "I understand."

"You're sure?" I asked, seeing she was shaken. A half nod, uncertainty looming. I reiterated, "The truth. In your words."

"Claire, what happened in the bathroom?" Tracy jumped on the opportunity, sensing the vulnerability. "In your words. What happened between you and Michael?"

"Um—" Claire started to say, swallowing dryly. She glanced

over at her father, her face red, flaming with embarrassment even. "Well—"

Her mother took the cue, the subject sensitive, and asked, "Coffee or water?"

"To the right of the conference room," I instructed. Claire's father hesitated to leave until the lawyer acknowledged he had the questioning covered. "There's just about anything you want."

"Thank you," Claire's mother replied. She leaned over, kissing her daughter on top of her head. "Tell them what happened like you told me. Okay?"

"Uh-huh," Claire answered, gaze remaining on her parents until the glass doors shut behind them with a clink.

"Claire?" Tracy urged. "Tell us about the assault."

"Assault," she muttered, focus drifting to her hands. "We went into the bathroom before the next class started."

"Did Michael ask you to go into the bathroom?" I asked, hating to interrupt already. How they got there had to be established though. When she didn't answer, I asked again, flipping it, "Did you ask Michael to go into the bathroom with you?"

"I think it was Michael who asked," she said, the top of her lawyer's pen swirling. She began to nod, more confident, adding, "Yeah, it was him."

"Was it by force?" Tracy asked, mocking an aggressive grab of her wrist. "Did Michael pull you into the girls' bathroom like that or with any kind of control?"

A frown. "Uh-uh. Nothing like that. I-I kinda followed him, you know?"

"No. We don't really know, Claire," I said, needing more. "The jury and judge, and the attorneys, will want you to explain it in full detail."

"Why? Like, this doesn't even have anything to do with the girls that got murdered," she said, growing annoyed. "I mean, like what happened in the bathroom was nothing."

Nothing? I braced the table. "Claire, it must have been something," I reminded her. "There was a claim of sexual assault made."

"Yeah, so what? Like nobody got in any trouble," she argued. "What's it matter now?"

I pulled a chair from the desk, rolling it near her, and sat. Calmly, I explained, "It matters what happened because of Jill Carter and Terri Rond. They can't speak for themselves about what happened. But you can, Claire." It was all I said, carefully selecting the words. The last thing a detective should ever do is influence testimony. Once that happens, the truth becomes almost impossible to find.

"So, like you want me to speak for Jill? For Terri too?" she asked, confused.

"Indirectly," I was quick to reply. She mouthed the word while I continued. "Your story will tell the jury and the judge and attorneys who Michael Gibson is."

"Because they'll hear what he did?" she asked, slowly nodding. "The assault?"

"Exactly. It'll paint a picture, tell them who he is," Tracy supported. "Does that make sense?"

"Sort of? And this is when I take the stand and do the oath thingy?" Her questions were coming faster.

"That's right," the Reynolds' lawyer said, helping explain it.

"Which has to be the truth or what?" she asked. "What actually happens if you get caught lying?"

She was as serious as the act of murder could get. Why would she ask or feel compelled to ask that question? "It's called perjury, and nobody wants that. But there's a way to avoid it."

"By telling the truth," she answered. With that she continued answering Tracy's question. "Yeah, Michael held my hand. Maybe he squeezed it a bit too."

"Did he squeeze it hard enough to hurt you?" Tracy followed up. "Or leave any kind of bruises?"

Claire frowned, scoffing a little. "No, nothing like that."

"Why wouldn't Michael have taken you into the boys' bathroom?" I asked, thinking it odd for a boy to go into the girls' bathroom, something boys are trained not to do from their first year of school.

The question bugged Claire and her lawyer too, who answered, "My client won't testify to what her attacker was thinking."

"Attacker?" Claire muttered.

"Understood," I agreed, wanting to be careful in the wording as well, not wanting to come off as intimidating a potential victim. That was the question though. Was Claire a victim? The way she balked at the word attacker had me wondering. "I'm just thinking that if Michael was the one to initiate this, he would have taken you into the boys' bathroom, or anywhere else. Not the girls' bathroom."

"Huh," she answered, considering it. "Well, we went into the girls' bathroom."

"Who went first?" Tracy questioned.

"First?" Claire asked.

Tracy made like she was taking notes, looking up to clarify. "Through the door, into the bathroom."

Claire searched around the table like the answer was waiting in one of the empty seats. "I, I don't remember."

"That's already been established. It was Michael Gibson since he took her by the hand," the lawyer answered.

"Right," Claire followed. "It was Michael."

"Excuse me, but it wasn't established," I countered, annoyed with what the lawyer had done. From this point forward, Claire was only going to remember it the way her lawyer said, that it was Michael leading her through the bathroom doors. The lawyer flipped through his notepad, paper rustling. When he saw his mistake, he made a face but said nothing. I don't know if it was calculated or not, but it wasn't helpful. "Let's jump ahead. Explain what happened in the attack."

"Attack," she muttered with the same questionable tone for the third time.

Before she continued, I leaned into the table, my eyes finding hers, and asked, "Claire, have you told anyone what happened? I mean, the details about exactly what happened to you in the bathroom?"

She looked away immediately, answering, "Some of it. I told my mom."

"If you're subpoenaed to testify, the court will require all of it to be told."

"What if I can't remember?" she asked, eyes bright. "Like, I blanked it out?"

This got her lawyer's attention and he shifted uncomfortably. "Is that what happened?" he asked. "Are you struggling to recall the events of that date?"

Whatever idea she had died like a candle flame, the brightness of it leaving her eyes. "No, I was just asking, you know?"

"Then start from the beginning," I said. "Would that be okay with you?"

Her eyes turned glassy, mouth twisting. "Uh-huh," she agreed reluctantly.

"Did Michael lead you into the bathroom?" Tracy asked, repeating the question.

The lawyer opened his mouth to object but stopped. Instead, he shoved his glasses up the bridge of his nose. Claire glanced at the table, her stare remaining. I held my hand up, quieting whatever the lawyer was going to say.

Tracy continued. "Claire, what happened in the bathroom with Michael?"

Her lower lip shook. "I couldn't get a suspension." She wiped at her eyes, annoyed, legs shaking. "There was no way that could happen."

"Did Michael assault you?" I pressed, seeking the truth to eliminate the he-said/she-said stories the DA had commented about. It was why no charges had ever been filed and why Michael was only transferred to another school. But the damage of the transfer, it had contributed to his arrest. Claire began to shake her head, and I asked again, "Was there a sexual assault? Was there any kind of assault involving Michael Gibson?"

She looked over at her lawyer who glimpsed the notes on his tablet. When she didn't answer, he closed the notepad and placed his hands on top. "I invited him. He didn't even want to go," she said, looking past us to where her parents were. "A suspension was going to look bad on my records. I couldn't have that."

"Michael didn't attack you?" I asked directly.

She shook her head briefly, saying, "I was only having fun."

"Was it your parents who told the school superintendent what happened?" Tracy asked. Her brow deepened with curiosity while searching her laptop. "They spoke for you?"

"Uh-huh," she replied. "But I should have told them. It all happened so fast and then Michael was gone. I didn't even know what happened to him."

"Thank you for explaining and for telling us the truth," I said, having heard enough.

"Ma'am, did Michael kill those girls?" she asked, drying her eyes.

I decided not to answer and asked her instead, "You know Michael. Do you think he could do something like this?"

Claire put on a scowl as if I'd said something offensive. "Never. He's the sweetest boy I know." She looked for her parents and when she couldn't see them, she added, "He didn't even want to go into the bathroom with me. He was like scared and all, you know."

I wanted to tell her where Michael was, that his life was going to be hell. I wanted to tell Claire Reynolds these things so she might feel just a little bad about having lied. Not lied. I don't think she lied. She just didn't come forward and had let her parents run with an idea which was meant to protect their daughter. But while it protected her, it did so with terrible and potentially tragic consequences for Michael.

TWENTY-FOUR

The ground was hard like ice, the grass brittle, a north wind returning to blow a chill into the day. I thought we were done with the winter, but we weren't. When I got out of the car, its frosty touch stung the tip of my nose and cheeks. Jericho held the door for me, his face hidden behind a white puff of breath while Tracy pulled up and parked. There were two funerals today, both coinciding only minutes apart, the timing unexpected.

The hearse was already parked across from us with Alice standing at the back, dressed in black from head to toe. To look at her, you'd think she was Karl Levkin's widow. And in a way, I think maybe she was. Without a doubt, she was his work-widow, but I'd begun to suspect there was a deeper relationship between them. They were both later in their lives and had been single. I didn't realize until after Karl's passing just how much time the two spent together.

Whatever they had was over, and now the grief of Karl's death was stuck frozen on her face. I'd been told that the grief we feel when losing someone is all the love we never had the chance to express for them. Well, to look at Alice, the sight of her putting sadness in my heart, I could see that the love she had for Karl must have been immeasurable.

Drying her face, Alice motioned to Jericho who was dressed in black as well. He said nothing, nodding quietly and wringing his gloved hands nervously. He'd been given the honor to stand as one of Karl's pall bearers, and squeezed my hand before moving to where the funeral director placed him. In a moment, the back of the hearse would open and the men lining up to receive Karl's body would hoist the casket into the air and carry Karl to his final resting place.

Tracy joined me without a word, and I looped an arm around hers to help steady us while we followed the casket and the growing parade. The cemetery grass was a dormant green-brown, the vast field pocked with headstones and mausoleums. The trees lining the hallowed grounds were bare, the branches clacking and rattling as if on cue for Karl's arrival. Evergreens lined the right side of the cemetery like dominoes, placed to hide Route 12, one of the barrier island's most traveled thoroughfares. People were filing in from between the bushes, dozens, young and old, some of them I recognized from Jill Carter and Michael Gibson's school. They were here for Jill's funeral, the gathering taking place less than two hundred yards from this one.

Terri Rond would have been there with the other students. I was certain of it. Her funeral hadn't been scheduled yet but like Jill Carter's, we'd attend, watching from afar. I nudged Tracy's arm, pulling her attention to the other funeral.

She saw the crowd forming, and we selected to stand in a place near Karl's service where we could monitor both. That's what we did when still investigating a murder. We monitored the attendees of the victim's services in hopes of identifying anything that might be considered peculiar. It helped that we'd interviewed so many people, the faces vaguely familiar, enough that I could marry the names to them if needed.

Jill Carter's parents were first, an elderly couple next to them. Grandparents perhaps. Girls and boys around Jill's age stood shivering, half of them without coats or jackets. The school administrator was there with a flower in hand, as were a few of her other teachers too. From where we stood, there wasn't anything out of sorts or alarming.

Family and friends gathered around Karl's grave, while Jericho and the pall bearers softly grunted while easing the casket down for the minister's passing words. I glanced at the other funeral again, leaning onto my toes, Tracy doing the same, the crowd building. A low mournful cry could be heard when Jill's casket appeared. It was white like snow, the sunshine bouncing off the top sharply. Pall bearers lined each side and carried her steadily, the approach slow. It was a mix of men and students, one of the older gentlemen a teacher we'd met in the hallway.

I jumped when the minister began to speak, Jericho leaving the casket behind. He weaved through the group, his shadow leading the way until he found my fingers with a gentle touch and stood next to me. He said nothing but turned to face the service, sunlight bright in his teary eyes. He'd known Karl most of his adult life, the two often going deep-sea fishing in the autumn months. I held his arm close and felt his sadness.

A few birds flitted across the treetops, their colors muted during the wintry days. But their songs didn't go unnoticed, turning more than a few heads, the feathery blurs jumping from branch to branch. I wasn't the only one who'd noticed: Jill Carter's science teacher was tracking them. He saw me watching and put on a sympathetic smile, glancing at Karl's service briefly.

Tracy nudged my arm, drawing my attention to where she was looking. It was the evergreens that lined Route 12, the sunlight casting shadows of them onto the cemetery lawn. But on the ground, there was another shadow between two of the bushes, someone standing hidden between them, remaining out of sight. Only they didn't know or didn't care that the sunlight had revealed them.

Whoever it was stood closer to Jill Carter's funeral, the sight of them making me suspicious. I craned my neck, stretching, pulling on Jericho's arm. His shoulder sagged and he looked at me, confusion in his eyes. I cocked a brow toward the bushes, but he turned back to the service and the minister's words about Karl which was carried on a stiff breeze.

"Who do you think that is?" Tracy asked, her breath warm in my ear.

I had no idea and shook my head, rising higher. It could have been another student or teacher. It could have been a distant relative of the Carter family. It wasn't though. My heart shot into my throat, the air squeezing from my lungs when the mystery person stepped forward. The doctor. The look of him as plain as the day of his overturned parole hearing. "Is that?"

"Casey?" Tracy asked nervously. Her voice rose then, fright in it, "Casey?!"

"I see him," I answered. I didn't wait for a response from Tracy, sweeping Jericho's hand from my arm. In that moment I felt like a predator, my eyes locked on the doctor's figure, approaching carefully while pushing through the crowd of mourners. I parted the sea of people who'd arrived at both funerals, desperation coursing through my veins when the doctor's figure disappeared into the trees.

It was the doctor, I was sure of it—thin and tall with jet-black hair which had to have been dyed recently. It had been salted gray before. I advanced faster, heels clopping the hard ground while I searched for my badge and gun, both absent. I was dressed for a funeral after all. We all were, including the doctor. He wore a suit, expensive and formal, dressed to be overlooked, the perfect attire for a funeral. Blending in with the Carter family and friends, it was the last place I'd think to see him. I had my phone though and dialed 9-1-1, an operator picking up.

"I need patrols at—" I stumbled, a heel catching in a divot, my phone cartwheeling end over end before striking a headstone. Members of the Carter funeral turned, heat rushing over my skin. A hand appeared beneath my arm, cradling softly and lifting.

"I got you," Tracy said, helping me up. She had her phone in hand as well. "I already called it in."

"Flank left and I'll come around the front of him," I instructed, having absolutely no idea what we'd do when we reached the doctor. His shadow remained between the bushes, oblivious to our approach. We were in his blind spot and advancing fast. I could barely catch my breath, my heart taking massive, walloping beats that felt like my chest was going to explode.

I kept an eye on Tracy when she'd taken to the other side of the tree line, traffic on Route 12 whizzing by. Each tree passed me as I got closer, the shadow I aimed for seeming smaller than it was before. When I reached the last bush, I motioned for Tracy to stop while I stepped around to block the doctor's escape. Sucking in a breath, I reached him. But he wasn't there, the shadow was cast by a smaller bush, dwarfed in the company of the taller ones.

When Tracy approached, I asked, "You saw him? Right?"

TWENTY-FIVE

"I-I did!" Tracy declared, breathing fast. By now more of the funeral patrons were turning, their curiosity unavoidable. I took her hand, leading her away, hiding us behind the evergreens and facing Route 12.

"Tracy!" I nearly yelled, seeing the doctor across the road, racing toward a market that had been abandoned years earlier. I knew the property, having had previous cases that required us to investigate it. The doctor shuffled along at a fast pace, cars and trucks separating us. "Call in the location!"

The doctor couldn't have been more than eighty yards from me. I raced across the lanes of Route 12, a truck slamming its brakes and laying on the horn as air whooshed behind a passing sedan, dust and exhaust fumes shooting up my skirt. When I got to the other side, I ditched the heels. I couldn't run in them, and the doctor was moving fast. He was older but spry and in better shape than I'd seen when we last met. The market's parking lot was crumbling and broken, the asphalt skittering painfully from beneath my bare feet.

In the distance, I heard a siren warbling, the unmistakable

trill reaching the doctor too. He stopped, frozen, turning to determine a direction. I was catching up and he noticed the distance closing. For a split second, I was sure he was going to stop and say something to me. Why was he here? Did he have anything to do with Jill Carter's murder? Terri Rond's? They were older girls which didn't fit his M.O. The questions peppered my brain like tiny migraines, bright flashing inquiries without any wisdom to answer them. The sirens were louder, closer now, and in a moment, we'd have the doctor in custody.

"Doctor!" I yelled when he reached the market doors. The building had been closed for too long, the structure growing derelict, dangerous even. It was scheduled for demolition soon with an open farmer's market planned to take its place. The doctor jerked on the door handles, chains rattling, and then he was gone in a blink, disappearing around the corner. I picked up the pace, running, struggling, the cold air stabbing my congested lungs.

Moving fast, adrenaline coursing through my arms and legs, ready to wrap them around him in a body tackle, I ran as fast as I could. I didn't know if he was armed but suspected he wasn't. Weapons weren't in his M.O. either. Though, who the doctor had been before prison and who he had become were two very different people. I couldn't trust my instincts around him.

When I reached the other side of the market, he was scaling an old ladder bolted to the cinder-block wall, paint chipped, welding rusting. His hands smacked the rungs, the metal ringing out, the doctor climbing it easily like a spider fleeing a flame. I followed, ascending the building's side, my muscles taut and burning, my feet hurting. I had no idea where he was going and yelled again, "Doctor, what are you doing? There's no place for you to go!"

It was a big market, the building spanning hundreds of feet, a thousand perhaps in every direction. He could reach the other side before I reached the roof. The doctor surprised me then, turning and looking down, wearing a frown, the hard look in his eyes stopping my ascent. "Detective, a game of cat and mouse wasn't in my plans. Not today."

"Tracy!" I yelled before he turned back, hoping she'd hear me as his body vanished beyond the edge of the rooftop. No response. She must have been on the other side of the building. I climbed over the lip, my feet landing with a crunch. The roof's surface was bubbling and warped, the tar scaly and broken. There were humongous air-conditioning units sitting near the middle, standing in a long row, one of them in a lean. I spotted the doctor racing around them, dodging back and forth. "Tracy, on the roof, heading south!"

A sheet of roofing asphalt turned slick, the soles of my feet sliding enough to lose my balance. When my knee struck the rooftop, a hole cratered around me, giving way in a dusty explosion. I heard a scream and felt its coarseness vibrating in my throat.

Before I could do anything, the roof beneath me was gone. The moment turned surreal, my legs dangling, my hands clutching the frail skeleton of what once made up the building's structure. A boom detonated below me, plumes of dust and debris shooting up. I dared to look down and saw the remains of the roof on the concrete below. The height was dizzying, my stomach vaulting into my throat like a gymnast.

"Tracy—" I tried screaming, my demise looming. This was bad on so many levels that I floundered, uncertain of what to do. I held on, the pinch of muscle aches ripping into my fingers and forearms.

Slipping. That cleared my head fast. I couldn't hold the old tar paper, a bunch of it knotted between my fingers but turning loose. I clutched the roof's wood framing in my other hand, but it had been plagued with rot, crumbling like the parking lot pavement. Termites, I thought wildly, suddenly itchy.

"Detective!" I heard, the sun gone in a blink, erased from

the sky like there'd been a full solar eclipse. My body suddenly turned cold like a ghost had come to take me home. It wasn't a ghost though. It was the doctor, his voice bellowing, "Take it!"

"Doctor," I squeezed out, my voice squeaking like a mouse. His hand jutted between my arms while I writhed and wiggled like a dying fish out of water. That's what I was, a fish out of water. Only, I was suspended high enough in the air to make a fall not survivable. I glanced up, the sunlight bleeding around his dark face. Breathy, my voice breaking, I demanded, "Doctor! You are under arrest. You have the right to remain silent. Anything you say can and will be used—"

"Tsk tsk, Detective. I didn't come here to see you die," he scoffed, the roof creaking loud enough to jar his attention. He flattened himself, distributing his weight like it was a thin sheet of ice. Another slip, the moment dragging long with fate tempting my death. My focus landed on his hand, his offer of salvation. His fingers and fingernails which were perfectly manicured. He shouted again then, yelling, "Detective! Take my damn hand!"

Reluctant and without options, I cried out with a scream and took hold, releasing the parts of the roof that held my life so precariously. The wood stud came loose without my weight on it and I watched it fall away, tumbling end over end for what seemed a horribly long time. It crashed with a thundering boom. I peered up into the doctor's eyes and saw all the power and control had shifted to him. All I could think of was Jericho and Thomas and Tabitha and Tracy. I confessed to him then, pleading, "I-I don't want to die today."

"I didn't think you did," he answered with a grin, struggling to wrench my weight over the broken lip. I rose from the roof's clutches, a rusting metal girder slipping into my side with the ease of a razor blade. When I screamed out, the doctor stopped and saw the injury and assessed the depth. He'd been a physician for many years before turning to psychiatry. And I suspected he was one of those types that never forgot anything. "Superficial. Some stitches and you'll need a tetanus shot too."

I rolled onto my back, his shadow gone, the air cold where he'd been holding my arms. The emotions were coming. They were welling up inside me like a geyser ready to blow after a long sleep. I rolled over and got to my knees and stood, ignoring the adrenaline playing games with my insides. Stars flashed across the rooftop with long tails zigzagging. I fell over clutching my side, struggling. The doctor was gone. He was nowhere to be seen.

Tracy approached cautiously, and I waved for her to stay back, "It's not safe!"

"It's not safe for you either," she yelled, waving hysterically for me to move. I made it back to my feet, the bottoms black with tar and rubbed raw in parts. She looked at the massive hole, asking, "The doctor? Is he... did he fall in?"

"He didn't fall in," I managed to say, taking hold of her, my hands and arms smeared black by the rooftop. "Would you believe he came back. The doctor saved me."

"He saved you?" Tracy asked, dumbstruck by the idea. "Why would he do that?"

I could only shake my head as the first of many patrols ascended the roof, police uniforms, fire patrol uniforms, a rescue squad too. I wanted off the roof. I wanted to get to the other side of the building and continue the chase. But the doctor had taken advantage of what had become my disadvantage.

My mind raced as I sat in an ambulance bay, Jericho asking one of the paramedics questions while another tore my dress and tended to my injuries.

Why did the doctor return to the Outer Banks? Why the risk? What was the thinking? Was it me? Was he here for me or

Tracy? My body drained instantly when Tabitha's small button face flashed in my mind. I grabbed hold of Jericho's hand, clutching it hard enough to make him wince. When he saw the terror on my face, a nightmare registering, I told him, "We've got to get home! I think the doctor is here for our little girl!"

TWENTY-SIX

Route 12 had never seemed so cluttered, Jericho stomping on the gas pedal to weave between cars, even crossing over the double yellow lines at times. His words were grunts and shouts directed at the dispatch person on the radio, instructing them on our heading and time, requesting a half dozen patrol cars. It was the voice of the sheriff he'd been once before and the demand in it was powerful, acknowledgments spoken in response with reverence and assuredness.

The noon hour's cloudless sky brought the sun which beamed golden rays into my car, the visors doing little to help. Jericho slowed down when traffic clogged the narrow strip of asphalt. The road was flanked by dunes and the Atlantic Ocean on one side with Pamlico Sound on the other. But there were other streets we could use, the backroads taking us into the barrier island's residential areas and away from the commercial traffic.

"Hang a right up here," I yelled, my insides jumpy. "Then turn left to continue north!"

"Uh-uh!" he snapped. "We might get stuck back there."

"Trust me, I've done it before."

"And I know the roads!" His eyes grew wide, voice stern. "I grew up here! This is the safest path."

I tightened my lips, disagreeing, and swallowed my words while grabbing the seat when a ribbon of brake lights flashed ahead of us. The world suddenly came to a stop, tires peeling against the blacktop, smoke rising, our bodies lurching forward. I couldn't help myself and pleaded, "Jericho, see! Try the backroads!"

"Yeah, I see it!" he barked, cranking on the steering wheel to leave Route 12. The car's front bounced up violently, a curb passing beneath while we cut across the corner of the intersection to a crossroad that bordered the ocean. When he spun the wheel in the opposite direction, the tires screeched and buffeted, his control of the speed and direction leaving me in awe. There was a reason he was driving, and I wasn't. We were headed north again, passing million-dollar beachfront properties, blurs of beachy pastels that towered above us, stilted with some sitting empty in the off-season. We were moving again but slower, the smaller road lined with trash and recycling bins, cars and some children braving the winter cold to play outdoors. There was relief on Jericho's face. "We're moving again. Try calling home."

"Just did." I couldn't get hold of the sitter. There was no answer on her cell phone or the home line. The roar of the engine mingled with the tire's rhythmic thumping, the miles passing beneath us. When we reached an open stretch, the houses shedding from sight, I hit the phone again, dialing, my eyes fixed on the sea and waves crashing against the shore. I had to keep my focus on the horizon where the sky met the expanse of blues and greens, the winds dotting it with whitecaps that sparkled bright with the sunlight. With every unanswered ring, a little more of me was breaking. I couldn't let Jericho see that I was going to lose it entirely if anything happened. "Still nothing."

"What is he doing here!" Jericho asked, engine groaning under the heavy load of his foot. He looked sideways, glancing quick before his gaze returned to the road. We were back into another residential area, our apartment less than a mile away. When I didn't answer, he asked, "Casey, have you heard from the FBI or the Marshals office at all?"

"Watch it!" I screamed, a mother carrying a baby appeared from between two parked cars. We swerved around them, the driver-side tires clipping the curb with a rubbery chirp. Relieved, I answered, "Just get there without killing anyone."

"What aren't you telling me?" Jericho asked, insisting. His neck and cheeks were turning reddish-purple, the necktie causing his veins to bulge. As if hearing me, he yanked the necktie loose, the silky material slipping through the knot, the color in his face draining subtly. "It's that online sleuthing team? Isn't it?"

"A few of us have been working the doctor's case," I said, glancing at the road signs, eyes fixed on them while I counted down the distance to our apartment. "And-and as best as I can tell, the doctor was in the group. We just didn't know it."

"In the group?" Jericho asked. His lips trembled. It wasn't fear though. Or maybe it was. Deep down, I think it might have been rage and I was suddenly sickeningly aware of just how dangerous it was to have had any talks with the doctor. "You knew? Casey! Did you know the doctor was going to be in there?"

"God no! I had no idea until he made himself known to me," I answered, tears springing to my eyes. I looked at the map on my phone and the different ways of getting to our place. The doctor had a head start on us, but was that enough time to have gotten to our place and done something terrible? I couldn't know for sure. "I only talked to him to keep him online so we could trace his location."

Jericho's expression eased some, his asking, "So the team working his case, they're aware? FBI and Marshals too?"

"Of course they are."

A text message appeared, Tracy saying the search around the market was coming up empty. There were car tracks that could have been fresh, the sand blown into the parking lot. That was all though. The security cameras around the market were defunct, the property without power for more than a month. I dropped my hands into my lap. The doctor could be anywhere. He could have had a car and been on his way to our apartment the moment he helped me climb to safety.

How many minutes did we stay on the roof? How many minutes had passed while we searched? And how long was I sitting in the back of the ambulance? Was it an hour? Two? My head was about to explode realizing it could have easily been three or more since I was giving the officers a report? In my experience as a detective, I'd seen what can happen in only a few minutes' time. "Jericho, please hurry!"

"I am!" Jericho barked callously. I wasn't used to this side of him. I'd seen it a few times and felt intimidated. He must have sensed it and reached across the console to take my hand. "Casey, I'm sorry. I'm really scared is all."

With that I opened up and cried. "I'll kill him if he's there!"

"Look!" There were patrols pulling up as we got to the apartment. They'd come in from the north, reaching our place at the same time. Jericho threw the shifter into park, the transmission grinding with a metallic clunk. He had the car door open and was gone in a single, swift motion. I followed, running behind him, stopping when we reached the front door which we found locked. A grin of reassurance. "I don't think anyone has been here."

"Keys," I said, poking the lock with my house key. But my hands shook terribly, the tip of the key skipping over the hole. Jericho took my hand in his, steadying it. I turned the lock, its metal insides clacking as the tumblers freed the door. "Go go go!"

We swung the door open and ran inside. That's where we found Thomas standing on the couch, wide-eyed and smiling, surprised to see us. He did a double take when he saw my soiled skin and clothes, the wonder of what happened lasting a moment.

The room was a disaster, and I knew instantly what Thomas had been doing. Every pillow and seat cushion was missing, the sofa and loveseat bare. Even Jericho's recliner cushion was gone, along with the throw pillows and blankets. Next to the television stand, the children had erected a blanket fort, using the cushions like building blocks, the pillows and sheets from the bedrooms were included in the build. It towered above us, which told me their sitter had been enlisted to help them. It was the latest craze, a new fort built every day.

"What happened?" the sitter asked, appearing from inside the fort, eyes half-lidded, her cheeks ruddy and damp with sweat.

"Were you sleeping?" My voice was loud and abrupt, Thomas flinching. The suddenness of it woke the sitter: she went motionless, her stare fixed on us.

"Just a second, I think?" she answered, crawling nervously along the floor until she cleared the pillows and blankets. "Tabitha?"

"Tabitha isn't in there with you?" Jericho asked.

He ignored the sitter, hunching over to peer inside the fort, a seat cushion falling. He returned a moment later, shaking his head.

"Where's your sister?" I asked, not waiting for Thomas to answer. Patrol officers were behind me, filing into the apartment and splitting up to check the kitchen, bathrooms and our bedrooms. Thomas didn't answer, his light hazel eyes bugging out from his head while watching the police. "Thomas?"

"I dunno," he answered, shrugging. With that he leapt from the empty couch and crash-landed onto a pillow. It was another daily event, tumbling and somersaulting, using the living room as his own gymnasium. "She's around."

"Why is the backdoor unlocked?" I yelled, sliding it open, the smell of salt and the beach hitting me. "Tabitha!"

"She wouldn't have gone outside? Would she?" the sitter asked, and began to cry, overwhelmed by the sight of us, the police and the storming urgency. She joined me, yelling, "Tabitha!"

"Jericho, check around the other side," I said, going outside and shading my eyes to search the beach toward the ocean. The waves swelled and broke restlessly against a southeasterly wind. The silhouette of distant boats appeared alongside the marine patrol which raced up and down the coastline. Jericho had called them earlier, expanding the search for the doctor. If we didn't find Tabitha soon, he'd be making another call to them.

"Anything?" Jericho asked, returning, breathless.

I could only shake my head and went to the nearest dune, my feet breaking the golden and windswept surfaces. They rose and fell like the crests of waves, their slopes peppered with sea oats, the feathery plumes swaying gently. Was she behind one of them?

We'd played around them before, careful about where we stood, Jericho explaining to us about the birds and other creatures that relied on the dunes. Tabitha loved the smaller dunes as much as Thomas loved the blanket forts. The bare mounds were formed by winds, and she was small enough to hide from us. We'd found Tabitha out here before while playing hide and seek. My heart stopped when I saw the footsteps, the pattern unmistakable. Only, there were two sets. Small and large. Side by side. Tabitha wasn't alone.

TWENTY-SEVEN

Gulls circled overhead, their cries piercing my ears and rivaled by my calls to our daughter. I ran, yelling her name, adding to the symphony of waves crashing. It was high tide, a rip current cutting perpendicular through the white foam. God! Please let her be safe! I continued to yell, the screams loud enough to peel my throat raw.

When I circled around one of the larger dunes, Tabitha was there. She was kneeling and shoveling as though playing in the sand during a warm summer afternoon. But it wasn't hot. It was winter, the tail end of it, and though she had her winter coat on, I saw her shivering. I saw something else too and it was enough to touch my heart like a cold dagger. A thick, pink ribbon was tied in her hair. It wasn't one I'd ever given her, or any that we had in the apartment. But it was one I'd seen before on a few of the doctor's patients, the young girls that he preyed upon.

"Tabitha!" I said hoarsely.

"Playing," she answered, sands sifting through her tiny fingers. She looked at me briefly, then my clothes. My hands were still sooty from the roofing materials, my clothes too, and

I'd forgotten about it and the blood, and could only imagine the sight I must be. "Mommy dirty."

"Yes, I am, sweetie." I forced a smile and her gaze locked on mine while I picked her up, insisting, "Let's get you back inside where it's warm."

"Is she okay?" Jericho asked, rushing at us, sands spraying from the tips of his shoes. He peppered Tabitha's face with kisses, light sparkling in his eyes. It wasn't often I'd seen Jericho shaken. Not like this. It was as jarring as I felt. "What are you doing out here in the cold?"

"Playing sandcastles," Tabitha answered. She sensed the fright, concern filling her face.

"Who gave you this?" I asked, touching the ribbon.

"Mine!" she objected when I began to unravel it. She clapped her hand against it. When I let it go, she added, "A friend."

"What friend?" Jericho asked, anger replacing the relief.

"Inside," I said, insisting, as I made our way back to the apartment, passing patrols while they scoured the area. I didn't know what they were searching for and didn't care. I held Tabitha close enough to feel her tiny heartbeat drumming against my chest. My insides were bubbling with every terrifying fear a parent could have. I'd been through one parental nightmare before which was enough for one lifetime.

When we were safe and warming, I calmly asked, "Tabitha. Who is your friend?"

"You mean Doc," Thomas said abruptly, his head appearing from the fort, cushions tumbling. He'd revealed the identity of his sister's friend as plainly as telling us the weather report. The excited smile he'd appeared with disappeared in an instant when Jericho knelt next to him. "That's what he told us to call him."

"Doc?" Tracy held out her phone, the screen filled with the doctor's face. "Thomas, is this him? Is this Doc?" she asked, looking every bit as sick and frightened as I was feeling.

"Doc," Tabitha answered and smiled. It was the smile that did me in, my stomach squeezing tight, a hot gush rising into the back of my throat. She pointed a finger, saying, "From Mommy co-puter."

"Mommy's computer?" Jericho asked, seeking clarification. He glowered at the ribbon and then at me. I felt myself shrinking in the path of his glare, especially when he asked, "Without Mommy?"

"That's how he talks to us," Thomas said, brow rising with delight. "I like Doc. He says funny things."

"Oh God!" the strength ran out of me like water through a breached damn. I had to put Tabitha down, my knees buckling. I searched Tracy's and Jericho's faces, asking, "That's not possible, is it?"

Tracy knelt next to Tabitha and gently ran her fingers through Tabitha's hair, slipping the ribbon free while asking, "Does Doc talk to you from the screen?"

"Uh-huh," Tabitha answered, the innocence on her face heartbreaking. She was far too young to understand the danger. Both of them were. "Thomas, he help me too."

"Helps, how?" Jericho asked. Thomas cowered at the tone, retreating inside the fort. "No, no, it's okay, buddy. Nobody is in trouble."

"Sometimes, I turn up the sound so we can hear him better," Thomas answered. "Is that wrong?"

"You didn't do anything wrong," I assured him, wiping the tears from my face. The computer. How could the doctor talk to the kids? When I leave the room, the online forum is closed. So are any of the browsers. It hit me then—the how, that is. I looked at Tracy, blurting, "It has to be a virus. A rat."

"A rat!" Thomas shouted.

"Not the kind with the snaky tails," Tracy said, trying to add some levity.

Thomas disappeared back into the fort, the sound of plastic clanking as he returned to playing. I put my finger to my lips, telling everyone to speak quietly.

Tracy asked, "Do you think the doctor installed a remote access trojan on your computer?"

"He had to have, right?" I answered, realizing that the first time the doctor appeared on my screen, he'd found a path into my computer and installed an application to manage the camera and microphone. He'd literally bugged our apartment through the online sleuthing forum. And now, he's been talking to the kids when we weren't around. "It's the only way."

"I'll get it off of there," Tracy said gruffly, her voice carrying the weight of conviction. When she got up to leave the room, I waved my arms. Jericho saw the response and frowned instantly but Tracy understood and stopped. With a nod, she said, "Right, we can use it to help trace it back to his location."

"And right now, the doctor is local. He's been here!" I said, a toxic stew of anger and fright coursing through me like adrenaline. I had to watch my voice though, unsure of how sensitive the computer's microphone was. "The doctor can't help himself. He'll contact me again."

"Then let me add more tools," Tracy said, continuing toward the computer. She stopped again and turned to the sitter, asking, "Didn't you hear anything? Or see anything."

"I thought it was a video?" the sitter answered. But it was enough to get her crying again.

"Listen to me. Thomas. Tabitha." I waited for their attention. "You're never ever supposed to answer that door unless you know who it is."

"We know Doc though," Thomas answered, appearing again, his mouth turned down. His chin wrinkled as if he was about to cry. "Tabitha said he's your friend."

I didn't know how to respond. There was no undoing what Tabitha saw and how the doctor had infiltrated our lives. Instinct had me wanting to unplug the computer and throw it into the ocean. But if we had a shot at locating the doctor, this was it. "Listen to me. Doc is not my friend. He's not your friend or anybody's friend."

"Sad," Tabitha said with a whimper. She was a pure soul, empathetic at heart, caring for the doctor. "He, my friend."

Jericho's eyelids shut tight. He'd been quiet and I knew it was anger, the circumstances bad and getting worse. "Tabs, honey." She went to him, arms and legs wrapped around him in a hug. "It's okay. Sometimes it's okay not to be friends with everybody."

"Don't want him to be sad," she said, voice squeaky like a mouse.

"I know." Jericho looked over, the angry eyes gone. He spoke in the same voice he used when speaking to the children, maintaining the calm that was settling. "If you and Tracy need the computer on, then we'll keep the door closed."

"That'd be best," I agreed. Before it was swept away while cleaning the floor, I grabbed a plastic bag and carefully secured the ribbon. The material didn't lend to lifting any fingerprints but there could be a hair or other fibers of value. When I looked down at myself, I grimaced at the mess and felt the urge to get cleaned up. Those plans would have to wait, the DA appearing outside, her hair buffeting in the wind. I slid the backdoor open enough for her to enter. Her narrow face seemed too thin in the cold, her lips chattering. "Come inside."

"Is everyone okay? I heard you may have had a visitor?" the DA asked, voice shaking. She glanced at me, head to toe, and then the kids and the room. "All accounted for. That's good."

"We're okay," Jericho said. Tracy and the sitter joined when he got up to leave and put out his hand. Thomas appeared from the fort, the dim shadows wrapping around his small frame before he took hold of Jericho's fingers. "I'll get them something to eat."

In the kitchen, the clamor of pots and pans broke the silence, the DA leaning in and asking, "I heard the reports over the radio. You really think it was the doctor?"

"The kids confirmed it—" I started to explain but she cut me off with the sharp edge of her voice.

"The balls on him!" Her eyes narrowed with a mix of anger and disbelief. "How did he get back here so fast?"

"I don't know," I answered, hating to have to admit it. It was a question that was apt to haunt me during the night's sleepless hours. "I think he'd already had a plan to be here. To be at the funeral too. The market, well, that was just an unfortunate missed opportunity."

"It was more than that, Detective," the DA said, her voice dropping to a grave whisper. She fixed her gaze on the floor, her stance widening as if to brace herself for what she had to say next.

"Ma'am?" I questioned, concerned. She looked like she was struggling, her strength waning. I reached out, gripping her arm gently. "Pauline? What is it?"

She could only shake her head, a deep sob rattling in her chest. I guided her to the bare couch. When I went to fetch the cushions, she clutched my hand and sat, insisting I join her. "After the rooftop, when the patrols were searching the inside of the market, they found something."

My heart pounded in my chest, a cold dread spreading through my veins. Whatever they found was tearing her apart, and that meant it was bad. "Pauline, what did they find?"

"It was inside the market, not far from where you almost fell." Her lips were trembling. "Casey, it's another body."

"Who?" I asked, my voice barely a whisper, the hairs on my neck standing on end, a chill racing down my spine.

"Shay Parker." She swiped errantly and wiped her eyes. She went on, "Michael Gibson. I should have listened to you. You had your doubts it could be him and now we have another body."

"She wasn't there," I said, realizing Shay Parker wasn't at Jill Carter's funeral.

"Huh?" Pauline asked. "Wasn't where?"

"Shay wasn't at the funeral. Did the doctor do this?" I said, asking. It was so far outside his M.O. though. I sat back, the couch's frame digging into me. I barely noticed it though, Pauline's voice carrying on again about Michael Gibson. "What about him? He's at the station's holding cell?"

"He's at the hospital," she said, a dark graveness returning to her voice. "Critical condition."

TWENTY-EIGHT

The sun was already dipping into the western horizon, the daylight ending while we raced back to the abandoned market. Headlights approached on the opposite side of Route 12 while ten people or more spoke on a conference call. Their voices rang loud inside my car along with me and Tracy and the district attorney. Pauline was beside herself with anger about what had happened to Michael Gibson following his arraignment. She was visibly shaken, her normally bulletproof exterior gone. I didn't place blame though. I couldn't, even if she was newer to the role of district attorney and had yet to establish all the nuances that came with the job.

For what might have been the tenth time, one of the voices on the call explained it was a simple mistake. Any calm I had was unraveling and I thumped the steering wheel hard enough to hurt. The sound echoed through the car, the microphone picking it up enough to quiet the meeting instantly. My car's headlights flicked on while I wove around traffic and hit the siren a few times. Tracy jabbed the mute button, to mute and unmute, timing it so we didn't blast the meeting attendees. I wanted to though. I really did.

"Inept is the word I'd use," replying in a yell at someone's comments.

Pauline's eyes found mine through the rearview mirror. She leaned in, fingers crawling onto my shoulder with a gentle squeeze. In her reflection, I saw her mouth the words, *soft skills*. I knew what she meant, my mannerisms ofttimes falling short when in the company of pay grades above my own.

"How is it that Michael Gibson's custody was mismanaged this badly?"

"We can't apologize enough about it. The best we can tell is that one of the court officers put Michael Gibson in the wrong group after the arraignment," a voice answered. "There were two dozen arraignments going on. That's how he ended up where he ended up."

"And the detention facility?" I asked, clenching my fists, knuckles white, insides boiling over the carelessness. The facility in question was a prison on the mainland where an empty wing had been repurposed, dedicated to holding men awaiting trial. The local jail normally used was being renovated, all traffic diverted.

The wing also housed inmates awaiting processing for entrance into the prison. These were hard criminals and Michael's arrest for murder in the first qualified him to be there. Nobody in the chain of custody gave it a second thought even though Michael was still more a boy than a man. There were four or more in his cell, the worst of the worst that could be imagined happening to him. He'd been beaten and may have even been sexually assaulted. The guards found him unconscious with life-threatening injuries. Michael was still alive, none of the physical injuries permanent, but he'd never be the same. Anger and rage pulsed through me like an open wound, the call getting nowhere.

"Let's table this for now, shifting efforts to how to make it right for Michael Gibson," Pauline said, trying to smooth things over.

"Is there anything else we can cover while on the call?" someone asked. To that, my eyeballs nearly fell out of my skull, the gravity of what happened being dismissed. "Anyone?"

"Yeah, someone over there better talk to legal. There's going to be a hell of a lawsuit coming your way!" It was a warning, but they were sure to already know it. It wouldn't surprise me if a few lawyers were already on the call.

I found Pauline's eyes staring again, brow furrowed. I hit the phone, hanging up, asking, "How's that for soft skills?"

She rolled the window down, replying, "I need air."

The cold hit me like a slap but felt good on my hot skin. "You still think he... that Michael did it?"

"There's no way," Tracy answered. She looked over her shoulder at the DA, asking, "What do you think?"

She shrugged, answering, "It's why I'm in this car with you. I need to be there with Shay Parker to figure out what to do next."

"Pauline?" I challenged. "You didn't answer the question?"

"Michael Gibson could have an accomplice?" she said plainly, shrugging. She dipped her head and cradled her face, mumbling, "I-I just don't know."

"For the record, I think Michael Gibson is innocent," Tracy said, speaking up over the wind. She prepped her camera gear, firing the strobe into the seat, testing the batteries charge. "Especially after listening to Claire Reynolds."

"Yeah, I think he's innocent too." I turned into the parking lot, broken pavement crunching beneath the tires. "Michael Gibson is another victim now."

The abandoned market was the last place I expected to be when the sun dipped in the late afternoon, the season inviting the dark early. It wasn't late yet, but the winter months had the shortest days of the year. What it meant though was that I should've been home with Tabitha and Thomas and Jericho. Selfishly, I should have been in a warm bath soon after bedtime, hot steam rolling across my neck and face, the water tending to the bruises from the rooftop fall. Instead, I was shielding my eyes against the flashing blue lights from five patrol vehicles sitting alongside the medical examiner's van. I slipped latex gloves over my fingers, a pair of booties in hand for when we reached the doors to enter the market. There were a thousand questions spinning in my brain like a tornado that wouldn't settle.

There was Michael Gibson's condition. There was Tabitha too, though she seemed fine, having no idea who Doc really was. And the doctor. What was he up to? He could have taken Tabitha but he didn't. Was it a warning? Was he showing me what he could do? That he was in control?

"Hold it a second," I told Tracy, leaning onto her shoulder while sliding the booties over my shoes. Pauline did the same, eyeing the market's weather-beaten facade. I wondered when she'd last been to a crime scene. I didn't ask though and helped her balance instead, her hand on my shoulder again while Tracy perched herself against the market's door. The chains on the front were heaped in a pile, cut and dropped during the search for the doctor. While they didn't find him, they did find Shay Parker. "Thanks, let's get to it."

"You could have died," Tracy said, her gaze on the hole in the ceiling where I'd been dangling from. A wide blade of dim sunlight jutted from the hole, dust shimmering faintly in the remains of the day.

"You may want to wear masks, guys," I commented, having no idea what pollutants we were breathing. The market looked sad, resembling something out of a dystopian novel, a relic of the busy commerce that ebbed and flowed with the day's hours. The off-season in the Outer Banks could be a struggle. Add in a pandemic and a lot of places that relied on the busy travel season were forced to shutter their doors. That's what happened here, the busy market a hub for beachgoers and locals alike was now a sad reminder of what happens when surrendering to the relentless march of time.

I pushed past what had once been the automatic doors, now covered in faded plywood marked with graffiti, some of it more like artwork than vandalism. We walked beneath an Exit sign hanging precariously from a pair of copper wires which had turned green from the salty air. Inside, the aisles which had once been lined with goods, the shelves brimming, were now bare, shadows falling strangely in the emptiness.

Dust motes danced in the shafts of light beaming from patrol officers' hands, the harder lights catching our eyes with apologies from the holder. I put a light on the path in front of us, following a thread of yellow crime-scene tape, the linoleum floors worn smooth by countless footsteps. Even with a mask on, I caught the faint smell of stale cardboard which tickled my nose and threatened to make me sneeze.

"You're lucky," the district attorney said, shining her flashlight near the ceiling where fluorescent lights hung askew. We snaked our way through a checkout counter, the conveyor belts frozen, some of the cash registers still in place, their drawers opened, any money long gone. "Gosh, what if the doctor had left you?"

"I don't want to think about that," I answered, pushing through the flimsy police tape, broken glass crunching under my shoe. The echo of our footsteps resonated through the hollowed-out space, punctuating the distance and size of the supermarket.

"Over here," I heard, recognizing Derek's voice.

"Follow the tape," Samantha Watson added, voice methodical, the pair already working.

"Coming," I told them, winding around what might have been the produce section once, the wall thick with fake garnish which had faded, an old water-mister lying in ruins atop it. "That is if we find you—"

The sight of the body stopped me. I saw the girl's gray feet first, bare like the rest of her, lifeless, a small butterfly tattoo just above the left ankle. Shay's face held a serene look, despite the violence that had claimed her life, evidence of it in the bruising around her neck. I stopped at the ligature marks, the number of them twenty, pocked by what I thought to be the killer's fingers and thumbs. They told the grim story of the victim's last moments—the girl strangled, her breath stolen by a pair of violently cruel hands.

I stepped closer, noting the disarray around the body—fallen cans that had been emptied long ago, a tipped-over mop bucket, and scattered pieces of paper that fluttered slightly in a draft. Samantha was crouched beside the body, her expression steeped heavy in concentration. Derek stood nearby, taking notes and preparing tools from one of the medical examiner cases, his thin hair draped in his eyes. The air was already riddled with the stench of the old market but was joined by death, the odor telling me it had been more than eight or so hours.

"Detective," Samantha acknowledged somberly without looking up as her gloved hands carefully examined the bruises, the focus of the examination's attention. She peered up at me, saying, "The cause of death is clear, but you know that we'll need to do a full autopsy. Though this bruising is consistent with that we saw on Jill Carter and Terri Rond."

"Understood," I nodded, surveying the scene in search of anything else resembling the other crime scenes. That meant looking for collections or anything that resembled them. My heart fell to the dusty floor when I saw what was hidden in the shadows. Victim first, I told myself, asking, "The time of death?"

Derek flipped through his notes and put a thumbs up. "Thinking it's approximately eighteen hours. From the body's temperature, death occurred somewhere between ten o'clock and midnight."

"Give or take," Samantha added.

Camera clicks punctuated the stillness as Tracy shuffled around the body, capturing every angle. It was good to see the look of determined focus on her face, the camera whirring and flashing as she documented the scene. "Casey," she asked, pausing around the victim's neck. "I'm not seeing any signs of a struggle."

I lowered myself over Shay Parker's face, her eyeballs bulging, red tendrils forever fixed in them, graying behind the mask of death. "There's no scuffle marks on the floor either and with the victim's clothes missing, we won't know how the killer got her here." I moved to the victim's arms and hands, searching for a torn fingernail or any evidence of a fight. When I didn't see any, I told Tracy, "Make sure to get close-ups of the marks on her neck. They may be the only visible injuries."

Samantha looked up at me, her face as serious as I'd ever seen it. "The victim may have put up a fight after she was initially attacked."

"Where?" I asked, unable to find anything. Tracy joined me near Samantha, readying her cameras, batteries cycling for another picture. On cue, Samantha raised the victim's arm, red welts and scratches beneath her forearm. "Defensive wounds. How about her fingernails?"

"Same nail polish as Jill's," Tracy commented. It was how we first found Shay, identifying her in the high school's hallway when interviewing students and staff. A flash cycled near my head, batteries whining abruptly. Tracy motioned to Samantha, asking, "Hold her arm, please."

I crouched down next to Shay's right arm, lifting it and seeing more defensive wounds. "I think we can assume that the defensive wounds occurred when the attack began?"

Tracy half nodded, uncertain. "Why?" she asked, moving to capture detailed images of the victim's fingernails. A can scuttled across the broken linoleum, skittering with clamoring echo. My heart jumped into my throat, Tracy and Samantha flinching as the district attorney stepped into the light, waving an apology. She'd been on her phone since we got here, every other word carrying Michael Gibson's name. Tracy shook her head, exclaiming, "Gosh this place gives me the creeps."

"Yeah, it does," Derek agreed.

"The creeps or not, it's our job to give Shay Parker a voice now," I told them. Inside, I was feeling every bit as creeped out by the market as they'd expressed. I couldn't show it though. Especially in front of the DA. "Tracy, we've got defensive wounds but no signs of a struggle. There're no marks on the floor to indicate the victim was dragged here. What's that tell you?"

"She knew the killer," Tracy answered almost before I could finish. Derek straightened, whisking his hair back, the combover growing haggard. She clarified for him, "The killer invited Shay here, leading her here with the promise of something. Could have been drugs or money, something to entice her to come willingly."

"Very good," I answered, Derek and Samantha continuing the examination while I walked around the perimeter of the scene, my flashlight sweeping over the floor's broken pieces. I wanted to see the collections. The beam from my flashlight landed on a pile of stones like what had been discovered at the previous two crime scenes. They were the same, smooth and rounded, nothing at all like the jagged debris scattered throughout the rest of the market. It was how they were piled too, like a pyramid, the balance of the ones near the top precarious. Next to the stones was a collection of whiteboard markers. There were no less than two dozen, stacked to form the same shape as the stones. Feathers were next. A hundred of them. Different colors and shapes and sizes, the shallow draft buffeting the soft edges. "I think the killer enticed Shay Parker with a promise to show her something."

"Whoever they are, they went through some trouble bringing that stuff in here," Derek said as Tracy's camera flash stung his eyes. He winced and shook it off, adding, "They probably made a couple trips."

"Trips?" I said, recalling the front door being chained. The market was inaccessible until earlier today. I glanced up at the roof, the cavity left behind in the chase. The doors had been chained. "Officer?"

A patrol officer approached, his eyes glued to the body. He couldn't have been more than a few years out of high school, the crime scene bothersome. "I need a perimeter assessment. That's every window and door. I want to know every single entrance that's possible. If a mouse can get inside, I want to know how and where."

"Yes, ma'am," he said, disappearing behind a dilapidated Campbell's Soup display.

"Tracy, when we're done here, let's visit the neighboring properties," I instructed.

"Video footage?" she asked. "Like from a doorbell camera?"

"One of them has got to have some sort of security camera that'll have this building in its background." As I spoke, I saw Samantha concentrating around the victim's midsection, some abrasions between the victim's legs. I don't rattle. Rarely anyway. But looking at Shay Parker, the young woman lying so still and seemingly peaceful, it was hard to imagine the nightmare she'd endured. "It's what I think it is? Am I right?"

Samantha stood up, brushing dust from her knees. "Well, I'll know for certain when I get her back to the morgue."

"May I?" Tracy asked, kneeling down where Samantha was concentrating her work. The camera's flash highlighted the victim's skin showing scratches and welts. "Casey? You want to take a look at these?"

"Her clothes were forcefully removed," I said, urging Tracy to continue with the photography. A cold knot sat in my stomach like a rock. "She was sexually assaulted?"

"Yes. It's likely," Samantha answered, confirming, her voice tight to temper any emotion. "Like I said, we'll know more after the autopsy."

"Shit," I mumbled, hands on my hips, turning away. The weight of the scene, of two other victims and the shared M.O. was heavy. And as I looked around the abandoned market, the silence of the place became crushing. This was no longer just an abandoned building in the Outer Banks. Not anymore. It was a crime scene, a place where Shay Parker's life had been brutally ended.

"What about these?" Tracy asked. My focus returning, she was working the area around the victim's neck, the bruising considerably more than what was seen with Jill Carter and Terri Rond. In her upturned face, a question loomed. "This is different."

"It is," Samantha said, working around Tracy to carefully lift Shay. Grunting, she said, "Get a picture of the ones behind her neck."

"There are so many," I commented, shining my light on the bruising. Shay was fair skinned, the petechia pronounced, especially around the eyes. The ligature marks were peppered over the front and back and even the sides of her neck, each standing out like a storm cloud in a perfectly blue sky. What happened to Shay hit me like a truck and I stood up, sickened by what she'd gone through. "It's control. All of it is control."

"Why so many?" Tracy asked. "I mean, not to sound crude, but if Shay was dead then why continue?"

"The dead don't bruise," I answered immediately.

"Oh God!" Tracy's jaw dropped open.

"Control?" Samantha asked, uncertain what it was Tracy had understood. "What do you mean?"

"The killer seeks control over the victim. I believe he is strangling the victims repeatedly." I approached Shay Parker's remains and made like I was facing her. "I think the killer straddled her, hands around her neck, his face in hers so that Shay could see that he had total control. Then the killer choked her until she passed out."

"Why would they do that?" Derek asked. It was the one question nobody except the killer could answer.

Speculating, I answered simply, "It's part of what gets him off."

"The killer revived her?" Tracy asked, grimacing, the color in her face pasty. Instinctively, she had a hand up around her throat, guarding. "And then does it again?"

"How many times?" Derek asked, appalled by what was described.

I motioned to the ligature marks, each one an affront to Shay's pure skin. Some overlapped though, my answering, "I don't think we'll be able to figure that out. As for how long this went on?" I shook my head, sharing in the disgust of it. "Samantha?"

"If the time of death was last night—" Samantha began to answer and searched around the abandoned market, "alone, in this place, it could have gone on for hours. The human body can endure a substantial amount of punishment."

"We'll piece together more with a timeline once we have a report of when Shay went missing." Tracy held up her phone as a cue. "You heard back from the station?"

"Shay Parker's parents reported her missing this morning." Tracy put on a frown. "That's all night. Maybe her parents thought she was in bed?"

"Must be something like that. Likely, she snuck out of her bedroom. And then was taken?" At this point, we were guessing what happened and had no idea. It meant we'd have to investigate the victim's home. "Does the report say anything else?"

"Just that they found her room empty when they went to wake her to get ready for Jill Carter's funeral." Tracy looked up from her phone, shaken. With her hand to her chest, she exclaimed, "Damn, that got me."

"It's awful," Derek commented, lowering his head. It was an impromptu moment of silence, the distant sound of feet shuffling, a breeze funneling through the roof to twist the crime-scene tape. Derek asked, "You think this was the doctor?"

"The timing says it is. The doctor was here too."

"Casey, you don't sound convinced," Samantha questioned, gathering equipment. "He was at the funeral and then he came to this building with you following."

"It's like he wanted to show you what he did," Tracy said, supporting Samantha's comment.

"I know what it looks like and maybe that's why I've got reservations." Maybe it is the doctor, his M.O. changing, his targeting adolescent girls. I thought back to the murder charges looming over him and the victim in that case. She wasn't much younger than the victims here. "You know, it very well might be the doctor, those collections over there nothing more than a game he's playing with us."

"It fits," Derek said, commenting with his shoulders raised. He looked at me with wishful eyes and said, "You'll get him, if it is."

"Derek," I said, wanting to say more about the doctor but choosing not to. "Let's get the body bag ready. Preserve every bit of evidence we can, and we'll resume this at the morgue."

He looked to Samantha who nodded in agreement, him and Tracy moving together to set the necessary equipment while Samantha and I carefully placed Shay Parker's body into the bag. Tracy got up and searched where the body had been, and continued to take photographs, ensuring nothing was missed. As we finished helping the medical examiner, and prepared to transport Shay, I glanced back at the stones and whiteboard markers, along with the feathers. The placement was chillingly deliberate. More than a game the doctor was playing.

"Tracy, get more close-ups of these," I said, my mind racing. "When you're ready, we'll bag them as evidence."

Her camera still flashing, I felt the abandoned market closing around us, the quiet aisles and empty shelves and strange shadows watching our every move. Instead of canned goods and produce and eggs and milk, the market was holding dark secrets now—it was the name of the killer. It was our job to reveal who they were before another girl was murdered.

TWENTY-NINE

I couldn't sleep, the computer screen's pixels burning into my eyes with glowing afterimages of the mouse cursor. I'd been staring for what felt like an hour or more, waiting for the doctor's return. After today, there was doubt we'd ever see him again, but I'd like to say I knew him by now. That we had a rapport which was unique, and that he'd call me. It was already late and if a call was going to happen, I hoped it would happen before the sun's first blink in the east. The kids were asleep, totally oblivious to the dangers that occurred this afternoon. Jericho was sleeping too, his soft snores stopping and starting, the bedsprings creaking whenever he flopped restlessly from one side to the other.

Restless. That's the real reason I couldn't shut my eyes and find a place in my dreams. I was achy and overloaded by the day. Between the funerals and the chase and the market's rooftop, my death staring up at me from the cracked linoleum below, I should be sleeping.

The doctor was at Jill Carter's funeral too, but why? Maybe he was like the arsonists I'd compared him to before. Maybe he was like the firebugs who watched the disaster of their own making, seeing it come alive, flicking sparks and igniting disaster. I wanted to doubt it and dismiss it. I mean, the doctor literally led us to another body. If not for the rooftop chase and the extensive search of the property afterward, Shay Parker would have become a missing person. With the abandoned market scheduled for demolition, there was the risk her body might not have been found at all. I'd like to think inspections were done before leveling a building, but I don't know that for certain.

By now, the FBI and US Marshals were filling the Outer Banks hotel vacancies, the rooms sitting empty in the off-season. No less than a hundred had arrived, all of them with the same agenda—find Dr. P.W. Boécemo. I sat back, sipping a chamomile tea with wishful thoughts for it to add some weight to my eyelids. I was too wired though and clicked around the online sleuthing forums to see if anyone else was as awake as I was. A few were. They were already working another case that involved a missing seven-year-old girl from Missouri. She'd be eight now, turning nine in less than six months. While the girl's case remained open, it had gone cold, the detectives likely working something new. I couldn't let the same happen with this one.

A text message chirped on my phone, the district attorney saying that Michael Gibson's condition had been upgraded to serious. He was no longer in critical condition, having suffered a serious head wound, his skull fractured. He'd been placed in an induced coma to stave off seizures and arrest incurring additional injuries to his brain.

I texted the DA a thumbs-up reply, my insides roiling about what had happened. No amount of apology from those in charge of Michael Gibson's custody could correct the wrong that had occurred. The evening news broadcasts had reported what happened too, the reporters running with the stories about Michael Gibson and Shay Parker's murder and the doctor's sightings of course. Tomorrow morning was going to be the mother of all shit-shows at the station. It was the only way to describe the mess this case had become.

I opened my eyes and flinched, the doctor staring at me. We'd left the computer as is, untampered, the remote access trojan, the RAT, the doctor installed still in place. Tracy found the digital evidence indicating it was installed during one of my earlier contacts with the doctor. Assuming the worst, that the doctor has been watching my family, listening to us all this time. The idea of it soured my gut and made me sick to my stomach.

I glanced at the icon Tracy placed on the computer's desktop. It was a remedy to the doctor's rat infestation, and worked like a kind of kill switch that could wipe out what the doctor installed on our computer. She'd even made the icon a giant mousetrap, playing on the acronym, RAT. I loved that she could find a humor in all of this.

I couldn't laugh about it though, the smug look of the doctor's face had me wanting to reach through the screen and ring his neck. He'd touched our little girl, holding her hand and God knows what else. I was speculating of course and Tabitha gave no indications of anything more happening. Still, I knew who this man was and the idea of him being close to our children was as dangerous as dangerous could be.

Finger hovering on Tracy's RAT trap, I moved the cursor away, leaving it in place for now. We needed it installed, along with a second computer that was accompanied by additional programs to help seek out the doctor's location. Outside the apartment, there was a police van, a bundle of wires slung loose from its rear and wired directly to our apartment. Inside the van, two officers worked a panel of humming computer gear to sniff network packets, tracing each of them, identifying headers and all the network breadcrumbs that are never fully sanitized.

"What the fuck were you doing at my place?" I said, hushed, voice strained and grating. "Why were you at my home?"

"*I wanted to visit, is all,*" he answered, holding up his hands and mouthing, *c'est la vie*. He picked up a brandy glass and swirled the liquid. He took a sip and slowly placed the glass down like this was a television interview. The doctor moved closer to the camera then, warning, "*Detective, if I wanted more, I would have taken it.*" He annunciated the word, taken, the sound indicating pleasure. It snatched my heart like a handful of cold fingers.

"Don't you threaten my family!" The day's rage spewed from every pore. I was livid and unsure I could stay composed long enough to keep him online. But I had to. There was the team of FBI and US Marshals online with us. Every keystroke and mouse click, every computer bit and byte packaged for travel was being taken apart, inspected, reassembled with tracking attached before it was sent on its way. I could see the activities on the other computer screen which was undetectable to the doctor. Or so I thought. He was far more tech-savvy than any of us had expected.

Reviewing the case which ultimately sent him to prison, none of us should have underestimated his technical abilities. While the charges of attempted abduction of a minor was thrown out, the child-pornography ring was more than enough to get him sentenced. The computer and networking systems he'd put in place, along with the broad distribution of materials, was both sophisticated and highly complex. That investigation required a technical team to disassemble and summarize the design to help the prosecution make their case. "If you ever come near my family again, I'll kill you."

"*Tsk, tsk, tsk,*" he replied, wagging a finger. He made like he was looking to my left and right, then up and down as if I were surrounded by a team. In a way I was, their digital ghosts hovering around our conversation. "*You shouldn't make threats with so many listening.*"

"It's not a threat," I assured him. "It's a promise."

Disappointment appeared with a genuine hurt in his eyes. *"And here I thought we had a better relationship than that."*

"The ribbon?" I scolded, images of his patients wearing the same color and style. "What? You thought I'd forgotten about them. I remember, Doctor."

"I never hurt those girls!" he shouted, hammering the table hard enough to jostle his screen. *"That accusation was unfounded. That's why it was thrown out!"*

We never did have evidence of harm against minors. Only the intent. "Well, you might not have been convicted for it, but we know what you were planning."

"She's a lovely child, Casey," he said with a sneer, the shape of his mouth warped by the brandy glass. He finished his drink, eyes warming. *"Casey, I do not want to hurt your family."*

"What? Are we friends here?" I barked, growing annoyed. Was that what this was? He was lonely? I didn't waste another minute, knowing he'd cut and run soon while his location was being searched. "Why did you kill Shay Parker?"

"Another accusation?" He flashed a coy smile. I could hear the soft gurgling of brandy being poured. He sipped it slowly, the smile returning. It was a tell of his whenever I challenged him. But there was more. For a killer who had the upper hand in the case, the doctor looked peaked. Tired even. His cheeks were sunken and the bags beneath his eyes pouching. Long strands of his salt and pepper hair fell in front of his unshaven face, the smile fading as he shook his head. *"Will you try to pin Terri Rond's and Jill Carter's murders on me as well? I thought you had that boy in custody. No?"*

"He couldn't have killed Shay Parker while he was in custody."

"I did not do anything to that girl or any other girls." His accent ticked the syllables in his reply. He usually did well to minimize it, but not tonight. Brushing his hair back, he said something to himself in French, one of the officers translating it

and flashing it on my screen, the words reminding me of a prayer, *"Find me peace in my time of need. The peace of freedom from the bondage of self."*

"Bondage of self, Doctor?" I asked. He looked ten years younger in an instant, his face filling with pleasant surprise. "What is the freedom you seek?"

"Detective, I'm disappointed. If you truly believe I killed these young women, then you haven't gotten to know me at all. Not really." He poured heavy and drank fast, slurring, *"Not even in a forensically viable way as should have been done when you'd initially profiled me."*

"Profiling?" I said, half asking.

"Those listening have the profile. Ask them what I like." The doctor sarcastically focused on his camera with a viciously animal look, leering. *"They'll tell you what age I like my girls."*

"I know what you like," I commented, terrified of his M.O. and his having been to our apartment. "Is that another threat?"

"It's not a threat," he said, composure falling over him like a softly spreading sheet across a bed. He fell back into his chair, seeming to grow tired of the banter. He combed his hair out of his face, asking, *"What was there?"*

"There? Where is there, Doctor?" I replied, answering with a question. His brow popped and he lowered his head, locking eyes.

"You know what I mean. Tell me what you saw at the crime scene. Were there more river stones? Was there anything new?"

I knew what he was referring to and wanted to see if I could slip him up. "Yes, the stones were there, like before."

He pondered this, finishing the brandy. *"And what else? There would have to be something new."*

"Why do you say that?" The doctor had me curious. The feathers were new. So were the whiteboard markers. He stared off, tapping his chin, thinking. "Doctor?"

"Your killer?" he began, pouring again. The doctor didn't

just look tired. He was drinking more. That was out of character, even for him. Squinting with concentration, he continued. *"The killer would have included something from the first murder?"*

"You already established that."

"The river stones," he answered, raising his glass in a mock toast. *"It's the new things. Those are your clues."*

"The entire crime scene is a clue, Doctor," I said, stating the obvious. "What is special about the new things the killer added?"

"Detective, this is a serial killer," he said, guzzling the brandy. Words listing, he continued. *"And contrary to what some believe, they may experience remorse for their actions."*

"Are you saying, they want to be caught?" I asked, seeing the feathers and stones and whiteboard markers in my mind like they were parts of a puzzle. "Like it's a game?"

The doctor shook his head, lips shiny with spittle. *"Not a game,"* he said, pointing his finger at the camera. Pouring again. I wanted to tell him to stop drinking. I wanted to tell him that it wasn't helping. *"Look at the history of serial killers. More than a few have self-surrendered, the remorse for their acts becoming too much. They also know they cannot help themselves and will do it again if not imprisoned."*

"The collections, the killer places them to show the victims," I said, the doctor listening and nodding. He urged me to continue. "Rather than take them away with him when the act is complete, the remorse builds, and the killer leaves them with hopes of being caught."

"Yes! This is a killer who satisfies a hunger, but once sated, they're wracked by remorse." He waited until I nodded in agreement. *"This killer is like the fable of a werewolf, secretly wanting to be stopped but unable to do it on their own."*

"The clues, Doctor," I said, hurrying my words, watching him finish another glass. "How do they fit together?"

"Wrong question," he scolded. He pointed at the camera like before, finger wagging, eyes swimming as he attempted to focus. *"Keep going. What else is at the crime scenes?"*

What else? When it hit me, I nearly shouted, "It's the victims. The question I should have asked was how do the victims fit together?"

"Excellent," he said, sloppily burping. He waved clumsily at the camera, urging me to continue.

"The victims, they knew their killer—" I began, thinking of all the other things Terri Rond, Jill Carter and Shay Parker had in common. There were none. They shared zero physical attributes, their eye and hair colors different. Their heights different. Even their builds were different with one being taller and another heavier, and the last more physically fit than the first two. They came from different socioeconomic households and participated in different school activities. When I saw it, I blurted, "The school classes!"

"School classes," he said, head shaking, surprised by the answer. He toasted the camera, *"Kudos, Detective. Their school is what they have in common."*

"Doctor—" I began to say, wanting to thank him, his asking questions helping me see what was right in front of us. I dipped my head, acknowledging quietly, emotions mixed and even conflicted. I said nothing though, thinking of his prayer, the bondage of self. What evils were lurking behind his drunken gaze? As if he could hear my thoughts, shame entered his eyes, the screen went black, the pixels dimming like the stars at sunrise. The doctor was gone. Deep down, I suspected I might not be seeing him again for a long time. If ever.

THIRTY

It was early in the morning, patrols following me along Route 12. Classes at the high school were already in session, the sun just making its appearance, the mornings starting late during the winter months. The early rays were orange and yellow and cast buttery hues over the two-lane highway that made the world look warm and soft even though the thermometers barely nudged forty-five degrees Fahrenheit outside. I parked my car in the lot, wondering which of the parking spaces Michael Gibson had used the day Jill Carter was murdered.

That was the last time the first victim had spoken with one of her classmates. The moment seized me, the quiet almost deceptive given the gravity of my task this morning. When I opened the car door, the patrol cars parking on each side followed. I motioned for them to wait, not wanting to spook the student's science teacher. I also didn't want this to be a disruption to the school if I was wrong about who killed Shay Parker, Terri Rond, and Jill Carter. Although it was school property, I slipped my gun into its holster and slid my badge around my neck. It was preparation for anything, never taking anything or anyone for granted. If I was right about the teacher, I'd be making an arrest this morning.

The wind picked up, the scent of the sea carried on a stiff breeze that whipped around me, blowing through my hair and into my eyes. It carried the cold that reached my bones and I longed for the summer days to return with the promises of hot afternoons that were doused by thunderstorms in the evenings. I glanced at the sky, the streaks of pink and orange blending into the blue, a canvas of pastels that was as beautiful as I was hopeful in bringing this tragic case to an end.

I swung the heavy metal door open to peer down a narrow, straight hallway lined with classrooms, most of the thick wooden doors closed, a few open. The air inside was a mix of cleaning solutions, chalk dust, and the faint lingering scent of cafeteria food. The walls were painted a drab beige, and the tiled floors worn smooth from decades of student foot traffic. The pictures memorializing Jill Carter and Terri Rond were gone, replaced with the face of Shay Parker. They were in the same locations like changing the picture of a billboard.

The collection of markers discovered at Shay Parker's crime scene had been a key clue, the doctor helping me to focus on them. While I'd had a hunch they meant something, I didn't see or connect them to the school until he challenged me with his questions. The chance of being wrong was still a possibility, the specific type and brand of markers matching those used in the school and any number of business offices, including the station. I had to trace their origins to confirm my suspicions.

My footsteps swept across the floor, moving quietly as though I were back in school and cutting class. I moved from door to door, peering inside while carrying one of the pictures Shay Parker posted online, the one that showed Michael Gibson. In it, he sat at one of the classroom desks and in the background, slightly out of focus, was the student's science teacher with Jill Carter. That detail had slipped by me initially, but now it seemed significant. I just needed to find the same classroom.

When I reached Jill Carter's locker, the white rose and other flowers and cards and mini teddy bears were gone. Terri Rond had a white rose in her bedroom. And when questioned, Shay Parker's mother mentioned her daughter having received a white rose too. A secret admirer, she'd said, the idea of it sweet and innocent. Only, it wasn't. It was from the killer. I was certain of it.

A memory of another white rose hit me and I suddenly recalled where I'd seen it last. It was at Jill Carter's funeral, an image of the science teacher flashing in my mind. He'd been carrying a white rose. Or was I imagining it? I'd become distracted by the doctor's presence and everything that happened after, but I'm sure I saw a white rose, the symbolism too strong to overlook. His classroom was directly across from Jill's locker, and I spun around and headed straight for it, my pulse racing with each step.

The door was open, slightly ajar, and I nudged the thick wood hard enough to make the hinges creak. Inside, the science class was empty, the tables and chairs were perfectly squared, row after row. The teacher's desk was equally organized, pencils and pens lined up, test booklets stacked without a single corner out of place. At the front was a placard with his name, the initials stealing my breath.

We'd never figured out what Jill Carter was trying to write in the snow, but looking at the science teacher's full name, David Gantry, with the initials D and G, I believed the DA could easily introduce this as evidence. But there was the heart shape with initials "M.G." at the top of Jill's science exam. Those were legible and clearly showed the initials. At the time of finding, we'd thought Jill had penned the heart and initials with reference to Michael Gibson. But the M wasn't for Michael. It was for mister. Jill and her classmates would have referred to their science teacher as Mr. Gantry, initials M and G.

Behind the desk was a chalkboard that looked as clean as if it was newly installed. And in the corner, a whiteboard with every color marker perched on the sill. It was there I found the confirmation needed, the whiteboard marker brand the same as what was in the abandoned market. Was the science teacher the werewolf the doctor mentioned, with remorse working against his anonymity? Did he want to get caught?

I ventured deeper inside, careful not to bump or nudge anything, recognizing the painstaking work that went into straightening and aligning every desk and chair. On the other side of the teacher's desk was a table, everything about it continuing to speak academia. There were more piles of graded exams with notes scribbled in the margins, a stack of unused blue test booklets, an inventory of unused whiteboard markers and chalk, the room catering to both. And in the corner of the table was a smaller wooden frame with a picture of a man and woman.

It was the teacher, younger, maybe by fifteen years or so. The woman was old enough to be his mother but the wedding bands on their fingers were matching signaling a union between them. The woman's face was pale, sickly, and maybe a little sad. Her hair was thinning and her skin loose like she'd lost weight recently. In her closed hands, she held a single white rose that matched the roses we'd found. I didn't know the motive for his placing it there and I didn't need to know it. What the picture told me was that I was in the right place.

The walls were a testament to the teacher's passion for ornithology. Or was it an obsession? Another collection openly shared with the public. There were pictures of birds covering every inch of the wall. My eyes were drawn to a few feathers pinned to a corkboard, their colors matching those found at Shay Parker's crime scene. That was two solid pieces of evidence. I'd brought latex gloves and empty evidence bags to collect whatever was needed for the district attorney to make a case.

Looking closer at the photograph Shay had taken inside this classroom, I figured out the vantage point she'd used. It wasn't hard to find where she'd been sitting at the time, and I eased into her chair, cold air rushing through me as if a ghost was in my presence. It wasn't, of course. Not in a paranormal way. But Shay was here just as much as Jill Carter and Terri Rond was too and I felt them in this classroom, watching intently, waiting to see their killer brought to justice.

I raised the picture from her cellphone, angling it until the classroom background lined up exactly as it had been when she captured the image. There were several birds in the picture, one particular species standing out from all the rest. In it, there were odd collections of small, brightly colored objects arranged around a nest. There were pebbles and sticks and grassy chutes of straw, the arrangements oddly similar to what was found at the crime scenes.

The species of bird was called a bowerbird, the index card beneath listing it in the family *Ptilonorhynchidae*, not that I could even pronounce it or spell it for that matter. I snapped a picture of it with my phone, along with the whiteboard markers and the loose feathers tacked to the corkboard. No matter what happened to me, these pictures were in the cloud now and shared with Tracy and the district attorney.

I read on, learning that the bowerbirds were renowned for their unique courtship behavior, the males building elaborate structures and decorating them with sticks and other colorful objects to attract a mate. Was that what the science teacher was doing? Trying to attract Terri Rond, Jill Carter, and Shay Parker to be his mate? I shuddered at the idea, certain that somewhere deep in his sick mind, it might have been how the thoughts started, his selecting victims. But courtship was not the teacher's true intention.

The door to the classroom creaked open, and I turned to see the science teacher entering. He was a tall man, broad-shouldered with a solid build that he carried shyly with a quiet strength. His brown hair, though slightly receding, still had enough fullness to side closer to the age of his student's than their parents. His face was slightly rounded and had a gentle warmth, and his attire reflected the intellect of someone deeply rooted in academia—an old tweed jacket with leather elbow patches, a crisp dress shirt, and well-kept pants. His pale blue eyes were full of character and framed by stylish glasses. That changed when he saw me and stopped cold in the doorway. A growing intensity appeared in them before he continued to enter.

His expression shifted from surprise to concern. I stood up, chair legs screeching. I held up my badge, the lanyard warm against my skin. "Detective Casey White," I said, keeping my tone even. "Apologies for the interruption. I'm investigating Shay Parker's murder and wondered if you had a few minutes?"

"Shay was a good student," he replied, his voice tinged with sadness. "It's a terrible loss."

"Yes, it is." I nodded, glancing at the bird pictures behind him. When he took a step, I glanced at his feet. They were large, about the size I'd seen at the creek where the pebbles were found. Pointing to the picture of the bowerbird, I added, "I noticed this bird in one of Shay's pictures from her phone. It's a bowerbird, right?"

The science teacher stepped closer, a flicker of interest sparking in his eyes. That's what I wanted to see, the tension in his frame easing slightly. I wanted him to be comfortable. With comfort comes a kind of complacency that frees your mind to speak openly. "An exceptional, fascinating creature," he began, his tone animated. "The males build these intricate structures called bowers which are used to attract the females."

"A bower? That's what they call it?"

"A bower, and in them, the male collects objects for the female to inspect."

"What kind of objects?" I asked, gaining more of his interest and trust while he moved closer.

"They could be anything from flower petals to twigs, even small stones, arranging them meticulously to appeal to his prospective mates."

"Small stones?" I asked. He'd made a grave mistake mentioning one of the collections from the crime scenes. He didn't notice and continued to speak. I steered the conversation toward another similarity. "How about items like feathers?"

"Oh yes." An enthusiastic nod.

When he was close enough, I asked point-blank, "The bowerbirds' collections remind me of what we found at Terri Rond's, Jill Carter's, and Shay Parker's crime scenes. Do you think there's a connection?"

His face turned a shade paler, sweat beading on his forehead. "I-I don't see how that would be relevant," he stammered, shifting nervously. Turning to the pictures, he quickly dismissed them, saying, "I mean, these are just birds here."

"Maybe," I said, taking a step closer. "But all of the crime scenes had collections of objects, arranged almost artistically. It's a peculiar coincidence, don't you think?"

He swallowed hard, his eyes darting toward the door. "I suppose... but I'm just a schoolteacher. I wouldn't know anything about crime scenes."

Sensing a growing discomfort, I pressed harder. "You were at Jill Carter's funeral. I saw you there with a white rose. That color. Do you think it's a bit unusual for a funeral?"

His breath hitched and he took a step back, his eyes wide with fear. "I-I need to get back to my other class," he muttered, turning to flee.

There was no revelation of guilt. No announcement of what he'd done. Instead, a chase was immediate and chaotic. Air whooshed past me as it followed a chair flung at my head. He picked up another and tossed it, a leg striking my forearm. I jumped clear of the third, knocking over two more desks, tossing and clearing a path to him. The science teacher was spry for his size, flipping desks, sending them to tumble end over end with books and papers flying.

I lunged after him, slamming into the whiteboard, my shoulder aching from the impact. He was surprisingly strong too, breaking free of my hold with little effort, the smell of sour sweat filling my nose. I'd gotten hold of his belt, the leather cutting into my hand, my fingers looped like a buckle as I held on while our entangled bodies burst into the hallway, the struggles spilling into the open space.

With the calamity came the noise, its thundering through the school, violence clapping against the distant walls. Students poured out of their classrooms, and I was vaguely aware of their forming a circle around us, their shouts and jeers blending into the grunts of punches and wrestling moves. I had him. I did. But somehow the teacher spun around and wrestled free enough to put his large hands around my neck, making like a vice and squeezing. That's when he pulled me up until we were nose to nose. In that moment, the ghosts of his victims came to visit. I was them and saw what they saw in their dying moments. Their teacher was in control, and he was squeezing the life from me.

Smaller arms were on him, a few of the students tugging and pulling to help. I rifled a knee into his middle and watched as the air shot out of him like a cannon ball. With it, the strike stole his strength, and I broke free, stars zigzagging. I tackled the science teacher to the ground, choking to catch my breath, squeezing out the words, "Stay down!"

"Get off me!" he roared, shoving as hard as he could. But I held on, adrenaline fueling my strength.

The principal appeared, his face punctuated with shock and awe. Another administrator appeared, pushing through the crowd. "Break it up! Break it up!" a teacher yelled, believing we were a pair of students tussling between classes.

With their help, I managed to pin the science teacher down, snapping handcuffs onto his wrists. "You are under arrest," I said in a wheezy and labored voice. "You have the right to remain silent. Anything you say can and will be used against you in a court of law..."

As I recited his rights, the reality of the situation settled in. The students, who had been spectators to a display rarely seen, now watched their teacher's arrest in stunned silence. The principal, a tall man with graying hair and a stern expression, helped me lift the teacher to his feet. "Detective! What's going on here?" he asked, demanding answers.

I glanced at the science teacher, whose face was now a sickly shade of white, sweat dripping from his brow, glasses knocked askew, a shiny bruise rising on his cheek. "This man is being arrested for the murders of Terri Rond, Jill Carter, and Shay Parker," I said, loud enough for those around to hear. I motioned to the classroom, thinking of the evidence. "His classroom has evidence we'll be collecting. I'll expect it to be secured."

"Certainly," the principal said, staring hard at the science teacher, disgust and shock on his face.

As I escorted the teacher out of the school, I felt a wave of nausea, the adrenaline peaking. But it was eclipsed by the grim satisfaction that came with the arrest, the pieces of the case finally coming together. The whiteboard markers, the feathers, the bowerbird-like arrangements. It all pointed to the science teacher and was a big step closer to getting justice for the victims.

THIRTY-ONE

Morning frost crunched underfoot as I walked across the parking lot, the cold air biting at my face. Like Terri Rond's, Jill Carter's, and Shay Parker's murder cases, winter was ending soon. Even now, my breath a puffy cloud in the morning air, there were ribbons of warmer air weaving its way up the coast from the south. Soon it would be spring again and then summer and that was fine by me.

As if on cue, the front of the station was being tended to by a landscaping crew, shovels in hand while preparing for the coming season, one of them batting their arms, the winter holding firm. When I reached the station doors, I flipped my badge shield side out, catching the faint glint from the overhead lights. Alice looked perkier this morning, better than she did at the funeral. She held the door, waving me through, her own breath visible in the morning's frigid air.

"Do you need boxes too?" Alice asked, nudging her chin toward my desk.

"Boxes?" I had no idea what she was talking about. "What boxes?"

"Then it's just Tracy," she answered herself, the tip of a pen and pencil sticking out of her hair. It caught my eye, but it was her comment that had me wondering.

"Any word on Michael Gibson?" she asked. "I feel so terrible about what happened to him."

"He's home," I said, putting on a smile, the news good, but my attention was drawn to Tracy. I could see the top of her head moving around her desk, the early morning silence revealing the screech of a packing-tape gun.

"That's good," Alice commented as I walked past the short wooden gate. The sun was barely over the lip of the ocean, bands of morning light blasting against the windows facing the beach. Bright yellow streaks raced across our workspace, highlighting Tracy's activities. She looked up, her eyes puffy. Was it lack of sleep? The case? Wish as I might, I didn't think it was any of those things.

"Morning, Casey." It was all she said and twirled a cable around a keyboard.

"Morning," I replied, dropping my bag onto my chair with a satisfying plunk. I made small talk, asking, "You got here early?"

"It was more of a late night," she replied, managing a tired smile as she zipped up her laptop bag. Her cubicle had become an extension of another office, which, under her direction, had been converted into a small forensic laboratory. I glanced over to see more boxes stacked in the doorway there. "I wanted to wrap up the report on Jill Carter's mother, the embezzlement. The district attorney is weighing options on charges to be filed."

"Wow, that's great news," I said with a nod, appreciating the effort. Tracy had a knack for detail that often brought clarity to the most convoluted cases, including the one aspect of this case I'd shown little interest in supporting. "Coffee?" I asked, continuing to make small talk, unnerved by her hurried activity. If I asked what was going on, I was sure I'd break down in a cry. She was my daughter first, a coworker second. And it was becoming clear that Tracy was leaving.

"Yeah, sure," she replied and returned to the laborious task of packing.

"I'll get us a cup," I told her, my insides shaking as I made my way back to my desk. The familiar hum of the station rang in my ears while the Outer Banks woke up. The phones came first, Alice answering, the news broadcast from the overhead station televisions turned on came next. I shrugged off my coat, the fabric stiff from the chill, and hung it on the back of my chair before following the scent of freshly brewed coffee that held the promise of a brief reprieve.

When I returned and handed Tracy a cup, she said, "Thank you." She took a sip and then handed me an envelope, saying, "Casey... it's my resignation. It's... it's effective immediately."

"What? Why?" I asked, watching her continue with the packing, more methodically now, her actions deliberate and careful. Rigid concern crept into my voice, I insisted, "Tracy?"

She paused, looking up at me with a mix of apprehension and determination. "Casey, I've accepted a job with the district attorney's office." She forced a smile. "I'm the new investigator for the district attorney's office."

I felt the frown before I knew it was there, my blurting, "You mean the job Pauline offered me?"

"Wow, what a way to say, congrats, Tracy," she snapped. She turned her back and kept working, tape screeching in revolt while mumbling something I couldn't hear but assumed was bad.

"Of course, yes congratulations, Tracy." For a moment, the world seemed to tilt, the right words slipping off the edge. "When did this happen?"

"The other day," she said softly, swiping light-brown hair from her face to show her eyes. A blade of sunlight caught them, revealing they were red-rimmed. I didn't see that until now. "I'll be out of here soon enough."

Shock, surprise, and a pang of hurt hit me all at once. "Why didn't you tell me sooner?"

"I don't know." She looked down, avoiding my gaze. "Maybe I didn't know how to tell you."

"I really am happy for you," I said, taking a deep breath, trying to steady my emotions. Sometimes it was impossible to be professional when there was history, when they were family. I changed the subject, telling her, "Thomas and Tabitha were asking for you."

"Huh?" she asked, her voice barely above a whisper. "Thomas and Tabitha?"

"Come over tonight," I insisted. "We'll order pizza with a glass of wine and talk more about it. The kids want to see you too."

"Sure," she replied, a small, relieved smile breaking a somber expression. "I'd like that."

The end of the day found me at home, sitting at the kitchen table, surrounded by the remnants of takeaway pizza. Thomas's lips smacked as he chomped on a chunk of crust, chewing loudly with his jaw slack. I tapped my lips, his seeing it and closing his mouth, tomato sauce smeared over his face. Tabitha was the same but had finished and was eager to escape the table to play. It was the second wind, both of them buzzing with the infectious energy only children seemed to possess. I gave them the go-ahead, their laughter chased by the patter of bare feet as they ran to the kitchen to clean up.

Jericho sat across from me, finishing the last bite of his slice. I looked down at the cold pizza slice staring back at me, untouched. "She'll be here soon," I said, insisting that Tracy was just late. But the words were more for my own reassurance than for Jericho. I looked at him, adding, "She's just running late. A meeting with the DA probably."

Jericho chewed slowly, his blue-green eyes soft with concern. He swallowed before speaking. "Casey, I don't think she's coming."

In that moment, the statement hurt me more than Tracy's absence. Perhaps because he was saying what I didn't want to hear. I looked up sharply and defended her. "Of course she's coming," I said, my voice trembling.

Jericho set his pizza down and reached across the table to take my hand. "Casey, did something happen between you two?"

"Yeah," I said, pushing away the gnawing doubt. Tears welled in my eyes and spilled before I could stop them. The room fell silent, the kids' playful chatter in front of the television faded as though they were sensing a shift in the atmosphere. "It's that job the DA offered me."

"The investigator position?" Jericho asked, wiping his face, bits of paper napkin sticking to his whiskers. I picked them out, his adding, "Did you change your mind about taking it?"

"Tracy took the position. She's their new investigator," I whispered, my voice breaking. "I don't know how it got bad enough between us that she'd get another job."

Jericho squeezed my hand gently, his thumb brushing over my knuckles. "Casey, maybe it wasn't about you? It could be that Tracy needs a change? You know, grow in her career?"

"I know. I get it. We jumped on new opportunities when we were her age too. I don't think it's just that though," I told him, having thought through every scenario as if contemplating my next move in a chess game. I took a shaky breath, trying to collect my thoughts. "Tracy, she's been so distant lately. And then this morning, she was already packing her desk and didn't even tell me she'd been approached about the job."

Jericho's brow furrowed. "She didn't mention it at all?"

"Not a word." I shook my head, wiping away a tear. "I thought we were... I thought we were better than that. I thought we were close."

Jericho shifted, pulling his chair near mine, his eyes searching mine. "Casey, it doesn't mean she doesn't value you and the friendship you have."

"She's my daughter," I reminded him. I couldn't help but want more between us and thought we were heading in the right direction. I hated that the pain was evident in my voice. "I just don't understand why she didn't come to me."

Jericho nodded. "I know it hurts. But maybe she had her reasons. Maybe she was afraid of disappointing you or that you'd try and talk her out of it."

I let out a bitter laugh. "Well, if it was disappointment, she succeeded in that."

Jericho sighed, standing up and moving around the table to sit beside me. He wrapped an arm around my shoulders, pulling me close. Instantly, I fell into the crook of his body, the shape a perfect fit as if it was made that way just for me. "I think the best thing you can do is give her time, Casey. Give her space and talk to her when she's ready."

I leaned heavily into him, saying, "I don't want to lose her, Jericho. Not again."

"You won't," he assured me and kissed the top of my head. "She'll come around. You'll see."

Jericho held me close, his warmth a comforting contrast to the cold pizza and the chill in my heart. As the tears slowed and my breathing steadied, I sensed a shift in his demeanor. His arms tightened around me briefly before he pulled back, his eyes serious. I looked up at him. "What is it?"

"Casey," he began, his tone hesitant. "I hate to add to your plate, but I have news."

A sting of anxiety surged through me when I saw the look on his face. "Are you okay?" I asked, my voice trembling again.

The whites of his eyes grew briefly, his assuring me, "Casey, it's good news." He forced a smile, the tension remaining. "I'm going to be sheriff again."

For a moment, his words didn't register. Sheriff. There'd been a conversation but nothing concrete was decided. And if anything was going to happen, it'd be with the Marine Patrol. Confusion mingling with concern, I sat up to ask, "How? Sheriff? What happened?"

Jericho ran a hand through his hair. "There's been an emergency vacancy. The sheriff is taking early retirement because of some outside issues that came to light recently. It's at the mayor's request, the city council approved a special election. That means an interim and they want someone with experience to step in immediately. They've asked if I would come back."

The logistics of it swirled in my head, the news mounting. "So, the city council appointed you temporarily? And then there'll be an election?"

He nodded. "There's no transition and they need immediate stability. With everything going on, they think I'm the best person for the job right now. Case, I agreed to step in." There was a long pause and in the quiet of the moment I could hear my heart pounding in my chest. I knew what he was going to say and didn't wait.

"Jericho, you know there's nothing more permanent than something temporary," I muttered. He chuckled at that, his lips tightening when I put him on the spot and asked, "When they hold the election, you're going to run, aren't you?"

"I think I want to run," he replied, the nod slight enough I could have missed it.

"They already know that. And the council, they're assuming you'll win it too."

"Are you mad?" he asked.

I didn't know how to answer. I knew it was what he wanted, he was good at the stay-at-home role but he wanted more.

"I mean, it's a big change. For all of us."

I kissed him on the mouth, easing back to say, "I'm proud of you. They're lucky to have you." But the weight of his words were settling heavily between us. "But..."

"What is it?" he asked.

I squeezed his hand, the reality of the situation sinking in. "It's the change part," I said, managing a smile. "Thomas and Tabitha."

Jericho nodded, his eyes softening. "We'll handle it together, Casey. Like we always do."

I felt the familiar strength of his embrace. I couldn't help but think about the arrangement of the adoption, the stability of a parent at home. How in the world would we make this work? I needed to think on it before I said anything more. "Together," I echoed, drawing strength from the promise.

Huddled beneath the sheets and comforter, we shared a bubble of warmth in our otherwise cool bedroom. My legs and arms were flat against the mattress, Jericho's chest rising and falling methodically. I couldn't sleep and stared at the midnight shadows on the ceiling, cast by the streetlights outside and the occasional flicker of headlights passing by. The rhythmic ticking of raindrops against the window's glass was like a lullaby trying to soothe me to sleep. It didn't work. Nothing could calm the turmoil in my mind.

Jericho rolled over, his arm draped across my waist, his presence usually a constant comfort. But not tonight. What he told me about being sheriff again, held me and wouldn't let go. He stirred, his breath stiff. I could tell he was stirring awake, bothered by what was shared, the tension troubling. This wasn't about him or me or our careers. It was about Thomas and Tabitha.

"Babe?" I whispered, breaking the silence. "Jericho?"

"Yeah?" he responded, his voice soft but alert.

"What are we going to do if you're going to be sheriff again?" I asked, my words tentative, testing the waters carefully.

He sighed, a deep breath, its warmth brushing against my skin. "I think we can make it work, Casey. Couples do it all the time."

"Babe!" I couldn't help but blurt out a laugh. "We are not like other couples."

"No," he agreed and propped himself onto an elbow. A low grumble came with a yawn while he rubbed the sleep from his eyes. "I don't suppose we are."

"I want to support this but how can we both work full time? We made a promise when we adopted Thomas and Tabitha with one of us being a stay-at-home parent."

He looked up at me. "Casey, I don't know. But I have to think that we'll figure it out."

I sat up suddenly, my heart pounding with a sudden idea. Or maybe it wasn't so sudden. Maybe it was something growing in the back of my mind for some time, and I'd been too afraid to face it until now.

"Casey?"

"I think I might have a way." The words faded, caught in my throat. I hesitated, the enormity of what I was about to tell him pressing like a stone between my heart and my mouth. Emotions ran through me like a torrent river, the love for my career and my family colliding. I took a ragged breath, finding the strength to speak. "Jericho, what if it's time for me to step back?"

He sat up at that, his eyes searching mine, concern etched into his face. "What do you mean by step back? Casey, it's not a part-time job."

I was fully alert and felt the troubling questions drain like water running out of a bucket. It was freeing, and I told him,

"Jericho, I don't think I need to be a detective anymore." I'd never said anything like that before, but the words felt right and liberating. I started nodding my head. The sight of me must have been contagious. Jericho nodded too as I continued. "I can step back from the job and focus on Thomas and Tabitha. Let it be me, I'll be the stay-at-home parent they need."

Jericho stared at me, shock giving way to understanding and then to something else—relief perhaps? But there was also a sadness in his face. "Are you sure, Casey? You love being a detective."

"I do," I admitted, my voice trembling. "But I love our family more. And this way, you can be sheriff, and I'll be a mom to Thomas and Tabitha."

He reached out, taking my hand in his. His grip was firm, steady. "I never wanted you to give up your career for me."

"I know, but this isn't just about you," I whispered, borrowing his words from earlier. "This is the right thing to do. For all of us. Plus, I feel it. I feel like I'm ready to do this."

We sat there in the quiet, the rain patter soft as it joined our breathing. The enormity of the decision settled over us, the suffering of what we were going to do was gone. This was the path we needed to take, the path I wanted to take.

Jericho finally spoke, his voice thick with emotion. "Casey, whatever comes next, we'll make it work." He nudged me playfully, saying, "Side by side. Me and you."

"Me and you," I said and wrapped myself around him, feeling the familiar strength of his embrace. "Side by side."

A LETTER FROM B.R. SPANGLER

Dear reader,

I want to say a huge thank you for choosing to read *Gone in the Storm*, Detective Casey White book 12. Thank you to the amazing team at Bookouture and to the readers who have supported the series.

If you enjoyed it and want to keep up to date with all my latest releases, just sign up at the following link. Your email address will never be shared and you can unsubscribe at any time.

www.bookouture.com/br-spangler

Want to help with the Detective Casey White series? I would be very grateful if you could write a review. Recommendations also make a huge difference helping readers discover a new series and one of my books for the first time.

Do you have a question or comment? I'd be happy to answer. You can reach me on my website or Twitter (X), Instagram and Facebook page. I've included the links overleaf.

Happy Reading,

B.R. Spangler

KEEP IN TOUCH WITH B.R. SPANGLER

www.brspangler.com

facebook.com/authorbrianspangler
x.com/BR_Spangler
instagram.com/brspangler

PUBLISHING TEAM

Turning a manuscript into a book requires the efforts of many people. The publishing team at Bookouture would like to acknowledge everyone who contributed to this publication.

Audio
Alba Proko
Sinead O'Connor
Melissa Tran

Commercial
Lauren Morrissette
Hannah Richmond
Imogen Allport

Data and analysis
Mark Alder
Mohamed Bussuri

Cover design
Head Design Ltd.

Editorial
Kelsie Marsden
Nadia Michael

Copyeditor
Janette Currie

Proofreader
Shirley Khan

Marketing
Alex Crow
Melanie Price
Occy Carr
Ciara Rosney
Martyna Młynarska

Operations and distribution
Marina Valles
Stephanie Straub
Joe Morris

Production
Hannah Snetsinger
Mandy Kullar
Jen Shannon
Ria Clare

Publicity
Kim Nash
Noelle Holten
Jess Readett
Sarah Hardy

Rights and contracts
Peta Nightingale
Richard King
Saidah Graham

Made in the USA
Monee, IL
31 August 2025